OLIVIA HARVARD

handcuffs, kisses and awkward situations

Please feel free to send me an email. Just know that my publisher filters these emails. Good news is always welcome.

Olivia Harvard - olivia-harvard.awesomeauthors.org

Sign up for my blog for updates and freebies!
olivia-harvard.awesomeauthors.org

About the Publisher

BLVNP Incorporated, A Nevada Corporation, 340 S. Lemon #6200, Walnut CA 91789, info@blvnp.com / legal@blvnp.com

DISCLAIMER

Please don't be stupid and kill yourself. This book is a work of FICTION.

It is fiction and not to be confused with reality. Neither the author nor the publisher or its associates assume any responsibility for any loss, injury, death or legal consequences resulting from acting on the contents in this book.The author's opinions are not to be construed as the opinions of the publisher.The material in this book is for entertainment purposes ONLY. Enjoy.

Handcuffs, Kisses,and Awkward Situations

By: Olivia Harvard

ISBN: 978-1-68030-068-0

For my parents, Kaitlin, and Chloe.
You all inspire me more and more every single day.

FREE DOWNLOAD

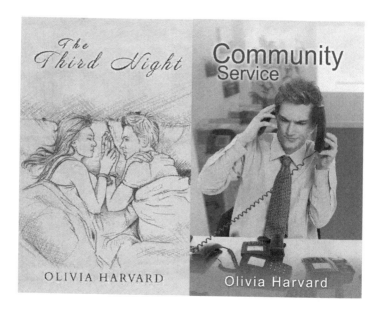

Read more about Nora and Ryderby reading the FREE chapter when you sign up for the author's mailing list!

olivia-harvard.awesomeauthors.org

One

If you have managed to claw your way to your last year of high school, I congratulate you. I really do. Not only is there the expectation that you have to provide a minimum number of hours per subject to study, but there are other expectations, too. Some of them are unspoken, like the fact that you're supposed to have kissed someone by the time you finish high school, or at *least* have been in a relationship. Because even though it isn't a written rule, the student body expects you to have completed it by the time you step up and take your graduation certificate. Other expectations are more vocal.

Like how you're supposed to demonstrate a particular level of maturity because you're suddenly given so much more freedom and opportunities. But when you're seventeen and still have to have a teacher's signature to go to the bathroom, it's arguably difficult. When you have to have permission to wash your hands, how does society expect you to decide what you want to do with your life?

Maybe it's the stress of graduating. Maybe it's the inner child in all of us, demanding release. Maybe it's all the expectations being thrown at us. Either way, the graduating students of Gregory High were definitely not acting like the mature and responsible individuals we were expected to be. "Would you rate his butt a seven or an eight?" Mel whispered.

Our school had been having huge career expositions for all graduating students, just to give us an idea of what our future options were. University professors and highly trained experts from various disciplines presented us with basic information on different courses. The lecture we were attending was hosted by the local police department. The two guys doing most of the talking looked like walking donuts, but at least they had brought along an undeniably fit rookie. "I don't know," I said as I squinted and leaned forward to get a clearer view. "His left butt cheek looks bigger than the right one."

Mel's jade green eyes widened as she leaned forward. "Hey, you're right."

Continuing our brilliant discourse on uneven butt cheeks, we compared it with other various human body parts. Before we knew it, the boring speech about Australian legislation and upholding the law seemed distant as we got lost in our own giggles.

"Officer Brandy, I think Miss Montgomery just volunteered for the demonstration."

Realising I had sunk half way down to the floor in my own laughter, I straightened in my seat, eyes wide. "What?"

Mrs. Coleman was this cranky, old woman, who allegedly had voodoo dolls stuffed in her teacher's pigeon hole. Her dull grey eyes seemed to taunt me with mocking satisfaction as she nodded towards the stage. Thin lips curled into a wicked grin as I grumbled something in gibberish and trudged onto the stage.

I stood between the officers and waited for further instructions. They both smelled like strong coffee and being so close up, I could see a collection of sprinkles on one of the policemen's moustache. My eyes fell down to his chest and caught sight of his golden name tag. His name was Officer Brandy.

"And we need one more volunteer." His deep, booming voice echoed through the large space of the auditorium.

Instantly, everyone tried not to make eye contact. Being up on the podium meant each and every student was exposed to my examination. Guys kept their gazes anywhere but in the direction of the supervising students; up at the ceiling, down at their shoes, across to their friends. The girls had the same idea, hiding behind curtains of hair or suddenly finding an interest in their pleated skirts.

"I think Ryder Collins is interested." The icy tone of Mrs. Coleman sliced through the tension.

At the start of high school, Ryder Collins' popularity came with his varsity jacket, the same way girls got their popularity from their bras. And now that I think about it, when you're twelve and just started high school, I'm not particularly sure how 'cool' you could get. At first, I didn't think it would affect our friendship. But after three months of being on the footy team, he decided to use his position to hoist himself up on the highest possible level of the social ladder. He'd been bathing in fame ever since, while I had been trying to avoid the smallest attentions.

Ryder tossed a filthy look of disgust to his friends, got up and walked towards the stage. He was one of the very few male students that could pull off his uniform. Who would have known clip-on ties and pinstripe trousers could look good on someone under twenty?

I'd like to think that I bloomed in high school too, that I developed into a sophisticated and beautiful woman. But really, I was just as awkward and average as I was when I first started. It was completely infuriating because Ryder was poster boy material. This only added to the uncomfortable tension between us.

"Great," Officer Brandy announced, clapping his meaty hands. "Now, as I was saying, the local police department has designed a new pair of handcuffs. They're made out of metal that is up to three times stronger than the original material, and as you can see, has thicker links."

I watched as he held up the handcuffs and the group of students eyed it in surprising curiosity. He had managed to capture the attention of the class as the jaws of the open cuffs dangled from his fingertips. Thinking it was stupid that everyone was so mesmerised by a pair of handcuffs. I snorted. Ryder must have had the same thoughts because he made an unattractive sound of dissatisfaction, too.

"This particular pair of handcuffs was designed for our plus-sized criminals, so it has more links," he continued, sliding his thick fingers down the long chain. The additional five links were hardly impressive, but by the way Officer Brandy was admiring them, you'd think they were solid gold. "The great thing about these new and improved cuffs is that they're just like houses. Only one key fits per pair. Now, this is only a prototype, so we're extremely fortunate to have the opportunity to feature it on this particular demonstration."

Excited murmurs came from a few members of the audience. Even Mel looked mildly interested. But then I realised she was only excited because Officer Brandy was now circling the stage. Before I could figure out what he was doing, he grabbed hold of my right wrist and snapped on a handcuff. The metal was warm from his hold as it clicked into place.

"What are you *doing?*" I asked, wide eyed.

Mrs. Coleman instantly scolded me for addressing a policeman in such an accusing manner. But I could hardly concentrate on what she was saying, because Officer Brandy had secured the other handcuff around Ryder's left wrist. Panic washed over me, drowning me in complete terror. I looked down at the piece of silver that connected us together and directed my gaze to meet Ryder's faded blue eyes. He looked just about as freaked out as I did.

"Garret, can you please grab the hammer?" Officer Brandy asked as he gently steered us towards a table. "Kids, place your hands on the table."

"We're going to die," I whispered, all sorts of terrible thoughts running through my mind. My stomach tightened to a squeeze and a bitter taste formed in my mouth.

When the hammer was in Officer Brandy's hands, the audience seemed to be holding its collective breath as he lifted the tool into the air. When he slammed the hammer down against the woodwork table with force, a loud, sharp bang of impact echoed through the room like a gunshot. It scared me so much that my heart could have just fallen straight out of my butt. To emphasise his point, Officer Brandy continued to beat the hell out of the metal links that joined Ryder and I together.

After another ten seconds of deafening hits, he placed the hammer down with a clatter and held up the undamaged chain. Impressed claps and a couple of cheers erupted from the students. Even Ryder's entourage seemed pretty impressed and didn't bother to conceal their interest behind their cool expressions. Admittedly, if I weren't contributing to the demonstration, I probably would have been attentive too, because other than the police, the most exciting thing that had ever happened in these career talks was when the science department from the local university made elephant toothpaste. It was something we were all shown in year seven, but that didn't make it any less entertaining.

The bell rang not long after; it was the sweet chime of freedom singing into my ears. As the teachers stood to keep the students tame and explain further instructions, Officer Brandy gave us a grin.

"Thanks for helping out with the demonstration, kids," he said, grabbing his foam cup of coffee and taking a quick drink.

Ryder, obviously getting impatient, held up his wrist, and the chain that bound us yanked my hand up with his. "Can we please go now?"

Officer Brandy lowered the cup from his lips and made a sound of agreement. He placed the cup back onto the table and fumbled around in his pockets. All his pockets. His bushy brows knitted together as he patted himself down and each time he reached in and came out empty handed, my stomach squeezed in both irritation and panic. "Garret, do you have the key?" he called, looking over at his partner. Garret, who had been talking with a few eager students, turned. Shaking his head, he answered, "You had them with you."

Officer Brandy nodded in agreement. "That's what I thought. Hey, Drew, have you seen the key?"

The rookie policeman shook his head as he strode towards us, hands digging into his pockets. "No, Sir."

When Brandy turned to us, he gave us a tight smile. I think it was meant to be reassuring but the way his lips curled, said otherwise. I suddenly felt light headed, my knees about to give way. He didn't have to say anything. His face said it all.

Officer Brandy had lost the key.

Two

I wasn't known for doing anything remotely badass, but being chained to Ryder was making me reevaluate my past motives. I considered doing a miniature protest in the principal's office. But I didn't have a sign and the closest thing available was someone's report card sitting on the desk. So, screaming like a mad woman with someone else's grades in your hands and doing a little *too* enthusiastic fist pump by yourself would have looked a little more ridiculous rather than empowering.

"What do you mean you can't find the key?" I repeated, my blood boiling in fury.

"We did not *lose* the key. It's just been *temporarily misplaced*," Officer Brandy corrected me for the seventh time, running a hand through his thick, brown hair. "We have a search party on the case."

In other words, Officer Garret was searching the police car while a few extra staff swept through the auditorium. I had been stuck with

Ryder all afternoon and we were seconds away from the final school bell. And though I was standing there, hand on my hips and glaring at the adults in outrage, Ryder was perfectly cosy sitting on the armrest of the small leather couch in the corner of the office. He had his third can of orange soda in his hands; complimentary from the police department because of the inconvenience.

"Listen here, you incompetent fool," I growled, pointing an accusing finger at him like a scowling mother, surprised at how sassy I was being. "I am chained to *Ryder Collins*. We have a past and I'm not particularly comfortable with the situation you have burdened us with. So, if I'm not released in the next hour, *I will sue you.*"

To be completely honest, I wasn't sure I was completely clear with the definition of 'incompetent' and I wasn't sure *how* to sue anyone, but with enough unspoken television show addictions, my vocabulary had expanded. Besides, out loud, it sounded pretty legit.

Mrs. Westfield, the principal, slid her glasses up her nose and narrowed her eyes at me. "Miss Montgomery," she warned, "watch how you address your elders."

Officer Brandy seemed more interested in what I had said, rather than what I had called him. His caterpillar eyebrows rose up to his hairline. "A past?" he questioned, eyes flicking from Ryder to me and back. "Bad relationship?"

I shivered in disgust and Ryder choked on his drink. Wiping his mouth from the orange splutter on his lips, he said, "As much as I'd like to date someone as predictable and petty as Nora Montgomery, it's with deep sympathy that I have *not* had the pleasure of being in a relationship with her."

"I think you meant *pretty*," I snapped.

"I really didn't."

My eyes met his raging blue ones and I gave him a look that could kill. But before I could shoot back a witty remark, the door to the principal's office swung open. Officer Garret looked flustered. His cheeks had bloomed into a rosy pink and his hair was tousled from the winter wind outside. He looked at us all, pulled his sagging trousers over his beer belly and marched into the room. My stomach tightened as I held my breath and waited to listen for the search update.

"I've thoroughly examined the police cruiser and there was no sign of the keys," he announced grimly.

I clenched my fists and narrowed my eyes at the officers. This was ridiculous. What kind of policemen were they? They couldn't even keep track of a key! Anger flamed inside me as I grinded my teeth together, trying to compress another round of harsh words threatening to slip out. Mrs. Westfield's lips pursed into a tight line as she exchanged quick glances with the police officers. Placing her hands on the desk in front of her, she pushed back the leather office chair and paced around the small space of her office. You could practically see the unspoken tension and frustration that simmered in the room as everyone brainstormed resolutions to our situation.

Then there was a knock on the door and the discomfort momentarily lifted as we all directed our attention to who it was. There was a moment of fumbling outside before a happy little boy walked in. He wore a dinosaur backpack and was carrying a small box of rocks. It was Sam, Mrs. Westfield's nephew. He was a mixture of strange and adorable and was going through an obsessive phase of being a palaeontologist. Really, it was probably just an excuse to get his hands dirty, but who was I to judge his childhood motives? Some kids liked playing dress-ups with their parents' clothing, some kids liked cooking mud pies in the kitchen and other kids liked collecting rocks –some of which were evidently mouse poop, but he was five and didn't know the difference.

Mrs. Westfield smiled at Sam. His mother constantly dropped him off for play dates and he was around the school a lot, usually accompanying Mrs. Westfield while she roamed the school halls in search of reasons to give out detention slips. However, that particular afternoon, she seemed clearly irritated by the added responsibility of looking after him and although she smiled, it didn't quite reach her eyes.

"Any suggestions on how to carry out the situation?" Mrs Westfield asked, directing her attention back to the policemen.

While the adults were talking strategies, Sam pulled out his rock collection. He popped the lid open and took a small rock, smaller than a fingernail, out of its compartment. Then, with complete and utter excitement, he held it up in his palm for us to examine. Up close, it looked exactly like a little chocolate drop. It took another few seconds of observation before I realised, to my delight, that Sam was showcasing a mouse dropping.

"Oh, look, Ryder," I smirked, "he's showing you his collection of faeces. You should be able to decipher which dropping comes from which species. You come from a family of animals, don't you?"

He lowered the can of citrus fizz and raised an eyebrow at me. "Gee, Nora, that's rich, coming from the bitch of the pack."

And that's when the claws came out. We snapped and hissed at each other, growling out insults and witty remarks. Ryder's denim eyes seemed to darken; intense fury stirring up like a stormy sea within his blue irises. And I guess we were so distracted, we didn't realise Sam was trying to get our attention.

Ryder opened his mouth to say something, but Mrs. Westfield beat him to it. "We're just going to have to pick the lock," she announced, rummaging around through her drawers.

She pulled out two little screwdrivers. The metal was long and thin with gold handles. Handing one over to each of the policemen, they examined the tools sceptically, doubt filling their eyes. I wasn't sure if it was because they were questioning why our principal had a small kit of tools in her office or if they were hesitant of the strength of them. But eventually, Officer Brandy exchanged a look with his partner and shrugged. Together they headed over to us.

Sam had trotted over to the bookshelf, innocently gazing up at the dark tower of novels. The slightly empty box of rocks sat on the floor of the office.

Drawing my attention back to the police officers, I said, "How long will this take?"

"Not long, Miss Montgomery," Officer Brandy answered, sounding like he was trying to convince himself more than me. "Just be patient."

I said nothing more as I watched him kneel down in front of me, taking the tiny handle of the tool in his big hand and wedging it into the keyhole. Well, at least, he *tried* to. Frowning, he attempted a second time to push it in, but still, something was blocking him off.

Tossing the screwdriver onto the coffee table, he leaned in and squinted at the keyhole. Instantly, I felt uncomfortable with how close his face was to my hand. I mean, what if my wrist smelled or something? It was possible; adolescents are known for sweating, particularly in weird places. What if he was secretly some creep with a wrist fetish? Some people have unbelievable fixations. It started creeping me out.

"There seems to be something wedged inside here," Officer Brandy called to his partner, scratching his head in confusion.

"Yeah, I've got the same problem here."

Fantastic.

At first, the policemen didn't say anything. They continued to squint and stare, probing at the keyholes, directing their flashlights to the handcuffs so they could see a little clearer.But after a few tense minutes of having no progress, Brandy sat back on his heels and scrubbed a hand down his face. His companion, Garret, was staring at the small, empty compartments of Sam's rock box.

"Sam," Officer Garret called, "is this your rock collection?"

looked up with wide Bambi eyes. He was as still as an animal in the headlights, waiting for the policeman to continue to determine his own reaction. Garret walked over and knelt down in front of him, looking at him with kind eyes, trying to silently convince him to 'fess up.

"Yes," Sam finally admitted, looking down as he gave a little nod.

"Have you been messing around with the handcuffs?" he pressed.

Sam looked up at him, eyebrows drawn together, bottom lip jutted out.

His face answered the question.

"Great." Ryder frowned in irritation, twisting the metal ring on his can until it came off. "So, there are rocks in there?"

"I don't even think half of those were rocks. Sam seemed pretty enthusiastic showing us bits of dried up poop," I piped up, cringing at the thought.

"Even better."

Ryder shook his wrist in an attempt to let them drop out, but they were jammed in pretty deep and nothing but a little dust came out. He groaned.

"Isn't there anything else we can do? The design and technology block has some saws. We could cut through the links and worry about the cuffs later," I suggested.

Brandy and Garret exchanged wary expressions.

"Thing is, it was a prototype," Brandy explained, looking at us sheepishly. I tried to tame the roaring wave of anger that was causing my cheeks to flame. "The *only* prototype."

"And you brought it to a *high school* demonstration?" I answered through clenched teeth.

My irritation was evident through my voice. Ryder's annoyance was showcased through his expression of displeasure. And Mrs. Westfield's temple-rubbing was self-explanatory. Being handcuffed caused numerous problems. But being handcuffed and not having a solution caused an infinite list of issues to arise. How long would we have to be stuck at school? How were we supposed to shower? Whose house we were meant to sleep at?

"So what's going to happen?" Ryder questioned.

"Chief is currently out of town so we aren't authorised to do anything more. Can you guys survive the night? I'm sure after a good night's sleep and some thinking, we can get you kids out of this mess in no time."

Ryder made a sound of dissatisfaction.

"I'm not happy about this either, Ryder, but being an ass isn't going to make this better," I warned.

"You're such a nun sometimes. Swear once in a while. We're teenagers; it's like our language," Ryder snorted in response. Tossing the can into the little bin in the corner, he added, "Speaking of language, nature is calling."

My eyes widened. "No. You *cannot* go to the bathroom," I shrieked in horror. "Cross your legs or something."

He gave me an exasperated look. "In case you haven't already noticed, *we don't share the same genitals.* Crossing my legs does nothing."

"Well, figure it out because I am *not* going into the bathroom with you."

I ended up going to the men's bathroom with him.

He half dragged me there by the handcuffs until I was breathing in the stuffy, clogged air of the room. The unpleasant stench hit my nose and suffocated me with its foul odour, making my throat close up and splutter for oxygen.

Ryder marched over to one of the urinals while I reluctantly followed. Then came the awkwardness. Once he had picked the urinal in the left corner, he turned and just stared at me. At first, I didn't meet his eyes. I looked around uncomfortably. But then I realised he was staring at me so I'd look away.

"Oh," I said, finally understanding, "right, I'll just... go over here."

I took a step away and turned in the opposite direction so my back was towards him. We were still chained together so that gave me limited escape space. There were a few seconds of silence before Ryder's zipper being pulled down broke through the silence like a fart. Even though I wasn't watching, I still felt extremely awkward.

And I suddenly had the urge to talk or laugh or burp. Anything to distract me.

"So, the other day, I heard this really great joke abo-"

"Nora, I'm busy right now," he said, cutting me off. "Can you annoy me with your jokes when I'm done?"

I opened my mouth to shoot back a reply when the sound of Ryder's pee shooting into the urinal made me stop. It was so loud in the deserted bathroom and I was going crazy, desperately needing a distraction. And it was as if my silent pleading had been heard by the universe and triggered some kid's bladder because a second later, a boy from the year below me walked into the bathroom.

At first, when he saw me, confusion washed over his face. His expression was giving off the holy-crap-did-I-just-walk-into-the-girls'-bathrooms vibe but his eyes were saying stuff-it-dude-you-really-gotta-go. Eventually, he realised he was in the right bathroom, but didn't dare question what I was doing there.

"What's up?" I asked, needing to talk.

He kept his gaze away and walked over, completely ignoring my question.

"Choose wisely," I continued, unable to stop myself. "This could change your life...*forever*."

Eventually, he looked over at me, completely pained. "You're really creeping me out. Who *are* you?"

"Toilet troll." I was really just making things worse.

"Seriously. *Who are you?*"

"I'm a senior. Do not question my superiority."

Digging yourself deeper, Nora.

"You know what, I think I can hold it," the kid answered, backing towards the door.

When he disappeared Ryder said, "You sure have a thing with the guys."

Then he led me towards the sinks. As he turned on the taps and washed his hands, I realised being handcuffed to Ryder wouldn't just be a pain in the ass, but would cause a whole lot of awkward situations, especially within the bathroom.

Great.

Three

When Mrs. Westfield announced she had a headache, they all agreed that it would be best to put the situation on hold until the following morning. The adults seemed to have no problem getting back to their normal routines, like none of the handcuff business ever happened. Ryder and I, on the other hand, weren't so fortunate to forget the issue.

"Suck in your butt cheeks!" Ryder ordered, awkwardly trying to push on my backside.

We were in a seriously uncomfortable position. There I was, my butt casually hanging out the driver's side of his little Porsche while he was screaming at me to suck my bum cheeks in. Since our wrists were still chained together, my hand was on the driver's side chair. Ryder's hand forced to move with mine, so we were pretty much cheek to cheek. Well, butt cheek to face cheek anyway.

We had been yelling at each other for ten minutes, just trying to squeeze into the compact space of the vehicle. The guy had obviously never been in the situation I was in, because he evidently didn't know how impossible it was to suck in your butt cheeks.

"Ryder," I said, attempting to clench my backside muscles together, "I'm trying to suck it, okay? I mean, I'm sucking in places I didn't even know I could suck."

He shoved my butt one last time and sighed, finally taking his hand off me. I crawled out of the little space of his car, ungracefully knocking my elbow into the chair and accidentally smacking my hand onto the horn. When I was out, I rolled my chained wrist, trying to relieve the pain it was going through.

"We need to take a bus," I declared. "Admit it, we aren't going to fit into your little Batmobile."

"We can't just leave my baby here," he argued, running his hand over the sleek, black coat of his car.

"How do you suggest we go home then?" I hissed, getting more irritated by the second.

Ryder looked over his shoulder just to glare at me before his fingers slowly slid off the car's edge. Reluctantly, he picked up his bag from the top of his Porsche and swung it over his shoulder. He looked extremely displeased, but he knew it was the only way to get out of there.

Together, we caught the next bus and started on our way home. Well, to *my* home. We agreed it would be best if we went to my house for the night, while my parents were on a week-long vacation for their anniversary. So, while they were experiencing the heat and beautiful cities of Europe, I was playing prisoner.

It was a short ride home, considering it was the last bus and didn't have many people. We departed the vehicle on the fourth stop, right at the corner of my street. A few primary students had gotten off the bus with us. As soon as their feet hit the footpath, they raced down the hill, squealing in joy. I watched and smiled, remembering when Ryder and I used to do the exact same thing.

"Remember how Mr. Nelson used to yell at us when we raced down this hill?" Ryder piped in, as if he had been having flashbacks of our childhood friendship, too.

"I remember," I answered, a grin stretching out over my face. "He used to come out in his bathrobe and fluffy slippers just to wave his newspaper around and scream at us."

Ryder let out a chuckle, the kind of deep, passionate laugh that rumbled in his throat and reached his eyes. "Man, that guy had problems."

For a brief thirty seconds, the popular, arrogant footy player I had gone through hell in high school with, dimmed down to the sweet, friendly guy I used to call my best friend. Not that I ever expected our friendship to rekindle, but it was a pleasant memory.

"Speak of the devil," I said, directing my attention back to the road and nodding ahead where Mr. Nelson was charging towards the kids in his white bathrobe, newspaper in hand. "He's probably going to yell the fun right out of those kids."

We watched as he waved the rolled newspaper in his curled fist like an angry member of a mob. His slippers slapped against the path as he ran towards the kids. But, to my surprise, he completely passed them, hardly acknowledging their 'annoying disturbance' -as he described it to us as kids- and charged on ahead. Eyes widening, I realised he was aiming towards us, determined, icy eyes glaring.

I froze just as Ryder did. "What's he do-"

And that's when Mr. Nelson tackled us to the ground. He screamed like a madman as he grabbed Ryder and threw him to the floor. Because I was chained to him, I went crashing down with them, rolling around on the grass of a random yard as our limbs tangled.

My face was pressed into someone's armpit, arms and legs intertwined with the other two bodies. Gasping for air, I popped my head out of the mess in time to see Mr. Nelson straddling Ryder and smacking him with the newspaper.

"Criminal! Criminal!" he yelled, as he continued to slap him.

"Nora!" Ryder yelled desperately. "I don't think he's wearing anything under that robe!"

"Mary! Call the police!" Mr. Nelson ordered as his wife came rushing up with a tray of cookies in her hands. "These must be the criminals they've been talking about on the radio!"

"George," Mrs. Nelson soothed, "those are high school kids, not jailbreak prisoners. Get off them this instant."

Her voice was soft, but compelling and Mr. Nelson found himself rolling off Ryder's back in a heartbeat. When he thought his wife wasn't watching, he smacked the back of Ryder's head once more before fully standing to adjust his robe. Mrs. Nelson shoved the tray of cookies into her husband's hands and hurried over to help us up.

Once we were on our feet and brushed the dirt off our uniforms, Mrs. Nelson grabbed a few warm cookies from her tray and handed them over.

"I'm sorry about him, dears," she said, as we took them from her fragile hands. "He's been obsessing over these silly police reports. It's been scaring all the kids around here for weeks."

I nibbled on the cookie while Mrs. Nelson complained about her husband. The dough was warm and moist, the sweet sensation engulfing me in a wave of delight as I continued to munch on the treat. Melted bites of chocolate oozed out of the cookie like sugary lava. Once I had finished, I licked the crumbs and chocolate stains off my fingers and looked over at Ryder; his cookie long gone.

"Well, we should be off," she said after ranting, pinching our cheeks before rushing off to Mr. Nelson.

As we watched them depart, Ryder mumbled, "Damn, that was one amazing cookie..."

I nodded in agreement and we continued on our way back home. We didn't repeat the Mr. Nelson incident. It was as if the cookies had washed away any weirdness and had settled with a reassuring calmness in our stomachs. It made me wonder what Mrs. Nelson had put in them.

The walk home was quiet and short, passing a total of twelve houses until we reached mine. Once we opened the door and entered, the soothing sound of an instructor on TV sang into my ears. Tugging Ryder along, we headed towards the lounge room where Eve was.

There she was, on her back, rolling around like a turtle that had gotten stuck on its shell. What looked even more stupid was her beach ball belly just poking out in all its eight-month-pregnancy glory. My sister made some weird sounds that resembled a whale dying before she looked up and spotted us.

She struggled to get to her feet, having to grab onto various bits of furniture so she could haul herself up. But once she was standing, she placed a hand on her lower back and the other on her stomach to keep her balance. Eve looked at us for a moment, her blonde hair falling out of her ponytail and her cheeks kissed with a rosy pink.

"Nora," she said, a little breathlessly, "you've kind of got a little something-something chained to your wrist."

Thanks for noticing.

"*Really?*" I replied sarcastically. "I didn't realise."

Eve rolled her eyes at me and approached us, waddling around awkwardly until she reached where we were standing. She examined Ryder for a second before poking him on the shoulder. "Hey, you're the Collins kid."

Ryder remained still, watching her with a mixture of curiosity and fright.

Before he could reply, Eve's eyes suddenly went wide. Her hazel irises blew up until her eyes looked like they didn't even fit her face anymore. She looked like a cartoon character you'd see on a Sunday morning TV show. Then, she did the weirdest thing.

She started *smelling* Ryder.

"Eve!" I hissed in embarrassment. "*What* are you doing?"

"I smell ham!" she replied, latching onto Ryder's bag like a crazed fangirl. "I haven't had ham in months."

He quickly shrugged off his backpack and tossed it over to my sister. Eve continued to rummage through his things until she found a ham sandwich. Shoving his belongings back into his arms, Eve cooed at the snack in delight and disappeared into the kitchen, inhaling the smell. Along with her weird cravings and ability to eat *a lot* of it, pregnancy meant she had to cut back on a lot of foods to ensure the best nutrition for her child. So, instead, she'd smell/sight hump the delicacies she couldn't eat.

"Your sister is so weird," Ryder grumbled, zipping up his bag.

"It's just the pregnancy. She eats everything now and acts like an animal."

"No," Ryder corrected, "she was weird before then too."

It was sad, but true so I didn't bother defending my sister. Once we had reached the top of the stairs, we entered my room. My really messy room. I cringed at the piles of clothes that covered the floor and the unmade bed. Realising there was a random bra hanging on the edge of my desk chair, I latched onto it, pulling Ryder along with me.

He grunted from the unexpected force and scanned my room. "You haven't changed."

I saw a flash of remembrance spark up in his faded blue eyes. And even though his lips didn't arc into a smile, I could almost, faintly, see the memory in his cerulean eyes. But once I blinked, his eyes were back to their normal; a casual stare of boredom.

"So, where am I supposed to sleep tonight?" he questioned, casually sweeping his hand towards my bed.

It was going to be a long night. A really long night.

Four

Eve used to hate tomato sauce... Well, that's until she got pregnant. Then she started drinking it like water. I watched in captivated disgust as she reached over, grabbed the bottle and squirted it over her chicken salad. Once her salad was no longer *green*, she placed the bottle back down and picked up her fork.

Patrick, Eve's boyfriend, looked down at her saucy bowl. "Honey, our baby is going to come out a tomato if you keep this up," he teased.

Eve rolled her eyes and shoved a fork full of tomato covered lettuce into her mouth. Since my parents were on holiday, they decided to give the responsibility of me to my sister. My mother insisted that it would be the perfect opportunity to practice taking care of a child, because apparently newborn babies and seventeen-year-olds are the same: we both eat, sleep, and cry a lot. Patrick was probably the only person that was keeping us all sane. He was a part time music teacher at the local primary school and spent his weekends singing for old people at the nursing homes. He didn't make much money, but he was happy, and he made Eve happy too.

As always, he started the topic at the dinner table. "So, why are you two handcuffed again? Is this some sort of high school partner-trusting exercise?"

"No," Eve answered before I could. "Police department handcuffed them together for a demo during their career speech, and then they lost the key."

Patrick sighed. "That's going to stir up some paparazzi, especially with all the advances in social media. Police never do that kind of thing and it's going to attract the public."

There's that saying that everyone gets fifteen minutes of fame. I had always questioned the statement, but being handcuffed to Ryder suddenly turned the tables. I wondered if the media would camp outside my house overnight and wait until morning to snap a quick picture of us like we were celebrities. Well, the word *celebrities* was a bit of a stretch. More like abnormalities.

I wondered if my parents would find out and how they would react. Just because they were halfway across the globe didn't mean they didn't have access to the internet. And because of social media, it'd take mere hours for the news to travel. Would they decide to come home? Would they sue?

How were parents meant to react to this type of situation?

Eve and Patrick seemed unaffected. I mean, I guess Ryder and I weren't exposed to any physical injury or anything. The handcuffs were just a nuisance, a constant discomfort. They appeared to have total faith that the issue would be resolved without their participation. I wish I shared that thought.

"So, do you kids know what you want to do after graduation?" Patrick must have sensed the discomfort and tried to switch up the atmosphere.

"I don't know," I answered truthfully, dropping half a cherry tomato into my mouth. "I want to travel, *then* go to university to study."

Patrick grinned in approval. He had been all over the world after he finished high school, from the busy streets of Tokyo, to the paradise of Fiji. "You have to go to Florida. It's beautiful."

I did some kind of half nod, half shrug at him. Just as I was about to scoop an uncooked noodle into my mouth, Ryder decided to pick up the salt shaker from the centre of the table and sprinkle his salad. And since I was chained to his left hand, his jerking wrist made mine jolt, too, until I looked like I was having a seizure.

My shaking hand flew bits of my dinner across the table. "Ryder!"

I watched as a piece of baby spinach flung off the tip of my fork and landed on Eve's belly. She must have mistaken it for something else, because she started screaming like a madwoman. I rolled my eyes as she flapped her arms. Seriously. It was a bit of spinach. Did she think the *vegetable leaf* was going to attack her?

"What the hell is that?" she squealed. "Patrick!"

"Honey," her boyfriend soothed, picking up my dinner from her stomach. "It's a piece of spinach."

"Oh." Eve stopped her flapping and reached over, eating the leaf right off his hand. "Why didn't you say so?"

Good God, my sister is weird.

Patrick coughed and wiped his hand on his work trousers before smiling at Ryder, continuing our conversation like Eve hadn't just eaten from his palm like a horse. "What about you, man? Any plans after graduation?"

Ryder placed the salt back down. "I got offered a scholarship to Oxford."

I nearly choked on a noodle. "*What?*"

Ryder looked at me like I was stupid. "Oxford. England. I dunno, I guess I'll crash with a few cousins."

"What are you gonna study? Alcohol and the female anatomy?".

"Nora," Eve warned, glaring at me from across the table.

I mean, Ryder wasn't the smartest cookie in the jar. In year seven, he decided to become an astronaut. He thought he could fart hard enough to blast him off to the moon—he was incredibly proud of his famous Silent but Deadly ones. And even though that was the same year our friendship ended, I didn't have much faith that his maturity had developed all that much since then.

"No," Ryder said, looking at me seriously for once. "I'm going to study law."

"I didn't know you were into that stuff."

He shrugged. "You don't really know me at all, Nora."

What Ryder had said at dinner replayed in my head like a broken record. I didn't even know why. I mean, it was true. We hadn't been friends for five years. He had changed and developed and so had I. But this distant storm of emotion stirred inside me, making me regret what had happened to us. And somewhere dark in the back of my mind, I wondered what we would be like if we hadn't fought that night.

"You're either thinking really hard, or you gotta go to the toilet." The sound of Ryder's voice broke me from my trance.

I frowned at him. "Shut up."

He raised an eyebrow at me, but turned his attention back to the flickering television. The faint, blue glow of the screen illuminated Ryder's face, casting shadows against his defined cheekbones. Realising I was staring, I frowned and tore my eyes away. I gazed blankly at the motion pictures that passed the screen and almost instantly, the remorse of losing our friendship dimmed until there was no trace of it left.

"When are you kids going to bed?" Eve had two boxes of Oreos in her hands, dark crumbs sprinkled across her face.

"Soon," I mumbled.

"Well, don't forget to fill up Marshmallow's bowl in the morning. He'll be out of water by then," she reminded me, before quietly shuffling upstairs.

"You feed your marshmallows?" Ryder asked, smirking.

"Marshmallow is my cat. Well, we think he's a cat."

"What do you mean you *think* he's a cat?"

"He's got too much hair to tell."

Ryder's lips arched into half a smile, but he didn't say anything. Slowly, he craned his neck back towards the television and ran a hand through his messy, dark hair. A yawn escaped his lips as he sunk himself deeper into the lounge, his eyes drooping as he gazed blankly at the screen. Sleepy Ryder was kind of scary. No witty remarks or childish insults. It left us in this awkward bubble of silence.

"I'm sleepy," I announced, shifting in my seat as I searched for the remote.

Ryder groaned sleepily in agreement.

Switching the television off, I stood and waited for him to follow. He lazily stood, stretched, and allowed me to lead the way. As we passed the lights, Ryder flicked them off, except for the motion-censored one in the foyer—we kept it on so people could find their way into the kitchen for midnight snacks. It surprised me that I didn't have to give him the instructions to do it. He had remembered the drill from years ago. I smiled slightly as we headed towards the staircase.

As we ascended up the stairs, Ryder's butt started making noises. And vibrating. I pointed to him. "Your ass is singing."

He tossed me a filthy look before he reached into the back pocket of his pants and pulled out his phone. He scanned the screen for the caller ID, and then reluctantly pressed the phone to his ear.

"Hey, Mum," he greeted, sounding less than enthusiastic. He paused for a moment, waiting for a reply. "I know. I'm at a mate's house."

I made a gagging sound when he said 'mate'. When we reached my room, his eyes narrowed into slits. Pushing the door open, I stepped inside, Ryder following close behind.

"I'm doing... a school project. No, not with Caine. No. Yes, a girl," he continued, then made an unattractive half grunt, half snort. "I guess. What do you mean that's not an answer?" Ryder groaned softly, then tilted his face away, whispering. "Okay, maybe she's kind of pretty. But what does that matter?"

I elbowed him in the stomach and he groaned from the impact. Then, as he listened to his mother's reply, he straightened, eyes widening. "Mum," he hissed, lowering his voice, "we aren't doing anything—*Mum.*"

Sounds like a pleasant conversation.

"Yes, yes, I know. Okay, yeah," he mumbled. He quickly looked up at me then lowered his voice again and said in a rush, "I love you too. Okay, bye."

Puffing his chest out, he glared down at me. Ryder was about a foot taller, towering at over six feet. Then there was me, the same size of a lawn gnome. However, after the phone call with his mother, Ryder seemed to think he just lost a thousand macho points, so puffing up like a cheese ball while doing his best manly stare at me was his attempt at gaining his lost masculinity.

I refrained from rolling my eyes and tugged him towards my bed.

We had set up Ryder's bed space before dinner. A spare blanket was sprawled out on the floor as well as my sleeping bag. Slowly, we carefully dropped into our places. My arm awkwardly dangled from the side of my bed, skimming against the floor as it rested close to Ryder's, fingertips inches away. It was an awkward position to sleep in and difficult to get comfortable, but I managed to find the most tolerable spot.

Closing my eyes, I instantly drifted into that lazy stage between consciousness and dreaming. It had been an extremely long and tiring day and I wanted to rest. But just as I was about to fall into a deep slumber, a loud snort erupted from Ryder.

Guess some things never change.

As predicted, it was already looking like an extremely long night.

Five

Sharing a bathroom with my sister is hell. But sharing the bathroom with Ryder is worse.

The following morning, we were in the bathroom together, shoving and pushing each other as we tried to get as much reflection view as possible. My muscles ached everywhere from having to sleep in the same position all night. My body was tense and I really needed a shower. But we were meant to get out of the handcuffs by the time school was over, so I decided I'd wait until I was alone.

When we finally stopped battling by the sink, Ryder rubbed some shaving cream onto the stubble that had magically grown on his chin overnight and picked up the new razor we had stolen from my parents' bathroom. While he was busy carefully gliding the razor over his stubble, I picked up an eyebrow wax strip and leaned in towards the mirror to get a better look at my eyes.

It was stupid and risky and I probably would have had better luck *shaving* my eyebrows into shape, but I wasn't thinking. I couldn't stop thinking that we'd be treated like the Kardashians and have journalists with microphones and cameras stalking us as soon as we left the house. I didn't want to be in the newspaper in general. But being in the newspaper *with one giant eyebrow* didn't sound very appealing either. A picture says a thousand words after all.

Tearing off the back, I slowly aimed the strip at the bush on my brow. But just as I was about to carefully put it in place, Ryder decided he wanted to feel how baby-butt-soft his jaw had become. His left hand shot out to stroke his face, causing my steady fingers to yank in his direction and accidentally plaster the wax strip halfway down my eyebrow.

"Ryder!" I squealed in horror as I squinted at the wax strip firmly planted in place.

He took one look at my panicked expression and burst out laughing. Frowning, I slapped his hand, causing him to lose his grip on the razor. It went flying into the air and landed in the toilet bowl with a splash. That would teach him to always put the lid down. He growled in annoyance.

"I wasn't finished yet!" he hissed.

Just at that moment, Eve burst in through the bathroom, a jumbo tub of Nutella in one hand and a giant spoon the size of an ice-cream scoop in the other.

"I can hear you guys fighting from downstairs. You're going to be late if you keep it up," she said, licking the chocolate spread off her huge spoon. When she finally got a good look at us, she added, "Why did you decide to wax half your eyebrow off? And why did you only shave half your face?"

Silently, Ryder and I glared at each other.

"Listen, if you guys want a ride, I'm leaving in fifteen minutes," Eve said before turning and strutting away.

"I can't wait to get out of these handcuffs," I grumbled.

Ryder took another quick glance into the mirror and sighed at his reflection. "Guess there's no time to finish shaving."

"At least your issue is resolvable. What the hell am *I* supposed to do? Glue on a new eyebrow?"

"If you're desperate." He shrugged and quickly rinsed the remaining shaving cream from his face while I looked at the perfectly bald space where my eyebrow had once been.

"It's not like I buy spare eyebrows on eBay and have them randomly sitting around my house in case one of my real ones goes missing," I hissed, rubbing my forehead. "What am I meant to do now? Just *draw* one? Oh my God. I can *draw* my eyebrow on."

I probably had better ideas but I was cold and tired and hadn't changed clothes for twenty four hours.

"What do you mean we have to wait a week for further instructions?" I snapped, my blood boiling in fury.

We had skipped half of our first lesson and wasted it on unproductive arguments in the principal's office. As always, the room smelt like strong coffee, an exotic mixture of freshly ground beans and stained breath. The office was warm and the seat I occupied was heated too, as if someone's butt had warmed it prior to our arrival.

Cool and collected, Mrs. Westfield, looked at us over her glasses. Her dirty blonde hair was tied up in a neat bun, a few silvery aged strands glittering in the weak, winter morning sunlight. Her lips pursed - an unconscious habit of hers, even if she wasn't frustrated - and she answered.

"Officer Brandy, Officer Garrett, and I have contacted the head chief and have been strictly notified to wait a week until he has returned from vacation. We are unauthorised to take any further action," she explained.

"Isn't it a legal requirement for policemen to help citizens in need? I mean, that's what they've been trained to do. It's their responsibility to resolve problems immediately, not postpone them!" Ryder, too, obviously had no shame in expressing his anger.

"Mr. Collins, as I have said multiple times, the police department has much more serious cases to investigate. It is expected, as young adults, that you handle the situation in a mature and sophisticated manner." Our principal effortlessly gave us an intimidating stare, almost challenging us to further press on the topic.

A challenge I accepted. "It's outrageous, though. Wouldn't you feel the exact same way if you were in our position?" I retorted, unable to control my temper. "I mean, look! I didn't sleep at all due to his snoring, I haven't showered in over twenty-four hours, and I only have half an eyebrow. *Half an eyebrow.*"

Mrs. Westfield briefly glanced at my drawn-on eyebrow, picked up her pen and started scribbling down on some documents laid out neatly in front of her. "You're late enough. I think it's time you went to class."

She picked up a pre-written late slip and tossed it over without looking up or lifting her pen from the paper. Snatching the note, we stood up from the rough leather chairs and stormed out of the staff's premises. The main block was on the other side of the school, so we made a shortcut through the quad.

"Damn, it's freezing. This day doesn't get any better, does it?" Ryder grumbled through gritted teeth as the harsh, wintery winds whipped our bare skin until it was tender.

"You look cold, Nora."

I looked over my shoulder at the sound of my name. There, standing on the other side of the quad, was Chris Baker. We had this 'thing' - a ridiculous noun Mel used to describe the situation - going on for almost a month. Mostly shameless flirting and little teases. Although he wasn't on Ryder's elite level of popularity, he was generally well known and loved. With his dreamy brown eyes and sandy hair, it was hard *not* to like him.

"Yeah, I am."

Chris shot me a heart-warming smile, sending shivers of pleasure running through me. As he neared, he probably would have noticed a few things. One, I was handcuffed to another person. And two, I had a drawn-on eyebrow. If he noticed, he didn't say - or even do - anything that suggested it.

"Here," Chris said, shrugging off his blazer, "take this."

I reached out and took his blazer. The fabric was warm as I slid an arm though and awkwardly tried to balance the other half on my shoulder. Although we were ages away from the beach, he always seemed to smell like the ocean. It was refreshing and comforting, the scent lingering on his jacket.

"Thanks." I offered a smile that he returned.

"We should go," Ryder grunted, his faded blue eyes meeting Chris' in a glare. They held each other's stare for a few tense seconds before Ryder tugged me along.

"Wait." Chris took hold of my arm, gentle but firm.

He looked over my shoulder at Ryder, his brown eyes almost challenging him. I didn't have to turn around to know that Ryder was returning the same death glare. Whatever was going on between the two was intense and I suddenly felt uncomfortable being in the middle of so much testosterone.

Chris' eyes swooped down to mine and they turned back into the warm pools of rich chocolate. He smiled and slowly removed his hand from my arm, fingers trailing a hot tingle down my skin.

"I was wondering what you were doing tomorrow night," Chris said.

It was the moment I had been waiting for. Pictures of luxurious dinners and romantic walks in the moonlight flashed through my mind, followed by one of those sweet, soft kisses you only see in the movies.

"There's this new pizza parlour down Main Street. They're meant to have the best stuffed crust," Chris continued. "Do you want to, maybe, grab a slice with me?"

Sure, pizza wasn't a part of the romantic picture I had planned out, but I wasn't complaining. I tried to bite back the grin that was threatening to spread across my face and strained to pull a casual expression.

"Yeah, sure." I tried to play it cool, but my high-pitch chipmunk voice kind of killed my nonchalance.

"Cool," he answered, grinning as he backed away and did one of those guy points at me. "I'll pick you up at seven."

I sighed dreamily as he sauntered away and slowly floated alongside Ryder. We walked towards the main building in silence. I could hardly notice the cold because the warmth of Chris' jacket resting on my shoulders. If I were in a normal state, the material of his blazer probably wouldn't have done any good in protecting me from the strong winds, but my happiness blocked out any negativity.

"He's not worth it, you know." The sound of Ryder's voice broke through the silence and bruised my happy bubble a little.

"Just because you guys aren't friends, doesn't mean he's a bad guy. In fact, seeing as he *isn't* your friend, means he's *definitely* not a bad guy."

Ryder looked down at me, all tall and built and even though I was much shorter, I tried to look just as intimidating. "Don't you know what kind of guy he is? He's going to play you, Nora."

"Jealous much?" I sneered. "Why should you care who I date?"

His stern face didn't falter. All he did was raise an eyebrow at me. "Don't come running to me when he breaks your heart."

There was seriousness in his tone and for a brief second, I saw my ex-best friend's soft, caring eyes. But it was probably just the weak winter light playing tricks on his sky coloured irises.

Six

"**I'll** have that, thank you, Mr. Collins," our history teacher, Mr. Kansas, snatched the note from Ryder's fingers just as he was about to slip it back to his friend. He gave Ryder a wicked grin of cruel satisfaction as he marched back up to the classroom. Ryder made a grunt and said a range of colourful language, to which our teacher scowled at in disgust. Mr. Kansas unfolded the thick piece of textured paper Ryder had ripped out from his sketch diary.

"Have you touched her boobs yet?" Mr. Kansas read out loud to the class.

This sparked up snickers and giggles chorusing through the class. Caine and Ryder exchanged cocky sneers, sharing some kind of best-bud telepathic bond. Mr. Kansas, on the other hand, wasn't as amused as the rest of us. He crunched up the note in his big hands and glared down at the boys.

"I'm glad you boys have a good sense of humour. I'm sure you'll find detention this afternoon just as hilarious."

That wiped the smirks off their faces. Ryder replaced his cocky grin with a scowl of displeasure, leaning back in his chair and as he glared at the teacher. Caine looked just as frustrated and decided to find entertainment in his click-y pen.

"Ha, ha," I whispered mockingly, jabbing him in the arm.

"Shut up, Nora," he hissed back, poking me with his pen. "If you haven't forgotten, you're still chained to me."

Dammit.

"Whatever," I scowled in defeat, sinking into my chair.

"And that concludes the history of the Russian Revolution," Mr. Kansas finished, placing the textbook he was gathering information from down onto his desk.

The bell rang seconds after his rant and everyone instantly started shuffling their things together to get out to lunch. Shoving some loose paper sleeves into my bag, I scraped back my chair and followed Ryder out.

"Remember to finish your essays for homework! We'll be starting a new topic tomorrow," Mr. Kansas yelled out to his students, but the excitement of lunch freedom had tuned him out.

As we all flooded out of the classroom and drifted into the sea of students in the corridors, heading for exits, Ryder and I made our way to the lockers. We had gotten a lot of stares since we got to class. Not because of the handcuffs. Apparently that was old news. It was because Ryder had only shaved half his face and I had a drawn on eyebrow.

We floated with the current of kids and we made a stop at Ryder's locker which, conveniently, was right next to Mel's. Her bright, green eyes lit up as she saw me and she slammed her locker door closed. She shifted the weight of her textbooks and grinned as she headed over.

Her vibrant, red hair was in a messy bun, a few short curls framing her thin, pale face. However, as she neared, she raised a perfectly shaped eyebrow at me.

"So, the rumours are true," she said.

"Yeah," I answered, "I *am* chained to an obnoxious jerk."

Mel looked down at our chained wrists, then back up at me. "No, I wasn't talking about that. I meant you really did draw on your eyebrow with a Crayola."

"I did *not* draw my eyebrow on with a Crayola."

My best friend gasped. "No way! Don't tell me Rachel Fawn was right. So it's true you drew it on with a permanent marker?"

I was seriously close slapping her. Mel became seriously interested in my face art. She leaned in closer to eyeball it and just when she was about to poke it, I leaned back and smacked into Ryder.

He frowned down at me, but said nothing, shifting awkwardly as he shoved something into his locker. I tried peeking over his shoulder but his broad shoulders blocked my view. Ryder pulled out his books for the next few classes and closed his locker, his face coming into view. Even though Mel knew we were handcuffed together, it didn't stop her from gaping at him. Girls like us usually didn't even come close to a five-metre radius with guys like Ryder.

"Wow..." she muttered. "Is it true that half a shaved face is what's hot in Europe?"

As always, Mel had no problem with asking people about gossip. It was just the way she was; shameless with her addiction to rumours. And what she said about Ryder's half shaved face was pretty insulting. I mean, he shaves half his face and it suddenly goes around that it's a trend in elite fashion. But my missing eyebrow sparks up a story, making everyone think I used my face as a canvas with a couple of crayons.

High school sucks.

Ryder raised an eyebrow and shrugged, which, apparently, was enough to pass as an answer, because Mel gasped in understanding and nodded. I, on the other hand, just stood there and watched them exchange telepathic messages through facial expressions. I seriously needed to get in with the whole silent conversation thing. "So, are we still sitting together?" Mel asked, walking along side us.

"Of course."

"Actually, we made plans with my friends," Ryder cut in.

"Since when?" I snapped as we exited the building.

"Since just now," he replied, nodding over at his friends that had gathered around the school fountain.

It was a large group, but although they all hung out together, they still split into smaller groups. Ryder's best friend, Caine, was sitting on the edge of the fountain, flexing for the giggly brunette who sat on his lap. They all had this superior aura around them and the guys shone like stars in their black and white varsity jackets.

I knew instantly I wouldn't fit it.

Mel must have been thinking the same thing because she paused. "I think…" she said, trailing off and hesitating as she stared at the group of populars. "I think I'll go find someone… Um, see you later, Nora."

"Hey," Ryder called, just as Mel was about to drift away. "You can stay."

Mel's eyes widened as she stared from the group of Ryder's friends, to me and back to Ryder. "Seriously?"

"Sure." Ryder shrugged. For a brief second, I thought Ryder was being nice. "I mean, it's not like any of my friends like Nora."

Nope. Still an ass.

We hardly took a step further before a group of giggling girls rushed over to him.

"Jessica, Hailee, Bree," Ryder soothed, giving each of them five precious seconds of his killer smile.

One of the girls reached up and touched his cheek. "Loving the new look, Ryder." Then she turned and saw me. "Nice Crayola eyebrow."

"Gee, nice to meet you too," I grumbled, feeling even more self-conscious about my drawn-on eyebrow.

I focused my attention on the fountain in front of me. It was painted coral blue, surprisingly clean, considering all the messy teenagers who loitered around it. In the centre of the fountain was a sculpture of a half lion, half human god. From its upraised palms, water, as clear as crystal, squirted and cascaded into the pool below. If you leaned in close enough and looked past the rippling sea, you could see glittering coins. And each of those coins held a wish.

It was a school tradition that each graduating class would surround the fountain, toss a coin and make a wish on the last day of their academic careers. I was exactly seventy-three days away from doing so. Suddenly feeling nervous, I stepped away from the water and back into safe grounds.

Although the fountain was reserved for the graduating class, any day that wasn't the last day of school, the fountain belonged to the populars. Rumours go around all the time about kids getting tossed into the fountain because they got too close. And even though I doubted it was true, I didn't want to get close enough to see if I was wrong.

"Man," Mel muttered, "I didn't know chilling here would be so intimidating. They're all so… mature. I'm scared to eat my sandwich in front of them."

My eyes flicked towards her. Her hair was dancing wildly around her porcelain face, like tongues of fire. "I know. I'm sorry I dragged you into this."

Mel's eyes widened as she gaped at me. "Are you serious? Do you know how much gossip goes around here? I can finally get some information right from the sources, rather than it being tossed around half a dozen times. This is great!"

I rolled my eyes at my friend. Mel really had no shame when it came to gossip. By the time lunch was over she had discovered that one of the jocks had a third nipple and one of the girls had a feet fetish. She couldn't stop chattering about the excitement, her enthusiasm oozing from her lips with every juicy word. I always thought she'd make a good journalist.

When we departed to go to class, Mel left in a happy flurry and I returned to my miserable state. Detention couldn't come fast enough.

Seven

Since Ryder and Caine were being distracting during detention, Mr. Kansas threw away his Sudoku puzzle from the newspaper and took Caine out for a "special job." In other words, he was going to be scrubbing the gym with a toothbrush. With a look of annoyance, Caine sauntered out of the classroom, hands shoved in his pockets.

In the meantime, we were put on chewie duty. Ryder and I were given two scrapers and a pair of gloves each and were expected to start cleaning immediately. But once we were under one of the desks, Ryder pulled his gloves off and tossed them away.

"I'm not cleaning anyone's gum from under those desks."

"If anything, *I* shouldn't be scraping gum off desks!" I answered. "It's your fault we're in detention."

Ryder raised an eyebrow. "Actually, *I'm* in detention. You just had to come along because we're chained together by these stupid handcuffs."

The thought had never occurred to me.

"Oh my God, so why *am* I cleaning?" I wondered out loud.

"Yeah, why *are* you?"

Snapping my gloves off and throwing away my tool, I nodded.
"I'm not." With that, I made my way out from under the table.

Only problem is, I forgot how close the table was to my head, so
when I was shifting around uncomfortably, I hit my head... right into a
big chunk of gum. Realising what I had just done, I tried to slowly pull
myself out, but the gum was fresh and it stuck to my scalp like sticky
glue.

Raising my hand, I placed it on the piece of hair and yanked
hard. All it did was break a few, blonde strands but a majority of my hair
stayed stuck to the gum. I scanned my panicked eyes to Ryder. He was
leaning against the chair, skilfully sending out a text with one hand and
grinning in cocky satisfaction.

"Ryder!" I hissed, poking his chest.

He grunted distractedly as he finished off the rest of his message
and finally looked up at me with a glower until he noticed that my head
was connected to the table. A grin spread out across his face and he let
out a deep chuckle.

"What the hell did you do?"

"Does it matter? Just help me out!"

Ryder laughed over my stupidity for another couple of long
minutes before he finally reached over to grab his bag. Drumming my
fingers impatiently on the floor, I waited for him to do something. When
he turned around, my stomach dropped. He had something in his hands.
The handles were a deep, sapphire blue and the blazes glinted in the
afternoon light.

Ryder was holding a pair of giant scissors.

"No," I said firmly. Then, to emphasise my displeasure, I
repeated,"No."

"What else am I supposed to do?" he questioned, skilfully
spinning the equipment in his hands.

"I don't want to have a bald patch," I cried.

But deep down, I sadly knew that this was the only way out.
Looking up at Ryder, I heaved a sigh and motioned for him to make the

snip. Shuffling closer, he ducked his head under the table with mine, scissors aiming for my head.

We were close, really close. So close that I could feel his warm breath against my cheek. I watched every even rise and fall of his chest, and saw his muscles tense in concentration. I could feel warmth radiating into me, from the heat of his chest to the warmth that flowed from his hands.

He leaned in closer, to see the gum, so close that his rough, unshavened cheek brushed against mine. I could hear my heartbeat thumping in my ears, and it drowned out all the other sounds to a point where I didn't notice Ryder had finished cutting.

He leaned back until his face was inches away from mine. His faded denim eyes glittered with rebellion, his lips slightly parted. I could feel his warm breath on my lips as his hand gently slid down to my elbow. Cerulean irises skimmed down to my mouth and they lingered there for no longer than a devilish second before he met my eyes again.

A full smirk grew across his face and his eyes shone with arrogance. "You have a booger," he whispered, taking his hand off my elbow.

Feeling flustered from embarrassment and intimacy, I did nothing but glare, feeling my cheeks heat up.

"Wow."

A sudden voice came from the door and Ryder shuffled away from me. It's not like he could go really far. Unlike myself, Ryder seemed to be calm and collected, no sign of colour blossoming into his cheeks. I, on the other hand, looked like an over ripened tomato.

"Did I just disturb 'a moment'?" Caine asked, crossing his arms across his chest as he leaned against the doorframe. A smirk danced on his lips.

"Just a disturbing discovery," Ryder snorted.

Caine stepped forward and grabbed a chair from the front row. He swung it back to front and sat on it, placing his long, muscular arms over the backrest. "As tempted as I am to ask what the hell that means,

I'm hungry. Want to break out of here? I feel like a double
cheeseburger."

"Sweet," Ryder answered, already trying to stand up. "Let's hit
Macca's."

When I followed Ryder, Caine took one look at me and burst out
laughing. "Were you that bored that you decided to cut your own hair?"
He chuckled.

"Shut up," I hissed.

Although Ryder and Caine ordered two double bacon
cheeseburger each with large, chocolate sundaes to devour afterwards,
they still ate faster than me. I had a happy meal, which, might I mention,
came with a really awesome stuffed Nemo toy.

Once we had finished eating, Caine dropped us back to my
house. Ryder told his parents that we were still doing our 'important
project' which allowed him to stay for another night. But, really, I didn't
know how long we could use the same excuse. Any normal kid would
have just told his parents, but Ryder's were... scary.

As we walked up the stairs, I hardly got to fish my key out from
my pocket because Eve swung the door open and glared at us. "Where
have you been?" she snapped.

I looked past her and towards the grandfather clock sitting by the
staircase. We had arrived home just after six. Eve blew away a piece of
hair that had fallen out from her low ponytail and continued to glare at us
with icy, hazel eyes. When I tried to brush past her, she slammed her
hand against the doorframe and blocked my entrance. Drumming her
fingers against the frame, she raised an eyebrow.

Sighing in exasperation, I said, "Ryder got detention."

"That's Ryder's excuse, not yours," Eve snapped. "Give me *your*
reason."

"How about that I'm handcuffed to him?" I answered, holding
up my wrist for evidence.

"That's not all," she replied, leaning in.

Then she did another weird thing. She licked me.

"You had a happy meal," she whispered in horror. "Where's mine?"

She did that weird eyeball thing at me, something she had inherited from Dad, and stared me down for answers. Just when I thought she was going to lick me again, I answered.

"I didn't get you a Happy Meal."

It was the wrong thing to say. You never tell a pregnant woman that you didn't get her a Happy Meal. Eve's bottom lip quivered and her eyes welled up. Honestly, if she wasn't in such a hormonal state, I would have smacked the back of her head. But since she was pregnant, and an emotional mess, I decided against it.

"But I want a Happy Meal!" Tears – real tears - burst out from her eyes.

Ryder just stared at her with bug eyes. "Uh..." he stuttered, stumbling over his words for the right sentence. "It wasn't even that great of a Happy Meal. Nora only got three fries or something. Plus, all she got was a stuffed Nemo. Five bucks is a rip off, I tell you."

That only made Eve cry harder. "I want a stuffed Nemo!"

I nudged Ryder in the stomach. "Nice work, moron."

Ryder frowned at me. "Give her your Nemo."

"No," I answered, a little too defensively as I patted my pocket. "I like Nemo."

Eve went ballistic. I didn't even know the human body could contain so many tears. It didn't take long for Patrick to come storming down the stairs in nothing but his boxers, and socks, baseball bat in his curled fists.

"Who's ass do I have to kick?" he yelled like a madman. He skidded to a halt and scanned the area.

"Wow," I said, eyes widening. I covered my face with my hands. "Let's keep this PG, shall we? This is *my* house, remember? Put some clothes on."

I mean, it's not like Patrick had man boobs or one of those scary, hairy chests. For a guy in his mid-twenties, he wasn't that bad. But he was my sister's boyfriend and seeing him in boxers and socks grossed me out.

Patrick scooped Eve into his arms and started stroking her hair. "Baby, what's wrong?"

"I want a Nemo," Eve whispered, sounding like a little kid.

Patrick looked over my sister's shoulder and gave us a clueless look. "She wants a Happy Meal," I translated. "With the orange fish toy."

Eve's boyfriend nodded and pulled back. "I'll get you one, okay?" he said reassuringly. He kissed her quickly, bent down to kiss her belly, and jogged upstairs to get some clothes.

"Pregnancy is scary," Ryder muttered.

Eight

I was completely disturbed.

"God! Oh, God! Put it away, just put it all away!" I shrieked,
stretching as far away as possible and closing my eyes.

Ryder reached out and smacked my forehead with his palm.
"Dork, I haven't even undressed yet."

I opened one eye and looked at him. "I know. I'm just preparing
myself."

It had been two days in the same clothes without having a
shower. I was pretty sure deodorant was no longer able to conceal our
smell. So, Ryder and I decided to finally take showers. We pretty much
had to cut out of our sweaty uniforms to peel out of them. Mum would
have killed me if she saw my shredded uniform lying peacefully on the
floor.

Ryder just gave me a filthy look and grabbed the hem of his
shirt, slipping it over his head. Since we had already cut a slit through the
left side of his uniform, he was able to pull it off easily. As he
effortlessly raised the material, my fingers moved with his, delicately
brushing against his warm skin.

His warm, *toned* skin. My eyes skimmed up his chest as he took his shirt off and lingered to the contours of his stomach. Slowly, I scanned up to his chest, then followed the distinct curve of the hollow of his neck towards his defined arms.

Ryder was *buff*. Last time I had seen him shirtless was when we started high school. And back then, his muscles were like any normal twelve-year-old's: non-existent.

"Like what you're seeing?"

Before I could let out a startled gag, he advanced onto his pants and that's when things got *really* awkward. I don't know why, but I just kept staring.Ryder must have felt the heat of my stare because after he unbuckled his belt, he just stared right back, waiting for me to turn around. Realising the creepiness on my behalf, I narrowed my eyes.

"Whatever..." It sounded weaker than I had intended.

Ryder laughed softly. "Just turn around, Nora."

His voice was surprisingly gentle. He opened his mouth for a millisecond after saying my name, his eyes gleaming with mischief, but he hesitated. His words were replaced with a smile.

His reaction caught me off guard and I felt my cheeks heat before I spun around on my heel, faced the wall, and closed my eyes. The sound of his zipper being pulled down echoed through the silence of the bathroom and the ruffling of his trousers being removed seemed to be the loudest thing I had ever heard.

I tried thinking of something, *anything* to distract me from the fact that the boy I was handcuffed to was naked in my house. Ryder shuffled around for a bit before stepping into the shower. The sound of the curtain being closed made me feel extremely uncomfortable, especially when the water started running.

That was when I *really* started thinking about the awkward situation. I mean, since we were handcuffed, my hand was in the shower with him. What if... I accidentally touched something? The thought haunted me, flashing like a horror motion picture behind my closed eyelids. Quickly, I opened them and stared at the wall opposite me, completely disturbed.

I needed a distraction...and fast.

"Why do boys have nipples?" I blurted.

Ryder stopped moving under the water. "What?"

"Why do guys have nipples? I mean, they have no purpose." I felt my cheeks heat in embarrassment at the most inappropriate topic of conversation to choose.

"Uh..." He went back to doing whatever he was doing in the shower. "Decoration?"

"Gross," I answered, cringing.

Silence fell between us as the room started steaming up. The mirror was starting to fog, drops of condensation pearling up on the surface. A thin, humid mist lingered through the air, heating up the room. Using my free hand, I reached up and wiped my forehead. I was seriously flustered and embarrassed and way too focused about what my hand was brushing against.

"Can you imagine if nipples were as big as Oreos?" I blabbered.

Ryder was silent for a moment. "Thanks for seriously ruining Oreos for me."

"Don't mention it." I laughed awkwardly.

Longest five minutes of my life.

The sound of sizzling came from the kitchen, wafting over a delectable scent. Although we were well into winter, the windows were open to circulate the smell. Frosty air blew through the room, harshly biting any bare skin it could find. The sunlight was weak, shining an icy bleakness to mix with the overhead lights of the dining room.

The following morning, Eve was doing her usual sniff at Ryder. He had quickly gotten used to it, so while we sat at the table with toast and eggs, he simply ignored her while she smelled him.

"Did you use my shampoo?" she questioned, picking up a piece of hair and running it under her nose.

Ryder shovelled a forkful of eggs into his mouth, then bit into his toast and shrugged. "Used whatever was in there," he said around his breakfast.

"Well, you smell like strawberries," Eve teased.

Ryder just looked briefly up at Eve who had started dancing around the dining room and returned back to his meal. Patrick appeared a moment later, two plates piled with eggs and toast and skilfully steered his girlfriend to the table before she started air humping.

Eve dropped down to her chair and licked her lips as Patrick placed her plate down. Once he had taken his own seat, he asked, "Do you kids need a ride to school?"

"That'd be -"

"Actually, we have a friend picking us up," Ryder interrupted, reaching for his glass of milk.

"We do?" I bit into my toast.

"Caine is giving us a ride," he answered, before tipping his head back and gulping down his full glass of milk in less than three swallows.

When he finished, he brought the glass down and made a sigh of satisfaction. Stained on his top lip was a layer of milk residue. He looked like such a little boy, completely oblivious to his white moustache hanging low on his upper lip. But the image was soon deleted once he used the back of his hand to smear it off.

"So, remind me again," Patrick said, "why I lent you guys a good shirt just for you to cut it."

I held up my wrist. "Hello? Handcuffed. It's hard to get dressed, you know."

Since we had destroyed our uniforms, Ryder and I were in casual gear. Ryder had to borrow some clothes from Patrick, which I'm pretty sure he was grateful for, especially after he saw what kind of clothes my dad was into. Patrick was only twenty-three and although most of his fashion choice was preppy for work, he had the odd shirt or two around. We had to cut a slit through the side of the dark T-shirt so Ryder could put it on. It was either that, or wear one of my tube tops.

After taking a quick sip from my orange juice, there was a honk at the door. Ryder scraped back his chair and picked up his bag. "That's our ride."

Grabbing my books and a jacket, I followed Ryder out the door, and there was Caine, music vibrating through his car. He leaned over and rolled down the tinted window, honking once more as he watched us walk out the door.

"Shut up, man," Ryder called. "We're coming."

"God, what's the rush?" I grumbled as Ryder tugged me along.

"We have to stop somewhere," he answered as he threw the door open.

I had a sickening feel in my stomach. "Where?" I dared to ask.

He just looked at me and said nothing, but the answer was clear in his eyes. I shook my head and restrained from his pull. Oh, no. There was no way I was going to go there.

Nine

June Collins. The woman could make nuns swear and cause full grown men to cry. She was a grade A bitch with the icy attitude to match.

Now, don't get me wrong. She wasn't always like this. In fact, she used to be one of those carefree mums who wore her hair in a lazy ponytail on the weekends and walked around barefoot in summer. She used to be the kind of parent that would hide behind doors, water gun in her hands, waiting for her children to walk around the corner.

June Collins was *fun.*

Then Ryder's dad cheated on her and she changed. A lot. After the divorce, Mr. Collins left the house and went to live with his girlfriend that looked young enough to still be in school. Mrs. Collins immediately dropped Ryder off at her mother's and disappeared for a few months.

And when she came back, she was a whole different person. I remember in year seven, before Ryder and I had broken up, I called her 'Mrs. Collins' and she looked like she was going to bite my face off. It wasn't my fault though. I mean, I was aware of the divorce and everything, but I didn't know what her maiden name was. I used to call her June. But when she came back looking like she'd just come back from boot camp, my confidence to call her by her first name dulled.

Ryder pulled out his keys and unlocked the front door. I was so scared. I *tiptoed* into the house and craned my neck like an ostrich trying to see if she was around. Ryder turned and saw me creeping around his house like a some sort of burglar, so he rolled his eyes at me and kicked the front door closed.

And that was all the noise he needed to make to have Mrs. Collins head towards the front door. The instant she started walking in our direction, I knew she was on the move. The sound of her heels clicking against the wooden floor echoed through the empty space of the house and a few seconds later, she appeared. Instantly, my back straightened, as if good posture would make me invisible to the woman.

"Ryder," she greeted, walking towards her son.

She paused for a moment, realising he wasn't alone. Her blue eyes flickered to me and quickly scanned my appearance. I suddenly felt extremely exposed and savage, wearing a tube as a shirt. Mrs. Collins adjusted her work blazer and smoothed down her pencil skirt.

"Nora," she said, her tone as cold as ice. Then she turned towards her son. "I didn't expect to see you here. Why haven't you been home?"

"We've been doing a school project," I answered for him.

"Excuse me, Nora, but I don't remember addressing you," she snapped, tone clipped.

I shrunk into the background.

"We're doing a school project," Ryder repeated, stepping forward to kiss his mother's cheek.

She arched her lips tightly, her lips thinning to a barely-there smile as she kept her eyes on me. When Ryder stepped back, she said nothing. She just continued to stare, her hand reaching up to her ear lobe to fiddle with her pearl earring. It was something she did unconsciously when she was thinking.

"When will you come home?" she questioned, after a moment of silence.

"Tonight, if you want," Ryder replied.

My eyes widened. Since Mrs. Collins had directed her attention to her son, I tried to catch his attention in the corners of his eyes. I kept my arms to my sides but waved my hands around in alert, probably looking like a penguin in a failed attempt to fly. When that didn't work, I started making faces at him, crossing my eyes, tilting my head to the side, frowning and sticking my tongue out but he kept his focus on his mother.

"Would you need a drink or something?"

Coughing awkwardly, I tried to act nonchalant.

"Nah," I said, racking my mind for an excuse. Then suddenly blurted, "I just need to pee."

Mrs. Collins raised an eyebrow at me. "You always did have a weak bladder."

"Um... Thank you?" I said hesitantly.

She waved a dismissive hand and walked away. "Please be quick, Nora."

God, that woman was so... intimidating.

When she disappeared, I muttered, "You got one scary mother..."

~♥♥♥~

After Ryder collected a few things, we went to school. We had about ten minutes to spare before first period started, so we headed towards the lockers. Ryder's first.

The halls were pretty empty, other than the random student or two huddling around trying to find a heater vent to cuddle up to. As we approached the rows of lockers, I saw shadows lurking around the corner, hushed whispers mumbling through the hall.

A moment later, a pretty blonde stepped out, taking one last glance at whoever she was talking to before walking briskly away. She looked like a junior student, tall, but with a young face. Eyes focused blankly in front of her, she brushed past us, hardly acknowledging our existence. After she had departed through the side exit, the harsh winds outside slammed the heavy doors back into place.

Returning my attention back in front of me, I saw Chris across the hall. Instantly, he smiled.

"Nora," he said, shoving his hands in his pockets as he headed over.

"Hey, Chris!" Instantly, my hand shot up and started waving dorkily. Quickly, I plastered it to my side.

He chuckled as he approached us, eyes shooting to Ryder's and darkening before focusing on mine and melting into something more sincere. His tie was loose, top button of his white shirt undone as if he had rushed to school that morning.

"Ready for our date tonight?" he asked.

"Absolutely." I tried not to sound so enthusiastic.

"I see your....situation still hasn't been resolved." He nodded towards Ryder.

I felt Ryder tense next to me.

"Unfortunately," I answered.

Ryder opened his mouth, eyes dark, but Chris was already making a move to leave.

"Well, I should go," he said apologetically. "Algebra just isn't the same without me." Then he leaned in and kissed my cheek. "I'm sorry, Nora. I can't wait to see you tonight." His gaze followed down my arm and towards my wrist where it was locked with Ryder's. "Can't wait to see you too, Collins. This should be interesting." He gave Ryder a look, then walked away.

Ryder continued to glare at him as he pushed past and disappeared down the hall. I heard him let out a grunt once he was out of view before we headed towards his locker. Dreamily, I rested against the one next to his. Ryder jerked open his locker so fast, I wasn't even sure if he spun the lock or just forced it open. The door swung open, nearly smacking me in the face. Quickly, I moved out of the way, barely avoiding a locker face-attack.

"Calm down, will you?" I said, watching as he pulled out some books and slammed the door closed again. "What's got you all worked up?"

"Look," he hissed, "he's trouble."

I laughed. "You sure have no shame in showing your jealousy, do you?"

Ryder shook his head, slamming his fist against the rows of lockers in frustration. With a loud, quick *bang*, he spun and looked at me. His usual faintly tinted blue eyes had darkened into something filled with passion and rage, like the sky before a thunderstorm. His jaw was tight. I was pretty sure he had just put a dent into someone's locker but I didn't dare keep my eyes off him.

"Why do you care?" I whispered, feeling small.

He narrowed his eyes at me. "I don't, Nora. I stopped caring about you that night at the game. I just don't want your girly mess when he breaks your heart."

Venom laced his words and I was stunned into silence. Looking down, away from his intense stare, I stared at the floor, suddenly finding a huge interest in the dirty ground. A moment later, Ryder spoke.

"Let's just go to class," he muttered, turning as he tugged me along.

I stayed almost silent through the rest of the day until my date with Chris, where I was determined to prove that he wasn't a bad guy. That Ryder had just misunderstood him. That Ryder just didn't know him and put so much hate on him because he wasn't part of the same group.

But in the end, was I trying to prove Chris' innocence to Ryder or to myself?

Ten

I had thought of this night over and over since the day I met Chris Baker.

I also thought I'd be wearing something a lot more... suitable for the occasion. Since I couldn't exactly wear sleeves, I had to squeeze into a strapless dress. The material was soft and silky, the kind that slipped between your fingers like delicate and icy waves. Tossing Chris' blazer over my shoulders, Ryder and I headed downstairs to where Chris was waiting.

Dressed in a pair of dark washed jeans and a grey button down, Chris stood at the door, engaging in small talk with Patrick. Eve was there too, completely convinced that Chris had brought her a ham. Eve really liked ham and according to her, Chris smelled like ham.

"If it's not ham, is it bacon?" Eve pressed.

Chris looked a little startled as she advanced towards his chest pockets. "I, uh, didn't know I was meant to bring a ham..." He looked at Patrick in desperation.

Patrick just wrapped his arms around Eve, placing his hands on her stomach as he pulled her away and pressed her against him. "We have some leftover ham in the fridge, baby," he soothed, Eve instantly melting.

We had reached the bottom of the stairs then. Chris suddenly looked so young and awkward as he watched my sister and her boyfriend contently wrapped in each other's arms. He looked away from the couple, suddenly finding the wall across the room extremely fascinating. Then, his eyes flickered towards us.

"Nora," he breathed, watching as we made our way towards him.

"Hey," I mumbled nervously, tucking a piece of hair behind my ear and wrapping the jacket around me tighter.

"You look beautiful," he commented, before looking over at Ryder. His tone turned to ice as he said, "How cute. You colour coordinated with my gorgeous date."

I looked over at Ryder. Patrick had lent him another one of his T-shirts and this time, it was grey. I hadn't realised how impeccably it matched the silvery material of my dress. Ryder and I exchanged quick glimpses, just a quick flicker before we returned our gazes back to Chris. Ryder stepped forward for a single second and briefly whispered something to my date. Chris narrowed his eyes in anger, lips tightening to a thin line as Ryder stepped back. Together, they stared each other down with a silent, raging intensity. Chris returned his gaze to me a moment later and smiled.

"You ready to go?" He held out his hand, tossing one last glare at Ryder.

Linking my arm through his, we stepped out into the night and towards his car. It was dark and sleek, glazed with a metallic coat of paint that glittered under the faint, golden glow of the streetlights. Ryder and I, since we were now conjoined twins, were forced to sit in the back seat. Chris still held the door open for me, but stepped away once I was in and let Ryder finish off what he started.

The serious tension between the two guys was starting to bug me and I had the urge to demand answers to avoid awkwardness for my date, but the way Chris looked through his rear view mirror every so often to sharply stare Ryder down made me pause. Sighing, I gazed out the window and into the night, as if I could really see anything.

The ride to the pizza parlour was short. It wasn't in town, which had surprised me. As Chris made every smooth turn and passed every streetlight, I started to become unfamiliar with the roads. I realised we weren't heading towards where the main shopping attractions were. In fact, we were just passing through streets full of houses.

After a few minutes of awkward tension in the car, we stopped at a house. Well, it looked like a house from the outside. The bright lights glowed from the inside, radiating the small building with a warm shine. But when Chris held the door opened, I was surprised to see what was inside.

The area was set up like small restaurant. I expected to walk into a house, but instead of seeing a kitchen and connected dining room, the place was just a wide floor of space. Small tables and chairs dotted the area and a few booths were lined up against the far wall.

It smelled wonderful. The delicious aromas of fresh vegetables and baking pizzas tickled my nose and teased me. My stomach involuntarily growled as we followed Chris towards a quiet table under the faint glow of a golden light. As we passed customers, the soft chattering of voices sounded, glasses clinking, and gentle laughs filling the room.

The welcoming warmth of the room made me shrug off the blazer resting on my shoulders as we sat down. "This place is amazing," I whispered in complete awe.

"This place was originally on the main street," Chris explained as he picked up the laminated menu and scanned through. "The place had different owners back then though. When they died, the Jones family took over and found that the main street rent was too expensive, so they decided to open here."

"In a house?" I questioned, picking up my own menu.

Chris chuckled and shook his head. "No. This is the old part of town, where some of the oldest houses were built. This place used to be a post office."

"Complimentary bread from the chef." A waiter dropped a roll of sliced garlic bread onto the table. It was only four slices, but it sure smelled heavenly.

"Free bread!" I cheered.

"Ah, Conrad is up to his old tricks. Be careful. This garlic bread is probably the most amazing thing you'll ever eat," Chris warned, smiling. "Chef always brings out complimentary bread just to encourage customers to buy a whole roll."

Picking up a slice, I broke my piece into two. The sound of the crunchy outer crust crumbling was just mouth-watering, especially as I watched the soft, fluffy centre tear effortlessly down the middle. The garlic butter had soaked deep into the soft bread, giving off the most amazing aroma.

I refrained from making an appreciative mumble.

When ordering came around, Chris told me to pick out whatever I wanted. Although there was just about every topping available, I chose a simple seven-cheese slice. Judging from the garlic bread, simplicity was delicious. When a giant pizza was placed in the middle of the table, each a different slice, I instantly dove for my cheese portion.

Ryder lazily reached out and snagged an all-topping slice, tormentingly glaring at Chris with satisfaction as he leaned back in his chair and took a big bite.

"You better be paying for that." Chris nodded at the pizza in Ryder's hands.

"What are you talking about?" Ryder replied, tipping his head back and shoving half the slice into his mouth. "Aren't *you* the one taking Nora on the date?"

"Yes," Chris answered coldly. "But I'm not taking *you* on the date."

Ryder simply held up the handcuffs. "Two or none, bro. We're a package deal now."

Chris just glared at him and picked up a meat-lover's slice of pizza. Then, before you know it, the guys were in a silent battle to see who can eat and shove the most pizza into their mouths. I was starting to feel like *I* was the third wheel intruding on *their* date. Within minutes, the boys were battling between the last slice while I was just finishing my first.

Looking at them glare at each other as they feasted their eyes on the last slice, I sighed. Reaching over, I snatched the last piece and shoved as much of it in my mouth. Chris looked over at me for a moment, crazy and wild, but as he kept staring, his eyes melted and his shoulders sagged.

Like a little boy, he muttered, "I'm sorry, Nora..."

While I was struggling to swallow all the pizza I had stuffed into my cheeks, Chris turned his attention away from me and looked distantly towards the back of the room. His lips twitched, then his eyes fell back on mine.

"Would you please excuse me?" he said, wiping the corners of his mouth with a serviette before scraping his chair back and walking away.

I watched him walk towards what I presumed to be the bathrooms.

"Prepare for disappointment," Ryder warned, picking his glass up and taking a swig, the ice clinking as the liquid in the cup stirred.

"Don't be so negative," I replied, picking up my own glass and raising it to my lips, but not drinking.

Chris wasn't that type of guy, right? Admittedly, I was a little worried at school after our encounter, but once the date progressed, I enjoyed myself. Sort of. The awkwardness with Ryder was tense, but putting that aside, Chris was a great guy... wasn't he?

Five minutes turned to fifteen and fifteen turned to thirty. All that remained were empty plates and bread crumbs. Couples, friends, and families.

"Excuse me, Miss, but we're going to have to ask you to leave," a waiter said, sounding sympathetic.

I looked towards the direction where Chris had disappeared. Sighing, I looked up and smiled wearily. "I understand. May I please visit the ladies room first?"

The waiter nodded and walked away. Dumping my napkin onto
my empty plate, I scraped my chair back and tugged Ryder along.
Twisting our way past chairs and people, we headed towards the
restrooms, but instead of going towards the ladies' room, I paused in
front of the men's.

"I don't need to go," Ryder said.

I shook my head. "Yes, you do. I know Chris isn't a bad guy. He
would never stand me up. I'm pretty sure he ate his pizza too fast. Maybe
he's sick."

"Nora..." Ryder's voice quietened and he gave me a half smile.
"I don't think..."

"Ryder," I interrupted, my voice sounding hurt and desperate,
although I tried to conceal it, "please..."

He sighed and pushed open the door, me following behind him.
The instant stench of seriously strong pee and some other unidentifiable
odour filled my senses. Holding my nose and breathing through my
mouth, we crossed the damp floors towards the urinals.

"Hey, lady! This is the men's room!" someone shouted from
across the room.

Ignoring the grunts and complaints, we stopped at the urinals.
Ryder just stood there, a hand in his pocket as he watched me. "Well, are
you gonna take your thing out and pee or something?" I hissed.

Ryder raised an eyebrow. "I told you I didn't need to go," he
answered.

I narrowed my eyes at him. "But you can't just burst in here
without a reason," I muttered. "Especially with a girl chained to your
wrist. Just pee, dammit, so we don't look like creepers looking around at
everyone else peeing."

Ryder just rolled his eyes and picked a urinal in the corner while
I scanned the area for Chris. He was in there. He *had* to be in there. In
the stalls maybe. Chris would never stand me up... He's not that kind of
guy. I mean, sure, Ryder was being a third wheel on our date was a pain
in the ass, but he wouldn't really-

And that's when I heard Chris' voice. "Slower. No, *slower*!"

It was coming from one of the bathroom stalls and instantly, images of bathroom hook-ups with waitresses flashed through my mind. Ryder was serious about not needing to pee, because in seconds, he was zipping his fly up and looking towards the stalls.

"Crap, man! What the hell is wrong with you? I said slowly or you're gonna drop me in the bloody toilet!" Chris hissed.

And that's when I realised where it was from. It wasn't *in* the bathroom stall. It was *above* the stall. There he was, legs and butt casually hanging out the little slither of a window as one of his mates lowered him down. Pursing my lips, I watched him struggle to squeeze through the gap.

I was mad. Mad that he felt the urge to ditch me. To use the oldest trick in the book and sneak out through the bathroom window. I didn't even want to think about what he was doing while he was gone. How dare he. How dare he even think he could get away with going on two dates at the same time.

Marching my way over to the stall, I poked his butt. That's right. I poked his butt. I heard Chris' head hit the glass as he kicked his legs and tried to scramble out to see who had just touched him.

"Uh, I really don't appreciate you feeling me up, dude."

"Oh, sorry, *dude*," I said, watching him tense when he realised it was me. "I thought you liked having hands all over you, you sick bastard!"

"Nora," he squirmed, "it's not what it looks like…"

"Save your excuses, you sad excuse of a man," I hissed.

This would have been the perfect opportunity to do something completely outrageous, like kick his ass. But I was too short for the window and I wasn't sure if I had the strength. Emotionally, I was all over the place and I'd probably end up hurting myself more than him. So, instead, I reached up into his back pocket, pulled out his wallet and dropped it onto the toilet.

"Have fun paying, jerk." Then I stormed out of the bathroom, pulling Ryder with me and ignoring Chris' explicit choice of language.

My whole body was shaking, so I had to clench my fists to
regain some control. I felt my cheeks flush as we pushed our way out of
the men's bathrooms and past all the staring customers. Once we exited
the restaurant, I was relieved to feel the cool air kiss my heated cheeks. I
tore Chris' blazer off my shoulders and threw it into a muddy puddle,
watching the expensive material soak up the dirty water.

Ryder called a taxi over and we hopped in. He hadn't said
anything. Nothing at all. And although I was usually begging for him to
be silent, this was the one time I needed him to say something. Anything.
Even if it was a simple, 'I told you so.' Because I didn't want to have to
put up with his humiliation later.

After a few minutes of silence, Ryder did speak. "You didn't
deserve this."

Of all the things he could have said, I didn't expect him to say
those four words.

I didn't look at him. I stared straight ahead, eyes glazed with
tears. It was so blurry, I could hardly see the road properly. My anger
had bled into embarrassment and hurt and once I blinked, the tears rolled
down my cheeks. It was dark inside the taxi so I hoped he couldn't see.

But I turned my head towards the window, just in case he saw
me cry.

Eleven

When the taxi pulled up at the curb, Ryder and I sat in silence for a few long minutes. I didn't move. I just stared blankly ahead, not wanting to look directly at the luminous glow of Ryder's house, knowing that he would see how broken I was. I didn't want to look out the window either. For one, I didn't want to get blinded by some random car's headlights, nor did I want the driver to freak out over my sad clown face. Noticing that Ryder and I weren't making any move to get out of the vehicle, the taxi driver turned around.

"You kids gonna go-" He paused, looking startled, probably because I looked like a seriously depressed squirrel with the makeup running down my face. "Oh... Is... Is she okay?"

The taxi driver looked completely terrified as he quickly switched his attention to me, to Ryder and back again. I guess I'd be pretty freaked out if some teenage girl started crying in my backseat. Of course, I'd be more concerned about the closest supermarket so I could buy her ice-cream, but I figured he was more worried about what to do with me.

"I think I have a tissue somewhere," he said, clumsily rummaging through his pockets. When he discovered he actually didn't have one, he frowned. "Oh, uh, sorry... I can't seem to find one. I swear I had one."

I didn't say anything. Instead, I just stared blankly at him. After a moment, he said, "Hey, don't even worry about paying, okay, darlin'?"

I managed a small, forced smile. But I guess I looked pretty scary because the taxi driver grimaced a little. I watched as he turned fully in his seat and looked at Ryder. His eyes narrowed at him.

"Wait a second... Did you hurt this young lady?" He glared at him.

Ryder simply shook his head and in his tone emotionless, said, "I didn't."

The taxi driver just kept his eyes on him. "You better be telling the truth, mate, 'cause I'll report you to the police if I find out you hurt this young lady."

I just wanted to go inside. So, to avoid any further conversation, I opened the passenger door and mumbled my gratitude to the driver. The icy air slapped my wet cheeks and blew through the flimsy material of my dress, causing me to shiver. A moment later, Ryder was at my side and leading us towards the house.

It was warm inside. And bright. I tried not to look at Ryder. I shifted my gaze to everything in the room other than him. Silently, I was preparing myself for the humiliating teasing that I knew Ryder was ready to do. But to my surprise, he didn't mock me or say anything insulting. He didn't laugh or give me a smart ass, 'told you so.' Instead, he did the most scariest and wonderful thing.

He hugged me.

With his free hand, he pulled me into him and just held me there. I tensed. His body was warm against mine, the hug tight, yet the way he held me was delicate, like my emotions had made my body fragile and I might have broken if he were rough. I rested my head against his chest and relaxed as he silently held me closer; the tears stopping, the pain easing, and at that moment, it felt like everything was going to be okay.

I had the comfort of a friend I had lost long ago... and at that
moment, I realised just how much I missed him.

~♥♥♥~

"Wake up." Someone poked me. "Wake up."

Throwing the pillow over my head, I groaned. Ryder continued
to poke the crap out of me until I opened one eye and looked at him. He
grinned, holding up a piece of clothing. At first, it was blurry. Just an
indistinct shape of green and gold. But once I rubbed my eyes, I saw the
familiar twenty-one printed on it.

"Oh, no..."

Training day.

We didn't have much time to get ready. Ryder had woken me up
at five because he knew I'd take longer than his usual ten-minute routine.
So sluggishly, I got ready. Slipping into a sleeveless summer print dress
and throwing half a jacket over my shoulders, we went downstairs for
breakfast.

Mrs. Collins took one look at me and said, "Honestly, Nora, I
doubt that will hardly keep you warm."

I scowled. It wasn't something I wanted to hear so early in the
morning. I didn't even bother arguing that it was the only thing I *could*
wear without reminding her of the fact that I was handcuffed to her son.
Brushing off her remark, I passed her and grabbed a bowl and the cereal
box.

Ryder, on the other hand, was busy cracking eggs into a blender.
Mrs. Collins watched us carefully, sipping on her coffee as her eyes
skimmed from her son to me. Ryder slid a spoon over to me as he
switched the blender on and waited for his protein shake to mix.

I leaned against the counter, shovelling cereal into my mouth,
trying to avoid the icy glare of Mrs. Collins. Glancing over at her son,
who now had a seriously weird coloured drink in his hand, I grimaced. I
swear his beverage was *moving*. Watching him swig down the shake
suddenly made breakfast far less appealing.

Mrs. Collins must have read my mind because while I was looking at the soggy remains of my cereal, she said, "You know, Nora, there are dying children out there that would do anything for the privileges of breakfast."

I refrained from showing how annoyed she was making me and instead, choked down the last few squares of berry-centred cereal. Once I was done, I dropped my bowl down into the sink and tugged on Ryder's arm, heading for the door. He protested, quickly disposing the glass as I led us out of the house.

"Slow down, tiger. Didn't think you were so enthusiastic to go to practice. You hate footy," Ryder said as the door slammed shut behind him.

"Yeah, well, practice sounds better than staying in that house with your mother," I hissed. "What's her problem?"

Ryder's mother had allowed Ryder to drive her Jeep as long as he was careful. It was a lot larger than Ryder's sports car, so with only limited struggle, I was able to get in and out of the car easier than expected. As he drove, I couldn't help but comment on his mother's snarky remarks.

"I mean, did you hear her comment about my dress? Does she really think I *want* to look like a wiener in a bread roll? Of course not!"

Ryder parked the car and looked like he was going to just straight out slap me, but all he did was flick my forehead and tell me to roll my window up so we could get out of the car. Pressing my finger to the automatic button, I watched it slowly ascend. But once it was almost to the top, a pair of fingers curled in and gripped the moving window.

I didn't realise I had kept my finger on the switch until someone let out a painful scream. "Nora! Jesus, Nora!"

Quickly pressing the opposite button to roll the window down, I saw Caine shaking his fingers, teeth gritted together as he glared at me.

"What the hell are you doing?" I demanded.

"Gee, an apology for nearly amputating my fingers would have been nice," Caine grunted.

"Sorry," I muttered. "But what are you doing? Couldn't you see I was rolling it up?"

Caine glanced through the window and looked over at Ryder. "What's her problem?" Caine jerked his chin in my direction as if I weren't listening. "Why is she so snappy?"

"Conflict with my mum," Ryder said, opening his side of the door.

Caine nodded in understanding and circled the car, reaching Ryder's side. Ryder used the driver controls to wind up my window without causing anyone's fingers to nearly fall off and once everything was secure, we hopped out of the vehicle. Ryder and Caine instantly fell into their typical boy banter while I trudged along like a third-wheel on their bromance catch up.

"Hey look, it's Baker's bitch."

I looked up to see the rest of Ryder's team pointing towards us. Or, more specifically, me. I was apparently Chris Baker's bitch. It troubled me knowing that my Friday night date disaster was now Saturday morning gossip to the footy team. The boys made immature noises and comments as we walked over and with every step I took, it just made it harder.

The voices got louder, remarks were clearer and if I wasn't chained to Ryder, I would have bolted by now. I felt stupid and insecure, and this was exactly the kind of humiliation I was expecting. But from fairy floss brains who thought football was a religion was something I wasn't prepared for. I supposed the Chris Baker's crowd would have been the main source of embarrassing attention, but from the guys at school who didn't really care about gossip unless it was football or boob related, I wasn't expecting them to care.

I fell a step behind Ryder, not wanting to show I was bothered, but I guess I wasn't doing a good job. Laughs and snickers sounded as we reached the group of testosterone. But after a moment, they all hesitated. Ryder was staring each one of them down, an intense fire burning in his faded blue irises.

"Nora is with me and while she's with me, I expect you all to treat her with respect. I don't have the patience for your crap this morning."

One of the guys, one that looked like he had eaten steroids for breakfast, stepped through the pack of guys and faced Ryder. They were about the same height as they stood head to head and glowered at each other.

"What are you going to do about it, huh, Collins?" The guy's voice was deep and challenging as he narrowed his eyes at him.

"Why don't you ask the last guy who tried to mess with her."

I presumed Ryder was referring to his most recent girlfriend when he said *her* and I was surprised to wonder who she was. I'd have to ask Mel about it.

A heavy tension fell between the boys. The muscular guy tossed me a dirty look before reluctantly stepping back and into the crowd. Ryder gave the rest of the team a warning look.

"Why are you boys still standing around?" he barked. "Are we a book club or a footy team?"

Instantly, the pack split, grunting and huffing as they jogged away to grab equipment and set up obstacle cones. Although Ryder wasn't captain of the team, he still had the leadership skills to throw a few demands that people would unquestioningly obey.

The random acts of kindness these past few hours had honestly kind of scared me. At first, I thought he was doing it to receive something seriously sick and twisted back in return. But deep down, a part of me ached thinking it was possible that we were slowly regrowing our friendship. And in that little moment of happiness, I felt like I could have tackled all the harassment and embarrassment in the world.

"Yeah, that's right." Caine smacked his chest. "Back off! You heard the man."

I couldn't help but laugh at Caine. He grinned at me, as if I hadn't nearly chopped his fingers off earlier, and swung an arm around my shoulders.

"Thanks," I mumbled, "to both of you…"

Ryder exchanged a look with Caine and they both chuckled. "Don't thank me," he said, a wicked tone to his voice as he pulled something out of his gym bag and threw it at me. "Trust me, you'll hate me."

Catching the green piece of fabric, I opened it up and saw it was a shirt. "Oh... God, please... No..."

"Welcome to the team. Hope you're ready to play your A game."

Twelve

Training day was hell. Mel and I used to sneak around some warm days and pretend we were doing art projects by the field, but really, we were just watching the footy team run around. Never would I have thought that one of these days, I would actually be *on* the team.

"Ow..." I sobbed. "Your stupid football smacked my chest."

Caine raised an eyebrow. "You were meant to catch it, Nora. Your boobs aren't hands."

"You didn't have to peg it at me," I pointed out.

Okay, so I definitely wasn't a football fan. Sure, I loved watching, but playing in an over eighteen men's team was scary. What Caine considered as a 'baby throw' was enough to knock the wind out of me. And my sprinting was considered as a 'dainty little stroll' to the guys.

Caine just chuckled at me, shaking his head as he jogged over and picked up the ball. We were doing the conclusion of our 'warm up' exercises, which included pegging balls at each other, running laps around the field, and push ups. Push ups was my favourite part. While all

he guys were on their toes, faces tense as they worked their muscles, I
got to lay there, face in the grass.

"Are we gonna have a quick practice game?" Ryder was talking
to the coach.

The coach, mean, muscular, and bald, nodded and soon enough,
the captain of the team split the boys into two groups: shirts and no-
shirts. Ryder and I had been put into the shirts category. Since I couldn't
put my team shirt on, I had just tied the material around my waist. All I
had to do was pull it off and toss it away. Ryder, who had been much
more prepared, had already cut a slit on the side of his so he could
remove it with ease.

Once everyone was in their positions and the whistle blew, it was
total chaos. Teams were yelling instructions to each other; members
cooperated and moved about the field as the ball swiftly moved towards
the far side of the oval. My legs burned as Ryder dragged me across the
turf.

"Get ready," Ryder warned.

I was still trying to catch my breath. "Ready for wh-"

A football smacked against my head and conveniently landed
right into Ryder's hands. His face determined, he raced down the field
while I staggered to keep up with him. Then, at the last minute, Ryder
threw the ball into my arms and I instantly freaked out.

"I don't want it!" I yelled at him.

"Just run," Ryder replied, completely cool with the fact that I
was now the next tackle-target.

So, hugging the ball to my chest with my free arm and closing
my eyes, I screamed like a mad woman and charged through. I didn't
open my eyes. I didn't listen to whatever everyone was screaming at me.
I didn't stop running. I just listened to the sound of Ryder's laugh as we
raced across the field.

Eventually, my warrior scream faded and when I opened my
eyes, we were at the touchdown line. Slamming the ball down and
watching it bounce around, I let out a victory cry. Ryder was bent over,

trying to catch his breath. Not because he was tired, but because he was laughing.

"Bam!" I said, throwing my arms up in triumph.

Caine jogged over to us after a moment, a smirk on his face, trying to contain his laughter as he said, "Sweet score," letting out a chuckle. Then, before I knew it, his hand was at my lower back.

I guess I freaked out with his sudden wandering hands because I scrambled back and sucked in my breath. "Watch what you're touching, Caine!"

Caine shook his head and plucked at the fabric of my dress. "Your dress was tucked into your undies," Caine said, stumbling back as he clutched his stomach and laughed.

I felt my cheeks burn. "Is that why you got me to run with the ball," I snapped at Ryder, trying not to hear the laughs from the rest of the team.

Ryder stopped laughing and turned insanely serious. "God, no, Nora," he said, sounding genuinely earnest, "I'd never take advantage of you like that. I handed you the ball because I knew you were safe with it. After the little mishap this morning, I doubted anyone would try to take it from you, despite your entertaining flash of your grandma undies."

I felt the colour branch out across my entire face. I was pretty sure my entire body was blushing with embarrassment. It was bad enough that I was already humiliated the previous night. It just made it worse that my mortification increased, running through a field full of boys with my dress tucked into my undies. Ryder just gave me a smile and cupped the side of my face.

"Come on, pink cheeks, don't give me that look," he teased. "Practice is over. We can do whatever you want for the rest of the day."

I let out an annoyed little whine, but let Ryder direct us towards the change rooms. The boys' change rooms. We were the last to reach the door. Caine had disappeared earlier so we were the only ones standing outside. I mean, the guys' bathrooms were one thing, but the locker rooms were a whole other thing.

However, before I could protest, Ryder pushed open the door and we stepped through. Any girl would be pleased to be privileged to go into the guys' change room, watching shirtless guys roam around the place. And, sure, I wouldn't have minded that. Except I could hardly see anything. Steam, thick and hot, fumed through the room, completely blinding me and clogging my lungs.

I had to keep my hands out in front of me, praying I wouldn't grab something or someone's inappropriate business. My only sense of direction was Ryder's hand at my back, gently steering me through the maze of lockers and benches. I don't know how Ryder had such a clear view of everything and it startled me when he applied more pressure onto my back and pulled me into him, keeping me out of the way as a guy blindly shoved his way past.

We were close, really close. Both of us were pressed against the lockers, his free arm around my waist, warm fingers pressed against my spine.

"Sorry," he muttered breathlessly, as if he had to control his words so they'd come out right.

I closed my eyes, feeling the warmth of his breath on my cheeks. I felt his breathing quicken, his chest rising and falling against mine. But after a while, I realised that it was my breathing that had spiked. I let out a ragged breath and tried to clear my thoughts.

Why was I feeling so weird? Was it just because it was so hot and stuffy in the room? I couldn't possibly be developing feelings for my old friend. It was Ryder after all; annoying, arrogant Ryder. We hated each other, ever since that fight almost six years ago.

Shaking my head, I tried to dismiss the weird feeling and wriggled out of his reach. "God, let go of me," I said, stepping away, looking away and hoping the mist could cover how my face said I wanted the exact opposite.

It was stupid. Was it just because I hadn't really gotten close with a guy in such a long time? Was it just a spark of remembrance of how nice it was to be held in such a way? Maybe I had just been smacked with so many footballs that morning that I couldn't think straight anymore. I could *not* be falling for Ryder.

Right?

Thirteen

Ryder said we could do whatever I wanted for the rest of the day. Honestly, I just wanted some space to think. The locker room incident had gotten me all flustered and now I was a complete and utter mess. By the time we got back to Ryder's house and gotten cleaned up, I had come to the conclusion that I had gotten too many footballs to the head and the locker room odours were making me feel funny.

Yeah. That's it. I think.

Ryder left me to come up with the remaining day's plans. In the end, we went out back. It was like a pergola, yet cased with glass so if you looked up, you could see the sky. It was one of many privileges Ryder had to his house. So, we sat out there for a while. I snuggled into some warm, comfortable clothes and curled up on the worn, backyard couch with a book. Ryder sat next to me.

He didn't seem to mind my choice of activity. He seemed tired. Within a few minutes of settling in, silence had fallen upon us. It wasn't a tense silence like the one we had experienced in the taxi ride home the previous night. It was... rather comforting.

When I opened my book, I didn't read it. I stared blankly at the jumble of words and thought. Absentmindedly, I'd flick the pages over once in a while, appearing to be reading, when really, my mind was racing with so many thoughts.

Say, hypothetically, if I were to fall for Ryder, what would be my reasons? We had been at each other's throats for almost six years and without that stupid handcuff demonstration we might have graduated with our silent loathing of each other. But Ryder and I had been handcuffed for nearly three days now. You couldn't possibly fall for someone in three days.

Maybe it wasn't love. Maybe it was just hate. I had read somewhere that there was a thin line between the two. Hate seemed like a more reasonable explanation, but I didn't think my hate for him was any more passionate than it was a few days ago. If anything, it had dimmed.

Perhaps I was just thrilled that Ryder was being nice to me. After six years of hate and a sudden change in attitude, maybe I was just pleased with the difference. Maybe I didn't like, *like* him. Maybe I was starting to like him as a *friend*. He was being extremely compassionate and supportive, especially with the recent disastrous events.

Looking over at Ryder, who was now fast asleep, I thought further. He sat there, eyes closed, lips slightly parted as he gently snored. His hair was a tousled mess, wisps of dark hair sticking out in all directions. My eyes skimmed through every line and angle of his face: the arch of his lips, the hollow of his cheekbones, the shape of his jaw. It was no doubt that Ryder was attractive, but that didn't mean that I actually was attracted to him.

That makes sense, right?

In the end, I just ended up back in square one. My thoughts had jumbled up so much that I decided since I had so many football attacks to my head that my brain had rattled up and was making me feel weird things. That, and the seriously foul odours of the boys' locker room.

I don't know how long we stayed outside for. Eventually, I just placed my book down and watched the sun set. Rich, vibrant colours

painted the sky, a spectrum of sparkling life. Slowly, the light dimmed
and the sky darkened; the faint glitter of stars appearing.

Ryder woke up at that point, right when the sky bled from
colour. He grunted, shifting on the couch as he stretched awkwardly and
slumped back into position. He turned and looked at me, rubbing a hand
down his face.

"How long was I out for?" he asked, voice slow and sleepy. His
words were pronounced with a deep huskiness which was
unquestioningly attractive. But then again, *all* guys' sleepy voice was
unbelievably addictive.

"A few hours," I replied, returning my gaze back at the sky.

Ryder didn't really seem interested in my reply. He regarded my
response with a smack to his stomach. "I'm starving."

I hadn't realised I was hungry as well until he mentioned it. So,
together, we went back inside in a hunt for food. Ryder walked towards
the fridge and opened the door, popping his head inside and searched
around.

"I don't see anything to eat," he groaned.

I peeked over his shoulder. "There's plenty to eat," I said, eyes
widening at the variety of foods.

"Yeah, but nothing *I* want to eat," Ryder complained as he
straightened and slammed the door closed, the sound of glass bottles
clinking from the impact.

He walked over towards the cupboards next and pulled out a bag.
"Now we're talking. I know exactly what to have for dinner."

I never expected to have s'mores for an evening meal. I had
always pictured myself surrounded by friends as we circled around a fire,
telling ghost stories as we roasted marshmallows. But never would I have
thought I'd be in Ryder's living room,, sitting on a pile of cushions as I
hunched over a fireplace.

I stuck my long fork into the flickering flames of the fire and
watched as the marshmallow slowly turned from a spongy ball into a
toasted hot mess. After I scraped the sticky remains of the 'mallow onto

a cracker and topped it off with a piece of chocolate, I shoved half of it into my mouth.

"Slow down, yeah?" Ryder said, raising an eyebrow at me.

Feeling slightly embarrassed, I snapped, "Shut up."

Ryder just shook his head, the corner of his lips twitching into a small smile. I slowed down my eating after that and went through another three s'mores without Ryder making any comments about my rude eating habits. I rested my head back against the couch and closed my eyes, feeling completely satisfied.

I don't know how long my eyes were closed for, but when I returned my gaze back down, I caught Ryder studying me. His expression showed nothing of interest. Instead, he seemed slightly confused as he tried to figure something out, searching my face for something, like he was lost and the contours of my face were directions on a map that would lead him to the right destination. His eyebrows knitted together as he concentrated further.

"What?" I said, being the first to look away as I reached over and cupped my mug of hot chocolate in my hands.

"I just don't understand anymore, Nora," he answered.

"About what?" I questioned, looking down at the rich chocolate pool of goodness before taking a sip. The warm liquid ran through my entire body.

"Lots of things," Ryder replied, eyes narrowing at me as he thought. "You, me, us…" He paused for a moment, then quickly added, "Just stuff. Okay? Stuff.Lots of stuff."

It had been a really long day. A really long and confusing day and it was comforting to know that Ryder was just as muddled as I was. Or did it just make it a whole lot complicated? If he was just as uncertain as I was about what had happened earlier in the day, was there a stronger possibility that he had considered that we experienced some sort of weird moment?

Oh, God.

As if we were both thinking about the same thing, we exchanged looks and quickly looked away from each other, cringing. "Look, Nora, what happened in the change rooms... It meant nothing, okay?" he said, as he looked away and seemed to think.

"Um, gross. Why would I think it would mean anything?" I quickly replied, flippantly tossing my hand in his direction for emphasis. I added a little snort just in case I didn't prove my point.

"Good," he answered, frowning as he let out one of his famous grunts. Grunts that apparently translated into English, considering it was now most guys communicated with each other.

"Yeah. Good."

We kind of just sat there in silence for a few minutes, the whole topic being dropped. Although the conversation had been dismissed, I still thought about it. It meant nothing to me. I knew that. It was just a stupid little incident.

Then why couldn't I stop thinking about it?

Fourteen

The next morning, I felt something wet brush up against my butt. Since the Collins liked warm nights, they had left the heat running and I had changed into a pair of cotton shorts before I went to sleep. And feeling something curl up under my shorts and lick the bare skin of my butt totally creeped me out. But what freaked me out even further was that once I felt it, I heard Mrs. Collins' voice extremely near.

Oh my God... Mrs. Collins just licked my butt...

But it wasn't her, of course. Thank God. It was just the family dog, Biscuit. He had gotten a lot older since the last time I saw him. Well, considering it had been almost six years, I didn't exactly blame him. When I used to go over to Ryder's house, Biscuit would always hang out with us in their backyard or come with us on walks, but now, the old Lab looked just about worn out.

Sitting up from my place on the floor, I scratched behind his ears. We had decided it was only fair that Ryder got to sleep in his bed because it was his house. He was reluctant at first, probably calculating whether I'd hold a grudge about it once I got a sore back or something, but I guess he was as sleepy as me when we finally agreed.

My movements to scratch behind his dog's ears made Ryder stir in his sleep and after a few seconds of shuffling, he let out a sleepy groan and looked down at us. He smiled weakly at his dog and he too reached over and patted the top of Biscuit's shaggy head.

"Glad you're up."

I had almost forgotten that Mrs. Collins was standing in the room. I instantly felt kind of undressed once I saw her standing dominantly in her ridiculously expensive-looking work heels, hands on her hips. She was wearing a black business dress, but it was classy enough to wear on a night out, completed with a string of gleaming pearls around her neck. I felt so unsophisticated and naked in my cotton ducky pyjamas.

"There's a street party being held tonight on the main road," Mrs. Collins said, looking at her son. "As you know, we have a certain... responsibility to participate in these events."

That was true. The Collins family always contributed to street parties and community events. It was mostly Mr. Collins doing. He loved socialising and entertaining the town. And a few years into their passionate response to their community service, the family was awarded a permanent position on the community organisation team. But when the word got out about Mr. Collins' outrageous affair, their enthusiasm to participate dimmed. Everyone was hesitant in suggesting to the family to retire their occupation on the team, but Mrs. Collins refused to withdraw. She knew the town was feeling sympathetic for her and because her husband left her for a younger woman and was aware everyone considered the family to be broken. However, with her high status and prestigious profession as a successful business woman, she regarded the loss of her husband lightly to her peers and insisted the family tradition to stay strong. Although she acted tough around everyone, I knew a part of her still felt uncomfortable about contributing to something her husband was so enthusiastic about. And I knew how much she depended on her son to keep up their reputation.

"I know." Ryder sat up and ran his fingers through his hair, making it even messier. He knew what his mother was going to say and was aware that it was a delicate subject. I suddenly felt awkward being in the room with the intensity of emotions stirring in the air.

"Thank you." Mrs. Collins did something between a constipated face and a smile and I figured it was as the closest expression she could get to thankful.

She turned and shut the door behind her, leaving a moody Ryder and a really awkward me. I didn't know what to say, so I just sat there with Biscuit and stared into his big, dark eyes. Since he had gotten so old, they looked slightly murky, like a mist had swept over his irises. There was no doubt that because of that, he was experiencing sight difficulty, but I wondered if the aged dog knew what had happened to his family.

Biscuit, watching me stare at him in thought, attacked my face with slobbery kisses. I squirmed out of his ticklish and sloppy grasp and gently pushed his nose away. He jumped on the bed after that to see if Ryder was interested in playing, but when he saw his master's face, staring blankly at nothing in particular, he walked to the end of the bed and just sat there, head in his paws.

I didn't know what to say. I wasn't sure if I was just supposed to ignore it or take it lightly and make a joke so he can laugh. I wasn't sure if I was supposed to comfort him or talk about it. Back when we were kids, I would have just hugged him. But now that we were older and different and *definitely* hated each other, I was at a loss. Besides, the handcuffs would have made the hug difficult.

Thankfully, Ryder turned and spoke. "We should get ready. We have a lot to do."

Ryder decided we'd make melting moments for the street party and sell them for a dollar each. So when we had gotten out all the ingredients and laid them out on the bench table, we decided we'd have a competition to see who could bake the best batch. It was pretty lame, but ve had quite a few batches to make and the thrill of a rivalry was exhilarating enough to keep us entertained throughout the morning.

"Three-quarter cup of plain flour," I read from the laminated recipe that rested between us.

Scanning the bench for all the bags and containers filled to their brims with white powder, I frowned. I had no idea there were so many things that looked exactly the same. I leaned over and tried to read their labels: cornflour, self-rising flour, barley flour, cake flour. I squinted at the row of buckets before me.

Ryder sighed, reached over and flicked me before grabbing a container from behind the rest and dumping it in front of me. All the time I had wasted on trying to find the plain flour, he had already measured his ingredients and was getting the electric mixer ready.

"I'm gonna kick your ass with this baking crap," Ryder said triumphantly as he plugged in the mixer. "I'm already dominating you..."

Ryder continued to gloat about how amazing he was and while I listened and snorted at the appropriate moments and pulled faces at his words, I hadn't realised that I was overflowing my cup with flour.

"Nora!"

I was so startled by his sudden outburst that I jumped half a metre into the air and let out a small scream, the bag of flour puffing out some of its contents as I leapt. I coughed as a cloud of powder blurred my vision and while spluttering like a cigarette addict, I tried dumping the bag back onto the table. But to my absolute luck, I missed and the bag dropped to the floor, flour skittering across the Collins' kitchen like dry snow.

Everything that came after that was a fast blur. Biscuit came charging to the rescue, looking fragile but determined as he sprinted into the kitchen. He reached us and noticed the flour on the floor, but it was too late. His paws struggled to regain his balance as he went sliding across the slippery floor and knocked right into the back of Ryder's knees, causing him to lose his balance as he buckled. Ryder let out a startled sound as he hastily grabbed something to help his poise. But instead of taking hold of the bench, he grasped his mixing bowl in his hands. It didn't do anything to help his posture so he fell to the dirty floor, taking the bowl *and* me down with him. He swore as he landed, letting out a grunt as I clumsily fell on top of him.

We were an awkward tangle of limbs. Due to the handcuffs, our arms were at the weirdest of angles and it was extremely uncomfortable. Looking up, I saw Biscuit whose casual gliding across the floor had stopped. He just lay there, looking exhausted.

Then my eyes returned back to Ryder. Flour had powdered throughout his hair and his face was covered in sticky, buttery batter. His eyes looked into mine and I instantly lost myself. I felt my heart spike and I wondered if he could feel it this time since we were pressed chest to chest. The beats quickened, pounding against me and my mind fogged until Ryder was my only focus and our surroundings had bled into nothingness.

It was the boys' locker room incident all over again, but this time, I didn't have any reasonable explanation. No footballs to the head, no indescribable smells, no hot steamy air to inhale. In the end, I had the most unthinkable, ridiculously impossible reason to why I was feeling the way I was.

I was falling for Ryder.

But why? That was my next question and I was determined to figure out why all these emotions were suddenly storming within me. We had spent almost four whole days together and that left no time for me to develop feelings for him. If anything, I expected to hate him more. He was irritable and stubborn and drove me absolutely crazy sometimes. But maybe I had been mistaking my hate for the complete opposite. Perhaps I was in denial and was only now realising the truth.

Ryder's hand on my waist broke me away from my thoughts. His grip was warm and gentle as his thumb gently drew circles on my side as he held me there, searching my eyes. All feelings of discomfort drained from me and suddenly, even though my arm was in a position that looked like it was totally broken, I felt completely content and safe. Like his embrace would protect me from anything.

Our hands that were handcuffed found each other, and slowly, even though it was a struggle with the restraint from the cuffs, his fingers fell between mine. His hand was warm and had a surprising roughness. I searched his face as he held me timidly, as if he were afraid I might just shatter if he squeezed too tightly.

It was stupid.

I could feel his racing heartbeat. Or maybe it was mine.

Really stupid.

His hand was just so damn warm.

Stupid.So stupid.

The way he smiled at me was unforgettable.

Stupid.

But I did it anyways.

I allowed myself to fall.

Fifteen

"Nora," he whispered, his thumb brushing the inside of my palm.

"Yeah?" It came out quieter than I had intended.

"We should get up."

"Okay."

Although I had agreed to his suggestion, neither of us moved. Instead, we stayed where we were, silently staring at each other, so many words unspoken between us. His thumb traced designs across my hand, warmth soaking into my veins and spreading through my body. I wondered if he was aware of his touch. I wondered if he knew what it was doing to me.

I could have asked. I should have asked.

But instead, Biscuit barked. He scrambled up and started to clumsily make his way toward the front door, paws still stained with dry ingredients. A moment later, there was a knock.

"We should get that," he mumbled distractedly, eyes focused on mine, rather than the direction of the door. "Okay, how should we do this?"

"Maybe--"

Ryder didn't wait for me to answer him. Instead, he tried moving us both, but all it caused was a head collision. We both let out pained groans and collapsed back onto the floor. And even though we both had throbbing heads, we laughed.

"Sorry," Ryder said through fits of laughter, "I'm so sorry."

He reached up and gently cupped his free hand against my cheek, leaning in and planting his lips onto my forehead. The kiss was the softest of things, but it ignited every nerve in my body.

Ryder must have realised the tenderness in the moment and the fact that he had just kissed me so casually, or maybe he had just acknowledged the fact that we hadn't exchanged a snarky comment all day. Either way, a combination of confusion and surprise crossed his features.

The knock got louder.

"One second!" Ryder called, frowning, as if he had just realised he had a visitor.

We didn't look at each other after that. Instead, we wordlessly managed to stand up, after a couple of painful twists and weird positions. Someone was still pounding on the door and Biscuit continued to bark. Ryder seemed irritated by the time we got to the door. He threw it open with more force than necessary.

"Check it out, dude," Caine said triumphantly, holding up a box of donuts. "Five dollars at Woolworths." Then he looked at us. "What the hell happened to you two?"

Ryder's eyebrows knitted together in confusion. He looked over at me, saw the disaster that exploded on my face, and reached over, gently running his thumb over the side of my nose to wipe off some flour. We were both startled by the gesture. Ryder quickly pulled away as we exchanged wide-eyed expressions, before we both faced Caine, who was now looking at us with raised eyebrows.

"Anyway," he said, pushing past us, "I bought these for the street fair." We followed him into the kitchen and watched him examine the mess. "And this is why I didn't attempt to make anything. What's it even supposed to be?" Caine picked up the bowl from the floor, stuck his finger into the remaining batter and ate it.

"Melting moments," Ryder and I said in unison.

We looked at each other like someone just told us we'd have to amputate a leg each.

"Aw, aren't you two just two peas in a pod," Caine said, laughing. It seemed a little uncomfortable, but I didn't get to see his expression to confirm my suspicions because he took the bowl away and clapped Ryder on his shoulder on his way into the living room.

"You have no idea," Ryder muttered under his breath.

Caine stuck around for another hour and even after he left, we continued and finished baking, cleaned the kitchen, and changed to get ready for the street party. Once on the main road, located by the lake, we were allocated a stall space that was set up in advance. All we had to do was line up our melting moments on the table provided and wait for tourists and community members to stop close by.

Stalls lined the closed street, glowing with vibrant colours and cooing customers. Next to us, a woman selling homemade woollen clothes items was helping a lady pick between two beautifully designed mittens and on the other side of our stall was a man retailing fresh fruits and vegetables. Each little stand had something beautiful and homemade. From people painting designs on people's converse sneakers to sparkling pieces of jewellery and warm, sweet treats, the street party had it all.

Caine turned up about half an hour into business. So far, we had only sold ten, but we were against some pretty tough competition. People were cooking everything: sweet and sour, hot and cold, soft and hard. So when Caine rolled up to our stall, he saw us, grinned and gave Ryder one of those ridiculously strange guy handshakes that I will never understand.

To me, he simply regarded me with a nod that I returned. Then he scuttled away towards Ryder and they started talking about pointless

tuff, like how many chillies they could stuff into their mouths before
creaming for mercy. I, on the other hand, kept an eye on the traffic of
people as their eyes scanned across stalls for anything of interest.

Ryder hadn't said anything about the kiss, or anything that
happened in his kitchen for that matter. We were both acting like it didn't
happen. I secretly hoped he'd bring it up though.

The same *what if* questions spun through my mind. What if
Caine didn't arrive at his doorstep? What if the kiss turned into
something else? What if he regretted it?

It was giving me a headache.

And what gave me even more of a headache was the fact that I
saw Chris Baker, looking high and mighty as he strutted down the street
with a giggling blonde. Cotton Dean. The girl really did live up to her
name, considering her brain consisted of mostly fluff. I frowned at them
as they walked together, watching as Cotton let out a little girly shriek of
laughter as Chris whispered something in her ear.

Seeing Chris with another girl wasn't a bother. I now knew that
he was trouble and was only using me for God knows what, but the fact
that he was *there* annoyed me. I hadn't really thought about our
disastrous date since Ryder had kept me seriously distracted, but now
that he was there and heading over to our stall, made me clench my fists.

Although Chris was wearing a pair of shades, I knew that his
smirk glittered in his eyes. I was kind of thankful that the dark, reflective
lens shadowed his gaze because I would have lost it. Ryder must have
sensed my tension and turned towards the couple, face hard.

"How much for a kiss?" Chris asked, leaning over the table so he
was closer.

"Don't make me slap you," I answered, trying to control my
temper as he reached out and brushed a piece of hair away from my face.

Although Chris was at the street party with Cotton, his date
didn't seem to mind that he was mocking me with his teasing flirtations,
mainly because Cotton seemed to be doing the same thing. She fluttered
her eyelashes at Ryder..

"So, what are these... things?" she asked, flipping her long blonde hair over her shoulder.

"Melting moments," Ryder answered distractedly, keeping a close eye on Chris and I.

Cotton leaned closer and adjusted her top. "What other kind of melting moments do you sell? I'd love to taste them all."

Ryder frowned, returning his gaze to her. "There's only one kind," he answered, clearly irritated.

"Are you sure there isn't any other kind of *melting moment* you'd like to share with me?" Cotton was determined.

"No."

"Nora," Chris whispered, making me turn my attention back to him. "We never got to properly finish our date... I think you owe me a kiss."

"I don't owe you anything," I snarled.

Chris reached over and cupped my chin. It wasn't in one of those heart stopping ways either. He grabbed my face with a strong grip and forced me closer. I glared at him and tried moving out of his grip, but his other hand had found its way over to my side and he was now digging his fingers into my skin. Fright consumed me, but concealed my horror with a cold, hard glare.

Before I could find out what was going to happen next, a cold voice growled, "Step away from her."

I had never heard Ryder use that voice before and honestly, it was rather startling. It was deep and commanding... but there was also something different about it. I realised what it was before I looked up.

It was Caine's voice.

It was nice of him to defend me, but I was more interested in the fact that he was actually doing it. I didn't exactly know Caine personally but I had witnessed characteristics of his reputation. He didn't exactly play anyone, but it was true that he was addicted to female attention. With his dark hair and equally dark eyes, it was impossible to not draw focus to.

Caine was slightly taller than Chris and although it shouldn't
have been very intimidating, it looked a hell of a lot scary. That inch or
so was daunting. Chris' eyes flickered to mine then returned to Caine's.
He narrowed his eyes for a second, then backed away. I was surprised to
see the same tension between the two that I had seen between Ryder and
Chris. That only made me more determined to find out about the
wickedly mysterious past Ryder kept shadowed.

"I'll deal with you later. Both of you," Chris hissed aggressively,
eyes scanning between Ryder and Caine. Then, he turned to Cotton and
barked, "Let's go."

Cotton looked irritated at Ryder for not acting upon her flirting,
but she seemed furious at Chris for using such a harsh and demanding
tone on her. She shot him a dirty look and stormed off. Chris, realising
he was being ditched, turned and started chasing after her, yelling out pet
names and pleas in attempt to calm her down.

"You okay?" Caine gently placed his hand against my arm and
scanned me over. His big brother protection was both comforting and
strange and I wasn't sure what to think of it.

Ryder didn't say anything. He just kind of looked at Caine all
confused and calculating as if he didn't understand something. I guess he
was as shocked about the whole helping-me-out thing as I was. I mean,
although Caine cherished the opposite sex's attention, he often targeted
the elite. Helping his mate's ex-best friend was seriously
uncharacteristic.

"I'm fine," I said, then my gaze returned to Ryder's. "Are you
okay? Cotton was ready to poke your eye out with a tampon in her ever-
so-subtle attempt to flirt."

Ryder laughed. "Yeah. I'm fine." His attention turned back to
his friend.

Ryder and Caine did their weird little psychic thing again that
consisted of a lot of stares and expressions. Eyebrows rose and knitted
together as they silently communicated with each other through eyebrow
movements. I just stood there, feeling awkward and excluded from their
brotherly bond.

After a moment, Ryder cracked a weak smile and nodded. Then with that, we proceeded with the rest of the day without saying much at all.

Sixteen

"**This** is probably the best sausage I've ever had," Caine said as he ate the last of his dinner.

As late afternoon rounded, the street party dimmed and people started packing away stalls and loading up cars. Only a few decided to stay and help with the last bit of cleaning. Most of the community were back home, in front of the fireplace and sheltered away from the cold evening.

But Ryder and I decided to stay, along with a couple of other kids from school, including Caine. We surrounded a little fire we had built on the sand, sausages on sticks as we roasted them. There was no doubt a bit of alcohol was going around because some people looked way too happy being there. And frankly, I didn't find anything about the harsh wind even the slightest bit cheerful. It just made me feel cold.

Caine had eaten about seven sausages and any normal girl would have been disgusted, but I understood he was a growing teenage guy. I also accepted the fact that he ate seven sausages because I almost beat him by consuming six. Although I hadn't thought anyone was keeping track, when I reached over to grab another one, Caine looked at me wide-eyed.

"What is that? Your third or something?" he asked, as he jabbed his sausage onto the stick.

"Possibly…" I muttered, feeling embarrassed that I had actually eaten double..

Ryder laughed from next to me and gave me a knowing smile, his expression telling me he knew exactly about my inner fat kid. That just made the colour in my cheeks turn a shade deeper so I kept my eyes on the flickering tongues of fire as they danced exotically into the early night sky.

Once I was pretty sure I'd pop, I placed my hands behind me, letting them sink in the cool, damp sand and sighed in satisfaction. It was starting to get darker, just the faintest bit of light over the hills as the sun made its departure.

A red cup was circling the fire and it was no doubt the reason behind the numerous choruses of giggles. When the cup came around, Ryder shook his head and passed it over to Caine, completely missing me.

"Hey," I said, frowning. Not that I was going to have a drink anyway.

"You're not eighteen yet, Nora," he said, glancing at me briefly.

"That doesn't stop anyone from drinking," I pointed out.

Ryder just looked at me and there was a mischievous gleam in his eyes. I groaned inwards. I knew that look anywhere. He was ready to sneer out an insult. But when he parted his lips, I was shocked to hear what he had to say.

"I care about you, Nora," he said, lifting his lips into a half smile. "Trust me, you don't want to get involved with alcohol. Besides, I really don't like being chained to sober Nora, let alone drunk and hungover Nora."

I stared at him with giant eyes. "What did you say?"

He sighed, irritably. "I don't want to deal with your complaining and throwing up if you drink that crap."

I shook my head. "The other part."

"What other part?" Ryder raised an eyebrow, honestly curious.

"You said you care about me," I muttered, feeling foolish.

Ryder frowned. "Really?"

His tone wasn't harsh, just surprised. He looked thoughtful for a moment as his eyebrows drew together in thought. He ran a hand through his hair and bit his lip, something I noticed he did a lot when he was concentrating. After a moment of silence, I spoke, not wanting to feel the awkward tension any longer.

"You gonna eat that?" I asked pathetically, poking the sausage that was speared into the end of his stick.

I was honestly stuffed, but I needed to put something in my mouth to avoid any more verbal diarrhoea. And since Ryder wasn't making any move to eat...

He handed it to me. I quickly took the biggest bite of my life and pretended to find the sandy floor extremely fascinating. The sausage wasn't even that good. It was all grainy and salty from the sand on my hands. And it was kind of cold and rubbery now since it had obviously been sitting out in the cold too long. It was no longer plump and flavoursome, but I just sat there and acted as though I hadn't noticed.

"How cute. Weenies in the sand."

I knew that voice. I didn't have to turn to know it was Chris. Shooting him the dirtiest look I could muster, I snapped, "They're good ones"

Sure, it was a pretty lame response. I was defending what he called *weenies.* But I was sick of Chris and seeing the smirk on his face didn't make me any better. I narrowed my eyes at him and curled my fingers tighter around the stick in my hand. I jabbed the air in front of him just to emphasise my sudden passion for defending my food.

Chris had brought a friend with him. I vaguely remembered his name. I only knew he hung out with the gang. Although he was a part of Chris' assembly, he had a minor role within the friendship group. He never really spoke up or anything, so you couldn't really remember him. So seeing him here to witness – or perhaps back up - the confrontation was surprising.

"Oh, I wasn't talking about your dinner," Chris snarled at the barbecued treat in my hand and nodded towards the boys on either side of me. "I was talking about *those* weenies."

Caine stood up at that and stood nose to nose with Chris, letting out a feral sound that stirred in the back of his throat. "Back off, man."

This time, Chris made no move to back down. His face was determined and mad. "You shouldn't have gotten into this, Wright."

Caine narrowed his eyes. "This is my fight just as much as it's yours. You mess with Nora, you mess with me too."

Well. That was an unexpected response.

"She's with us while she's handcuffed to Ryder," he continued, voice low and steady, scary and intimidating.

That was more like it.

Then, without warning, Caine struck at Chris' jaw. Chris stumbled back, startled as he cupped his chin. When he had recovered enough to react, he snapped his attention towards Caine who was making it evident that he was impatient with waiting for him to fight back. Chris lurched at him with a feral look in his eyes like an animal about to capture his prey.

All I saw were Caine's eyes widen as Chris tackled him to the ground and then, before I knew it, they were a tangle of limbs rolling around on the sand as they struggled to block and punch each other's hits. Chris had gotten the advantage of surprise so he gripped his opponent's neck in a headlock as he fought to place them into a position where he could truly hurt Caine.

Caine fought against Chris' iron grip and let out a grunt as he tightened the hold around his neck. I watched as he tried to knock his head back into Chris' nose, but the clasp around his neck was too secure for him to move. His fingers tried to pry his rivals arm away but when that was no use, Caine put all the force he could into his other arm, elbowing Chris in the gut.

Chris let out a spluttering cough and his grip faltered. With that, Caine threw a punch right at Chris' nose. I swear I could hear the bone crunch beneath his knuckles when his fist came in contact with his face. I cringed, watching as Chris stumbled back, gripping his nose as he tried to reduce the amount of blood gushing out.

"Stay away from her," Caine growled.

But apparently a broken nose wasn't going to make Chris back off. He lunged at Caine and again, they started fighting. I felt sick seeing them. I mean, was it even necessary? Chris was a jerk with the way he treated me on our date, but was that really worth the conflict? Especially from someone who hardly knew me.

"You'd think you would have learned your lesson about throwing yourself into places where you're not needed, huh?" Chris' friend was heading towards us, casually strolling by like he wasn't walking past a huge testosterone-filled fight.

Ryder's jaw clenched as he glared at Chris' friend. "You know nothing, Will."

Will let out a howl of laughter and gave Ryder a menacing glare. "Were you really that high that night that you can't remember that I was there the whole time?"

"Just because you saw doesn't mean you understand," Ryder replied, his voice level but serious discomfort masked his face.

"You had it bad, man. You were so deep into it."

God, Ryder had been experimenting with drugs?

Ryder's gaze flicked to mine for a second and I swear I could see pain in his eyes. But he turned back to Will before I could be sure I had even seen the slightest bit of hurt. He was close now, faint traces of food and alcohol lingering on his stained breath. Will looked from Ryder to me and a slow smirk grew on his lips.

"She doesn't know, does she?" Amusement laced his tone.

"She doesn't need to." Ryder's voice was low and scary, making me want to step back into the shadows and hide.

"You were addicted. Does she know it's the reason your friendship-"

He never got to finish the sentence, because Ryder swung back and hit Will right on the eye. I flinched, knowing that he would wake up with a colourful eye in the morning. Will stumbled back and Ryder hit him again. And again. He did it so effortlessly and carelessly, like he was just tenderising a piece of meat. I felt every force of his hits as he tugged me along.

"Stay the hell away from her!" Ryder shouted, something extremely dark and frightening about his tone.

"Ryder." My voice was quiet and breathless, the fear evident from the way I whispered his voice in panic. I placed a hand on his arm to try and calm him down but the way he jerked once I came in contact with him made me draw back.

He spun and looked at me, a wildfire burning in his eyes. It was terrifying to see blatant horror in such innocent coloured irises. Ryder studied me for a moment, confused about what was going on. I tried to picture what I looked like to him: small, puzzled, and frightened. His eyebrows furrowed in concentration and although it took more than a second, he finally started to relax until he was at this stage of complete vulnerability. Ryder looked so young, his eyes finally didn't look like a raging river, but more of a calm ocean, glazed with a wavering layer of fear.

I don't know what came over me after that. I guess, seeing someone so strong completely lose it to a point of helplessness made something in my heart ache. But before I knew it, my free arm was wrapped around him in the tightest embrace I could muster. Ryder was stunned at first, but after a moment, his free arm wrapped around my waist and he gripped me to him just as tightly as I was.

From next to us, Will rolled around in the sand, moaning in pain. But when he caught my eye, he winked and burst out in the most dramatic struggle I had ever seen. I didn't understand why he was making such a sudden big deal from all this, but when I finally listened hard enough, I knew exactly why.

Police sirens.

Ryder heard them at the same time I did. His grip tightened, orcing me to press closer. His body was tense against mine and his reathing had suddenly gotten rigid. Quickly scanning the beach, he ooked for Caine. When he spotted his friend, clothes dirty, he shouted.

"Caine!"

Caine whipped around and looked over towards the road where he police were racing closer towards the sand. He swore, kicked Chris ehind the knees so he went stumbling into the sand and quickly raced fter us. Ryder grabbed my hand and curled his fingers around mine as we made a run for it. The adrenaline was overwhelming, my heart was ounding, head spinning, breathing raspy as we ran to escape. But we never got far.

"Mind explaining what's going on here?"

Busted.

~♥♥♥~

Surprising how it was my first time to ride in a police car, but not my first time being handcuffed. All three of us were chained together in the back of a police vehicle. The police officer was no one I was familiar with. She was mean looking and tough, like she could effortlessly beat up any full grown man twice her height and weight.

However, the police rookie accompanying her I recognised as the guy who was there at school the day Ryder and I got handcuffed. I think his name was Drew. I scowled at him. It must have been a pretty menacing glare because he gave me a sheepish half-smile and turned around in his seat, directing his gaze away from me.

The ride was tense. Neither of us spoke. Ryder looked out the window, hands clenched, body tense. Caine sat on the other side of me, staring straight ahead. Although it was dark inside the car I could see his battered face. His lip was swollen and bloody, grains of sand sprinkled through his brown hair.

At the police station, we were held inside a room, with one of those long mirrors that ran across one side of the wall. I wondered if it were one of those reflective ones where people from a secret room next door could examine our every move. The room was warm, no windows and the only escape was the door, which was no doubt locked and guarded.

I wasn't sure how much trouble we'd be in and I wasn't even sure if we'd get special consideration for being underage, especially since both Ryder and Caine were recently considered legal adults. The fact that Caine had a bit to drink was also an issue I dwelled upon. The chairs we were sitting on were extremely uncomfortable, plastic and hard. Tipping my head back, I glanced up at the bright, fluorescent light above and groaned. I stared at the blinding bulb until blinding spots blurred my vision.

The heavy door creaked as it opened. Straightening in my seat, I directed my sight towards the policeman who walked into the room. Spots still covered the image that formed before my eyes, but once my eyes had adjusted, I saw a familiar caterpillar moustache and beer belly.

Officer Brandy.

He waddled into the room, hands on his hips, fingers hooked through his belt. The keys dangling from the compartment on his belt jingled with every step until he fully walked in. Officer Brandy studied us for a moment and when he realised it was us, his eyes widened.

"Fancy seeing you here." He smiled easily.

That earned him three typical teenage silent-death stares. Sensing his appearance hadn't exactly made us happy chappies, he grunted, put on a stern face, and held open the door.

"Head outside."

We stood lazily and shuffled towards the exit. I was sure it was midnight at the latest and wondered when we would be able to go home. A shower and bed sounded amazing at that moment. I really didn't want to have to deal with all this legal business.

We were led down the hall towards a little reception area where I spotted my sister. I had never been so relieved to see Eve. She was in her maternity pyjamas, leaning against the counter, her nose pressed against

he security glass that separated her from the police officer sitting behind
t.

"Listen... I have a butterfinger in my bag... What do you say we
nake a little negotiation? I'll give you my butterfinger if you give me
hat taco."

Eve didn't seem startled that she was called into the police
station in the middle of the night. She was more concerned with feeding
herself. I almost teared up seeing her hungry hippo side as she tried
anything to get her hands on the taco the policeman had in his hands.

Patrick placed his hands against her stomach, gently pushing her
towards him and away from the window. "We're here because we got a
phone call about Nora Montgomery."

A cool gust of wind blew into the room as the entrance door
swung open and Mrs. Collins strutted through the room. Her icy eyes
skimmed across the room and she scowled at her surroundings in disgust.
Then she spotted us and her death glare was enough to make me
spontaneously combust. Her lips pursed and her work heels clicked
against the floor as she marched her way over.

"Do you know how embarrassed I was when I received a phone
call in the middle of an extremely important conference telling me that
my son had gotten into an argument and was now locked up at the police
department?" Her tone was as sharp and cold as icicles, every word
slicing through painfully.

Ryder lifted a shoulder in nonchalance and kept his voice level
as he replied, "I regret nothing."

Mrs. Collins shot her son a look of disapproval and then tossed
me one as well. She didn't say anything to me though. I guess she didn't
want to start conflict with someone who wasn't her own flesh and blood
right in the middle of a police station. But I knew exactly what her
thoughts were: it was all my fault.

And I couldn't agree more. It *was* my fault. The only reason
Ryder and Caine had gotten into those fights was because of me.
Because I had gotten involved with the wrong guy and they were trying
to protect me. This burden of heavy truth hung on my shoulders and

suffocated me. I felt my stomach drop and my heart sink when the realisation sunk.

Mrs. Wright turned up at that moment, her husband trailing behind. Unlike Mrs. Collins who had greeted her son with dripping venom, she wrapped her arms around her child and held him close, muttering about how worried she was and how happy she was to see that he was okay. Caine, like any gruff teenage guy, tried to awkwardly pry her off, but I could see the affection in his eyes. If we weren't all handcuffed together, I knew he would have hugged her back, in one of those quick, secretive moments.

I felt really awkward. Between Mrs. Collins' hate and Mrs. Wright's warmth, I just stood in the middle of this seriously emotional reunion. I wasn't sure where to look or what to do. I tried avoiding Ryder's mum and I didn't think she'd approve if I looked at her son. I couldn't just stare at Mrs. Wright either, especially when she was in this really compassionate state. I didn't want to intrude on their moment. Staring at my hands wasn't an option either since I was still handcuffed on each wrist to the boys.

Craning my neck and stretching up on my toes, I tried searching for my family. Patrick must have noticed the commotion because he turned from Eve and caught my eye. I saw relief wash over his tired features and he gave me a weak smile, took his girlfriend's hand in his, and gently steered her away from her taco negotiation.

"Nora!" Eve grinned at me and practically skipped towards me. Well, as close to skipping as you can get when you're pregnant.

She let go of Patrick's hand and squeezed through the two other families, embracing me in a weird kind of way. It was hard hugging her when there was a giant ball in between. I was surprised to see her so cheerful, especially considering I was at a police station in the middle of the night. I supposed it was her pregnancy emotions. Realisation would probably sink in by morning.

"We've been so worried about you," Patrick said, reaching over to place his hand on my shoulder. Genuine concern was all over his face.

Eve, on the other hand... looked kind of happy. She held me at arm's length and grinned at me with pride. "Your first encounter with the law," she said, sniffling. "You are so ready for university."

This just left me speechless. She was... proud of me. "You're not going to tell Mum, right?"

I eyed her carefully. I wasn't sure if this was an act or if she was truly delighted with me having to go to the police department. Keeping a cautious gaze on my sister, I wondered if she'd suddenly turn ape on me and give me a lecture. But she didn't. She just dismissed my question and went on about 'this one time' in college.

It was weird how all three of our families acted differently. Caine's parents seemed happy and relieved, smothering their child with affection. Ryder's mother looked like she was ready to kill someone with her famous death stare. Then there was me, with my sister and her boyfriend. While Patrick reacted normally to this situation with worry and concern, Eve topped the weirdness cake with her honoured response.

Officer Brandy, looking just as startled as I felt, walked over and unlocked the handcuffs chaining Caine and I together. It felt good to have my left wrist breathe again and I shook it, reviving some life into it.

"You kids are allowed to go home, but you do understand that you are going to have to be punished," he said gruffly. "Nothing serious, considering no permanent or serious damage was done. Just ten hours of community service to complete, but if I see you starting any more fights around town again, the consequences will be severe."

"We were intimidated!" Caine burst out. "It was personal defence."

"Look, kid, we have no real evidence of who started what. So we're just going to be putting all five of you on community service."

Caine didn't look completely satisfied but I think the thought of Chris and his friend getting punished as well helped tame him a little. After a few more finalisations, we were released from the police station around two in the morning. We were all tired and silent by the time we walked out.

As we stepped outside in the night air, I gently touched Caine's
arm. It was a timid gesture. He turned and faced me, looking beaten and
sleepy. His parents headed for their car across the car park but he
lingered behind.

"Thanks... for defending me and stuff," I said in a rush. "I mean,
Chris was my business and you didn't have to get involved-"

I stopped because Caine had suddenly gotten hold of my hand.
He held it in his, warm fingers wrapping around mine and he smiled at
me sleepily. "Don't mention it."

He brought my hand to his lips and gently kissed it. I just stared
at him. Even when he was beaten up and exhausted, he still was the
regular Caine Wright who could charm the ladies with a single smile. His
eyes sparkled as he gave me a grin, let go of my hand and raised his in
one of those half guy-waves.

"Farewell, fair maiden." He winked and with that, he was off.

I looked up at Ryder, in a *what the hell* kind of way. He was still
watching Caine walk away, expression thoughtful. I sighed and tugged
him along. Perhaps the effects of alcohol and fatigue were finally taking
its toll on Caine, to a point where he didn't understand his motives or
actions.

Once inside the car, we were silent. The heater was running, Eve
was quietly munching on her chocolate bar and Patrick concentrated on
driving and not falling asleep at the wheel. My eyes had gotten heavy
and I knew I was close to passing out. The day's events had exhausted
me and rest seemed like the most heavenly thing in the world.

Before I knew it, I was resting against Ryder, our handcuffed
hands finding each other. His body was warm, his touch was comforting
and the feel of his chest moving with every breath made me relax. I knew
I should have gotten off, but I felt weak and I wasn't sure if it was
because of tiredness or because I enjoyed the feeling of being close to
him to a point where I didn't have the strength to move. Either way, I
stayed there, eyes closing completely.

I was in that hazy state between sleep and consciousness, my imagination right at the edge of my dreams, when I thought I heard him speak.

"Sweet dreams," he whispered, pressing his lips to the top of my head before I fell into a deep slumber.

Seventeen

As always, sleep was awkwardly positioned and uncomfortable, making my muscles ache with tension. I vaguely remembered falling asleep but as I gradually woke up more, I remembered. Feeling dirty and sticky lying in my bed, I shuffled and tangled myself further into the sheets. I felt the tug of Ryder as he stirred from next to me on the floor.

Glancing over, I saw him sleeping with his brow furrowed, eyes squeezed shut. An animal-like sound erupted from his lips and his body jerked. Pearls of sweat had formed on his forehead, dampening his hairline. Ryder was having a bad dream. Placing a hand on his shoulder, I gently shook.

"Shh, it's okay. It's just a nightmare…"

His eyes flew open, searching the room in confusion. His breathing was faster than usual but he tried to control it, running his free hand through his messy hair. He tilted his head to the side and saw me, then cracked a small smile. Ryder ran the same hand down his face and let out a sleepy groan.

"Morning," he greeted, tone slow and deep. He stretched – well, as much as he could, considering he was still chained to me - and

glanced around. "What time is it?" 'It's... Crap!" Panic rose in my throat
as I glanced at the clock and realised we were beyond late for school. It
was already ten in the morning and second period would have been well
underway.

On cue, Eve knocked and entered my room. "Oh, good, you're
up now."

"Why didn't you wake us?" I burst out, trying to kick the sheets
off.

"I knew you guys were tired. It's fine. I called the school in
advance, told them you had an appointment and that you'd be at school
around lunch," Eve explained, waving around a cookie.

"You lied to the school?" I was starting to really freak out.
"Aren't we already in enough trouble with the authorities?"

My sister just rolled her eyes and started backing out of the
room. "Calm down, Nora. God. I used to do it all the time. It's no big
deal. Look, I just came up here to tell you that Patrick and I are going to
the doctor for an ultrasound."

"Your baby must be heaps big now, huh?" Ryder said, nodding
at Eve's prized-sized belly.

She placed her hands on her stomach and unconsciously rubbed,
something she did whenever someone asked about her baby. I guess it
was one of those protective gestures that emphasised the attachment and
relationship between mother and child.

"Yeah," she answered, smiling, "but this ultrasound is for
Patrick."

"Imagine if boys got pregnant."

Eve walked over and smacked me over the head with her box of
chocolate chip cookies. "It's a soft tissue injury." The sound of Patrick's
voice drifted up the stairs as he called for my sister. Before leaving, she
added, "Have a shower. Both of you. You're filthy."

Then with that, she left. Ryder and I exchanged glances and
knew we both needed to proceed with our day. We had gotten
increasingly better with the whole bathroom situation. When it came to
showering, it was still pretty awkward, but anything beyond that, we

coped surprisingly well. I supposed we were both just tired and figured the situation of being handcuffed was difficult enough so cooperating sounded like the most suitable way to tackle it all.

From our first awkward bathroom situation, we had fallen into a routine and a set of appropriate rules and guidelines had been silently agreed between us. Things like when Ryder had to go to the bathroom, I didn't turn into a comedian. And when we were at the sink, we were careful that I didn't shave off my other eyebrow and that Ryder cleanly shaved off all the stubble that magically grows on his chin every night. Although these aspects of our bathroom routine were good, the thing I hated the most was peeing in front of him.

It was the most awkward and uncomfortable thing ever. As always, while I went on my morning pee break, Ryder had to squat awkwardly so that I could properly place my butt onto the toilet. After, there was the difficult wriggling and one-hand tugging as I tried to get my pants to roll down and then, there was the most awkward part of the entire thing: Me actually peeing.

Now, I'm seriously self-conscious about how I pee. I mean, it's not exactly a graceful thing to do. I can't just daintily do my business, particularly when there was a guy squatting awkwardly to the side. Especially a guy like Ryder Collins.

Oh my God... What if I'm peeing too loudly?

The same thought occurred to me and trying to casually block out the sound, I attempted a casual conversation, which was a complete failure, considering that there was *nothing* casual about having a friendly chat with someone while you're watering the garden or dropping raisins. And, as always, that morning wasn't an exception and I *again* tried talking to Ryder. However, I guess I had just about tried every single topic in the book of conversations so I was at a complete loss and I blurted out the worst possible thing ever.

"So... You have a pretty nice looking butt." The words were out of my mouth before I could even think about it.

"I have... I have a what?" Ryder asked, almost losing his concentration on maintaining his balance.

I knew there was no backing down now, so I decided to go with
t. "You have... a nice butt."

Ryder shifted uncomfortably. "Thanks?"

"I mean, I'd totally rate it a nine... Possibly a ten. You see, Mel
and I have a thing where we rate guys' butts. In fact, it was the reason
why Mrs. Coleman voluntarily picked me to be a part of this
demonstration. But yeah. You have a pretty nice butt. It's really... manly
and stuff." I realised every word was making it worse, but I couldn't
stop.

Ryder laughed softly. My cheeks caught on fire.

My tendency to make awkward situations even more
inappropriate and uncomfortable was such a charming characteristic.

~♥♥♥~

We were quiet after the bathroom incident. After we had exited,
we entered the kitchen where Ryder fried some eggs and toast while I
stood to the side and tried to distract myself with Biology homework. It
wasn't until there was a knock on the back door that I almost cried of
relief. Finally, a *real* distraction.

Ryder was just about finished cooking breakfast so he switched
the stove off, brought the pan off the heat and together we headed for the
door. I looked through the glass frame and saw Caine. He grinned and
pointed towards the lock. Realising I hadn't made much of a move to
open it, I mentally shook my head and reached for the door.

"Hey, thanks," he breathed, shrugging off his jacket once he was
inside and dropping it onto one of the stools by the counter.

Caine was just the type of person who could enter a stranger's
house and instantly feel comfortable with making himself feel welcome.
Although I wasn't a complete stranger to him, I might as well have
considered being one. Prior to the whole handcuff thing, Caine and I had
never associated before and now that some chains had imprisoned me
with his best friend, he started acting like we had been in each other's
lives since the start of time.

"Oh, breakfast," Caine said, grinning as he pinched a piece of toast from a plate and took a huge bite. "Man, I'm starved."

"Aren't you meant to be at school?" Ryder asked, a little more accusing rather than curious. "How'd you know we were home?"

"After last night? There was no freaking way I was going to wake up at six in the morning and go to school," he answered around a mouthful of toast. "Hey, did you fry up some eggs with this?"

Ryder just snorted, slid the plate away from Caine and directed it closer to us. "Hey, hands off the food, man."

Caine held his hands up in surrender and backed off a little. When Ryder cooled off, Caine swiftly reached out and grabbed a side of bacon, grinning wickedly as he dropped half of it into his mouth. I watched as Ryder glared at him from across the bench. I didn't understand why he was being so tense and weird. I know guys are really protective over their food, but they didn't go all ice-queen when it was their friends trying to steal a bite, right?

"What's up with you?" Caine raised an eyebrow at Ryder, asking the question I was thinking of.

"Nothing, just what are you doing here?" he answered.

"Don't you want me around?" Caine didn't sound offended, just confused. "Are you feeling alright?"

Ryder didn't say anything; he just stared blankly at his friend, body stiff. The tension between the boys was suffocating and the longer the silence stretched, the more uncomfortable it became. Although I knew my attention shouldn't be directed at them, I couldn't help it and gradually, my appetite dimmed and breakfast didn't seem so appealing. It was none of my concern to just jump into all the testosterone but I couldn't tolerate their behaviour any longer.

"This is intense." It was probably the stupidest and most obvious thing I could say in that situation. When I received the *oh-my-god-you're-a-moron* glances, I clicked my tongue and dragged out a low whistle. "Intense," I repeated, feeling like an idiot, but not knowing what else to do.

"Hey, you know what? Maybe I'll just head to school." Caine
looked at us briefly, swung around in his stool and stood. He showed no
sign of emotion and his tone was neutral. "See you guys there?"

"Bye..." I answered as he gave me a tight nod and slipped out
the back door. I waited a minute or so, just to make sure he was gone
before I whipped around and faced Ryder. "What was that all about?"

Ryder wasn't looking at me. He just picked up the plate full of
food and stepped around me to the bin, throwing away the contents.
"Nothing. I think he likes you."

I wasn't sure how to respond to that. I was glad Ryder was
keeping distracted by throwing the dishes into the sink otherwise it
would have been even harder to clear my head. This was way too much
for me to absorb in the morning, so I did the only thing that I could: I
dismissed the thought.

"I don't think so."

He paused and leaned against the counter to look at me but I
tipped my head forward, letting a strand of hair fall to hide my eyes and
pretended to be fascinated by a smudge on the floor. The heavy stare of
his eyes studying my face was almost unbearable, so I coughed and
looked up to slowly meet his gaze.

Ryder stared at the strand of hair with knitted eyebrows and the
muscles in his arm twitched as if he were going to reach out. But he
restrained and looked away, turning to the sink and picking up the
sponge. The sounds of clinking glass echoed through the kitchen.

"Do you," Ryder paused for a moment, slowing the movement of
the sponge against the surface of the plate, "like him?"

"Caine?" I questioned, almost barking out a laugh. "I hardly
know the guy."

Ryder seemed to think about my answer. "I mean, would you
give him a chance?"

Would I?

"I don't know," I replied honestly.

He thought for a moment while he turned the tap on and rinsed
the soapy residue off the plate. "I still think he likes you," he repeated

"Why are you telling me this?" I asked, picking up a cloth to dry the wet plates. "You aren't trying to hook me up with him, are you?"

"No!" Ryder burst out, with a little more edge than I expected. His face hardened. "No," he repeated, in a much calmer tone. "I just don't think you should date him if he asks you out. He's not right for you."

I stopped drying and gave him a look. "You don't think anyone's right for me," I pointed out.

A smile formed on his lips as he turned and looked at me a moment. He held his gaze for merely a second though before turning back to the running water to rinse off the rest of the dishes. I watched as his hands moved over the soapy surface of the glistening cutlery. Sunlight shone through the window above the sink, specks of dust floating around him like flecks of glitter disappearing as they travelled out of the light. His hair seemed a shade lighter, eyes brighter. And at that moment, I looked at him in a different way. I saw beyond the arrogant exterior and haughty attitude and saw him as someone…normal. Not the superstar senior who roamed the school halls like a lion in his jungle kingdom. But as someone who cooked breakfast and washed dishes and did *normal* stuff. It was wonderful. All ways I had seen him were wonderful. From his compassionate and caring side when I had my dating disaster, to protectiveness and courage when he stood up for me to half the footy team and to the vulnerability and fright after the fight at the beach. The more time we spent together, the more emotions he expressed and the more characteristics were visible, ones that weren't airbrushed with an artificial coat. It made me wonder if anyone else had seen this part of him…

…and if anyone else was falling in love with it too.

"I don't think *everyone* is bad for you. In fact, I know someone who is *perfect* for you," Ryder answered, snapping me out of my mental ranting.

"Oh, really? Who?"

He turned the tap off and looked at me seriously. He looked determined and encouraged, then…scared. Like he doubted his answer,

ethinking his response. He looked down, away from me and knitted his
eyebrows in concentration as he calculated something. But that flash of
questioning was replaced by a grin of arrogance and an entertained
sparkling in his blue eyes.

"Fred Grosby."

I blinked. Definitely wasn't expecting that answer. "He doesn't
even like physical contact."

"Exactly."

Eighteen

Seeing Mel at lunch was the greatest moment in history. I had spent the past few days with way too much testosterone, a seriously hormonal and pregnant sister and Ryder's moody mother. The sound of my best friend's chatty tone as she gushed out the latest gossip was like music to my ears as we met up at our usual lunch table outside.

"So," Mel said, as she cracked open her bottle of orange juice, "I heard that one of the students is having a scandalous affair with that really hot P.E. teacher. Apparently they've been having one-on-one lessons on something a little more physical than volleyball."

"No way," I replied, jabbing a piece of macaroni with my fork. Skipping breakfast was a bad idea because I had spent third and fourth period with a stomach that sounded like a dying whale symphony.

"Way," she exclaimed. "Trust me, she's totally seen his personal bat and balls. I bet it's that girl that transferred here from Jefferson. The poor thing is going to graduate with an STD rather than her HSC."

That cracked a laugh from Ryder, but he kept his head down, smiling secretly to himself and staring at the blank piece of paper in front of him. We had gotten an English assignment before the start of lunch and Ryder was determined to get his finished...or at least *started.*

"Ugh, is that the Shakespeare speech?" Mel wiped the orange moustache that had stained her upper lip and glared at the notification resting between Ryder and I.

"Seven minutes minimum." Ryder sighed in frustration, scratching his head with the end of his pencil. "*And* it's about old Elizabethan English."

"What play are you studying?" my best friend asked, picking up a perfectly cut sandwich sector.

Mel was the kind of person who could eat three times as much as the average person and still have supermodel thinness. She didn't eat because she was passionate about food or because it was a dietary requirement. She ate a lot because she claimed to be on "a hunt for boobs" to which she claimed, although she was seventeen, her boobs *will* come out of hiding.

She tried an assortment of different food groups, spices and flavours. Last week she was binging on the flavoursome taste of Indian food and the other day, she ate nothing but watermelon. But today she had settled with a dainty arrangement of food you'd find at a tea party. A cleanly cut cucumber sandwich sat in front of her, the edges removed and sliced into neat, triangular quarters. There was an assortment of colourful fruits, all peeled and sliced that sat comfortably in a little Tupperware container. Three ANZAC biscuits wrapped in glad wrap sat next to it and of course, there was her bottle of organically squeezed orange juice. It looked like a feast compared to my bowl of cold mac 'n' cheese.

"Othello," Ryder replied, popping the lid of his Gatorade. "It's depressing. They all die in the end." Mel disposed of the rest of her little slice of sandwich, brushed the crumbs away and gave him a sympathetic look. "Trust me, it's just as bad as Macbeth."

"I thought this was the cool table, but everyone seems to be talking about homework." I looked up from my lunch to see Caine sliding into the spot next to Mel and across from Ryder. He gave me a wink and threw his bag onto the table.

I smiled weakly. Mel almost had a heart attack seeing him there. I wasn't sure if it was of excitement or fright because she looked like she wanted to hug him but run away at the same time. Ryder, on the other hand, made it brusquely clear that he disliked his friend joining us.

"We're just discussing the assignment," I informed him.

Caine looked at the assignment notification and snatched it into his hands. He frowned down at it and studied intensely. After a moment though, he gave up and looked up at us. "This is the reason I do a standard level of English and not an advanced. I mean, we've been studying Shakespeare since the start of high school, but it's still like trying to understand Chinese calligraphy."

Mel let out something between a giggle and a screech of pain. I raised an eyebrow at her, and she mouthed: *oh my god, he's sitting with us.* Caine was still grinning, one of those boyish smiles, mischievous and playful. But he soon lost it when no one replied to him. Other than the animal-like sound made by Mel, he didn't get a reaction.

"I get the feeling I'm not wanted here," he said, looking between the three of us.

When his gaze reached Mel, she quickly looked away and busied herself with rolling around a grape in her fruit salad. She brushed a piece of fuzzy hair behind her ear, a pink blush slowly creeping its way up her pale cheeks. The way she tried to keep her interest on her salad was starting to creep me out. She was basically staring down at her lunch cross eyed.

"How about we all hang out this afternoon?" I asked, trying to start another conversation. "We could all catch an early-night movie or something? Or just rent a DVD and have microwave popcorn at my place. It'll be fun."

Caine didn't seem convinced. He looked at Ryder for support. "What do you think, man?"

Ryder was scribbling furiously into his notebook, his messy scrawl filling up the lines as he shrugged. He looked up to meet his friend's eyes and his eyes – eyes that had been so alive and sparkling that morning - turned as cold as ice.

"So you ask my thoughts about this, but not about *the other thing.*"

Caine scrubbed a hand down his face and looked at me. "Sorry, Nora, I don't think hanging out tonight is a good idea-"

"I thought I made it clear that you need to back off."

Caine suddenly didn't look so patient. "Look, I don't know why I like her, okay? I guess it never occurred to me to think of her in that way and once I started to, I liked it. A lot. I couldn't help it, alright?"

"You hardly know her."

"Neither do you, man." Caine looked angry now.

"I've known her for years," Ryder growled, a feral sound erupting from the back of his throat.

"No. You *did* know her. You had your chance and you fuc-"

Ryder stood up causing me to half jerk up with him, the metal of the handcuffs biting into my wrist. Fists curled, knuckles white, he challenged Caine with his eyes. His friend was up and ready in an instant for a fight and Mel just sat there with Bambi eyes and a dropped jaw.

Oh, God, I thought.

But before either of the guys could throw a punch or a snarky comment, a high pitched shriek pierced through the school. Instantly, I covered my ears, trying to block the sound but it did no good. The screaming alarm sent shivers through my entire body and yelled for attention.

"What's going on?" Ryder had forgotten his duel with Caine and pulled me close as if the alarm was going to grow legs and attack.

Then the familiar, commanding sound of Mrs. Coleman's voice yelled through the speakers. "All students report to the school oval and organise yourselves into year groups. A fire has been reported. This is not a drill."

And all hell broke loose.

Nineteen

Drills were always cooperative, mainly because most of our fire drills happened straight after fourth period and right before lunch. Students were usually calm and collected and we were merely gathered together for longer than twenty minutes. I guess going to lunch was a motivation. But now that the real thing was happening, havoc struck.

We were always told that in this situation, we were to always leave our belongings behind and to just continue down to the designated location in an orderly fashion. However, people were repacking lunches, shoving books into bags and running towards the football field like there was no tomorrow. Kids shoved their way past to race to safety and stressed teachers struggled to keep them in order.

Caine, Ryder, Mel, and I seemed to be the only calm students there.

Mel made a little excited squeak. "This is the most exciting news ever!"

Trust Mel to get excited over the gossip of a fire rather than the fright of getting, I don't know…killed. It reminded me how much I love her. Shooting her a grin, I calmly packed up my things and let Ryder guide us through the sea of students towards our specialised area.

"Ugh, I heard some year ten kid farted in front of his friend's lighter. I didn't even know that was possible," a junior girl said, tossing her long, dark hair over her shoulder as she fluttered past.

Mel's ears perked and she instantly followed. "Hey! What's this I hear about a lighter and a fart?"

When she disappeared, it was just Ryder, Caine, and I. There wasn't as much tension as there was at lunch, but you could tell they were still uncomfortable around each other and just the suggestion of conflict could influence them into a brawl. Ryder tried to ignore his friend and searched the school.

He inhaled deeply. "I can smell the smoke but I can't see the fire," Ryder examined, looking confused.

Caine let in a breath too and frowned. "I can smell it too."

Feeling kind of left out, I was the last to have an intake of air. "I smell…popcorn."

Ryder looked down at me but didn't say anything. In fact, he didn't say anything *at all* after that. Neither did Caine. Halfway through all the chaos, he disappeared into the sea of students and gathered around with the other guys from our year group.

Eventually, all the standing around was making me tired and I muttered to Ryder that I wanted to sit. Even then, he hardly made a sound. He just kept his focus alert as he dropped down to the grass with me and soon enough, we were surrounded with gossiping students trying to come up with solutions to solve the mysterious fire.

I don't know how long we stayed outside for, but it seemed like forever. All students and staff were to wait until the fire brigade came. Once they triple checked the premises for any more signs of danger and confirmed that the flames were put out, we were given permission to leave early. It was already two thirty by then and school would have been out in half an hour, so it wasn't much of an excitement, particularly when my phone buzzed while we were in the car on the way home.

~♥♥♥~

Officer Brandy called with our first task of community service: serving soup at the community kitchen. He notified us that it would probably be best if Caine, Ryder and I were split up to avoid any more trouble. But since Ryder and I were chained together, we had no choice but to stick together and service chicken-noodle soup to the homeless, lonely, and elderly while Caine disappeared to do his own specialised job. I guess I was relieved knowing that Caine wouldn't be there. It would have been extremely awkward because of the tension earlier at school.

"Just grab a hairnet, an apron, and a ladle," Mary - the woman who was in charge - instructed as she started scooping up soup into bowls and passing them to the line of people.

Ryder looked at the hairnet packed safely in a little plastic sleeve and pulled a face of disgust. "I'm not wearing one of those," he announced.

I, on the other hand, was already rolling my hair up into a bun so I could place the net over my head and amuse myself with how weird it felt. When we were all dressed up and had our spoons, we were directed to the end of the line to hand out bread slices.

It was only a two-hour shift, from three to five, but it was the craziest part of the day for the soup kitchen. A lot of old people turned up for an early dinner, most of them scattering into little groups to play chess, knit, and read as they ate their meals.

There was about half an hour left to go and a lot of people were finishing up their meals. As I was casually brushing crumbs from the bread onto the floor and sneakily pretending it wasn't me, the chime from the front door rang and in stepped a girl. She was about six or so, dirty dishwater hair in a sloppy ponytail and freckles dotted across her pale face.

"What's the kid doing here?" Ryder asked, looking at the girl as he walked in with a backpack that looked way too big for her slim figure.

Mary turned towards the door and waved at the little girl. "Hi Gracie. How you doing, hon?"

Gracie lit up like a firefly when she saw Mary and skipped up to the counter, reaching up on her toes. "Hey, Mary. Do you have chicken-noodle today?"

"Sure do," Mary said, grabbing a bowl and swiftly scooping in a bowl of soup for the kid. "How was school?"

Gracie reached up and took the warm bowl from Mary, shrugging. "It was okay. Is there any bread?"

"Of course.Just head down to the end. We have two new helpers today. Say hello to Nora and Raisin."

"It's Ryder," Ryder muttered under his breath.

Mary had been calling Ryder by the wrong name all day. He had been addressed as Raisin all afternoon and no matter how many times he tried to correct her, she still called him a shrivelled up grape. I could tell he was getting irritated, especially with the way his eyes shot daggers her way whenever she called him by the wrong name.

Gracie gave us a nervous smile and tried to move her way down without spilling soup all over her uniform. While she was struggling to make her way over, Mary shuffled closer.

"She's been coming here for the past four months. Don't think things are too well at home for her," Mary explained, shaking her head. "Poor thing."

Mary walked away then, to serve an elderly couple who had walked in and we were left with Gracie who had finally moved close enough. Ryder peered down at her and gave her a little half smile.

"Would you like some bread?" he asked.

"Yes, please," she politely replied.

She attempted to balance her bowl in one hand and reach out with the other, but it just made her wobble and her dinner swirled. Ryder held out a hand to stop her.

"I'll carry it for you. Where would you like to sit?"

Gracie cupped her soup in two hands and slowly shuffled towards an empty table. I thought Ryder was going to drop the bread off and go, but he didn't. Instead, he sat down across from her, placed the bread on a napkin beside her bowl and made no move of getting up. So, I slid into the seat beside him.

"Do your friends hang out here too?" Ryder tried making conversation as she scooped and slurped her soup.

She shook her head and tore off a piece of bread. "No."

"What about your family?" he asked.

Something about the way Ryder spoke to her was so... welcoming. Even though he was a complete stranger and the soup lady had introduced him as *Raisin*, even I felt at ease with all his questions. His tone and pace of voice was smooth and silky, a wonderful combination.

Again, Gracie shook her head. "I don't see my mum much."

Ryder smiled weakly. "Neither do I."

The kid looked up with a spark of excitement in her eyes. Excitement of Ryder's understanding.

"Sometimes she sends me cards on my birthday. If I'm lucky, she even gives me money," Gracie continued, seeming to ease into conversation.

Ryder's face fell for a second as he realised that he couldn't relate to her as much as she was hoping. The pain behind his eyes swirled like a whirlpool as he watched her eat. Gracie had barely said anything more than five responses and she had already earned a soft spot in Ryder's heart.

"I live with my sister," she added, dipping a piece of bread into her soup.

"I've always wanted a sister," Ryder answered, smiling.

The two seemed to connect after that. Ryder taught her things, fantastic things, like how to find your way home if you're ever lost at night. He taught her to look for a certain star and her eyes lit up as he fed her the magic of his knowledge. Then he taught her absolutely ridiculous

ings, like what the lines on your palms meant. Most of what he said
was utter nonsense but Gracie was mesmerised by his words, moved by
he power of his compelling voice.

All three of us sat there for an extra hour, Ryder and Gracie
bonded and occasionally I'd pipe in a comment or two. But the way they
related to each other just seemed too precious for me to disturb so I sat
there, watching Ryder in adoration as he made her smile more
throughout the night. He was gentle, funny and friendly through his
actions and words and soon enough, Gracie had fallen in love with him.

And maybe I fell for him a little harder too.

Maybe.

It was dark by the time we left the community kitchen with
Gracie. She claimed to live right down the road, but Ryder insisted on
walking her home to make sure she got there safely. When she paused at
an apartment block, she turned and without warning, threw her arms
around Ryder.

"Thank you," she mumbled against his jeans.

Ryder held her tightly and gently squeezed. "Any time."

Then she disappeared inside and he waited until she popped her
head out from behind the curtains of a window and waved before
leaving. The walk back to the car was quiet.

"You're really great with kids," I said, looking up at him.

Ryder got a cheesy grin on his face. "She's a sweet kid. Just got
a rough childhood, you know? I never really respected what I had until
meeting her. I mean, I thought *my* mother was horrible, but hers isn't
even in the same town."

"She's got it tough," I agreed, turning my attention to the
glittering road in front of us. It had rained earlier and the way the
streetlamps lit up the road made it look like an endless sea of sparkling
black diamonds. "What you did for her was amazing. I mean…
everything you do is… I just… It makes me…" My voice trailed off.

"It makes you what?" Ryder asked, pausing in the middle of the
road to turn and look at me.

"Nothing," I quickly muttered, feeling heat creep up my neck.

It makes me fall for you even more...

Ryder studied me in the shadows, just the faint glow of the streetlamps illuminating against our faces. I felt him gently pull me closer, his warm fingertips trailing up my spine, sending branches of warmth throughout my body. His free hand made its way to my neck and lingered there for a moment before he pressed his palm to my cheek and cupped the side of my face. His thumb gently stroked my cheek and I closed my eyes. Fingers brushed against my parted lips, ever so gently..

When I opened my eyes, he pressed his forehead to mine and I stared into those beautiful faded blue eyes. It was as if the whole world had gone blurry but he was in completely perfect focus. I could feel the exact beat of his racing heart. The warmth of his touch, tracing secrets and promises against my skin. The way his breath brushed against my lips.

We stood like that, in the middle of the road, for what seemed like minutes but it only lasted a few seconds before Ryder pulled back slightly, then pressed his lips against my forehead.

My breath caught.

It was so simple.

So gentle.

So god damned wonderful.

Ryder chuckled softly when I breathlessly exhaled. Then he laced his fingers through mine. I had no idea what this was. What *we* were or how he felt. I just knew that in that moment, I knew how *I* felt and I didn't want to lose the moment, so I held his hand tightly and walked as slowly as possible to the car, treasuring every heartbeat.

Twenty

"Is something wrong?"

Ryder sat behind the wheel of the car, gripping it like the world was about to swallow him whole. We had been sitting in my driveway in the dark for ten minutes and he hadn't made any move to get out. He just sat there, staring intensely at my garage door.

His eyes skittered towards my direction then looked back out the windshield. He didn't say anything, just sat there, jaw square, eyebrows drawn together. Ryder had gone from completely comfortable to seriously disturbed. Knowing he wasn't going to reply instantly, I sat there and twiddled my thumbs, waiting patiently for him to say something.

"I think we should talk," he said finally.

I tensed at his words. *We should talk* never ended well. It usually resulted in crying, yelling and throwing things. But that was usually in the movies. And often, the couple having the conversation were together. Ryder and I weren't together. But even though I tried to convince myself that he couldn't possibly have anything that could hurt me, I still couldn't untie the twist that had formed in my stomach.

"Um," I answered, trying to keep my voice level, "what do you want to talk about?"

Ryder rubbed his thumb along the plush leather around the steering wheel and took a deep breath, not looking at me. "There're just some things I'd like to clarify."

Oh crap, I thought. *Crap, crap, crap.*

I swallowed and tried to stop my hands from shaking. "Oh?"

It was the only word I could properly form. Even so, it was slightly breathless and shaky, but Ryder didn't seem to notice. He was too busy death staring at my garage. It shouldn't have bothered me: Ryder not liking me back. But it did. In fact, it *sucked.* I had just started to confess to myself that I did feel something for Ryder and he was going to turn me down before anything happened. He was going to tell me that all those little things didn't mean anything to him and it would crush me.

Because they meant more than everything to me.

"Remember when we were best friends?"

His words startled me, but I nodded and waited for him to continue.

"What do you think happened to our friendship?" he asked, turning to look at me in the darkness.

I couldn't clearly see him. There was a faint glow outside from the porch lights and it kissed one side of his face, but other than that, his features were mere shadows. The faint outline of his eyes was apparent but they didn't hold the usual confidence and tranquillity. Instead, they showed tints of something that looked like fear.

I thought back to the day that our friendship ended. Back when we both just started high school and Ryder was getting recognised for his athletic abilities which gave him a whole lot of pride and popularity.

"Yeah," I muttered.

"What happened?" he whispered and it went so quiet that I heard him swallow nervously.

I suddenly felt extremely uncomfortable. "You ditched me for popularity."

"Did I?"

The way he said it wasn't accusing. It wasn't a confused tone
either, nor was it amused. He didn't seem doubtful either. His tone
simply challenged me to think again and boy did it make me falter. I
back tracked my thoughts, brought back memories of that night and
suddenly, the events that had happened didn't seem so clear anymore.

Ryder took my hesitation as an answer. "Did you ever think that
it was the other way around?"

Normally, I would have laughed in his face and barked out an
insult or a smart retort. I didn't exactly agree with him, but I was
interested in what he had to say. I couldn't have possibly been the one to
ditch him. What was there to ditch him for?

"That's ridiculous."

"If I remember correctly, you were quite occupied with things,"
Ryder said slowly, choosing his words carefully. "Like Dan Fletcher."

Dan Fletcher was my first ever high school boyfriend. It wasn't
anything serious. We were both thirteen and still giggled at the word sex
so it wasn't one of those intense relationships. If anything, we were
together just for the hand holding and cute texts. We lasted a blissful four
weeks until he got bored and got one of his friends to break up with me
at lunch because he was way too chicken to say it to my face.

"Dan?" I repeated intelligently, not completely understanding.

"Nora, you were with him *all the time*," Ryder responded.

I frowned. "Yeah, like lunch at school."

He shook his head. "That's how it started. Then you started
meeting up before school and after. On weekends, you were always out
on your bike with him or at the library studying. You had no time for
me."

"No," I said, starting to feel a little offended now. "The only
reason I hung out with him was because *you* were never there. You were
always at practice and the only thing you'd talk about was football. Plus,
it's not like you needed me. Thirteen and you already had half the girls in
our year falling all over you."

"Nora," Ryder said calmly. "Stop."

"Why should I?" I snapped, irritation creeping in. "You're *blaming* me for what happened. I didn't do anything."

"Can you please stop?" he repeated.

"*Shut up.* You brought this up. I can't believe you have the nerve to blame me for our friendship ending. All I ever did was support you at every game and be there for you for all those injuries you had. I was *always* there for you and now you're accusing me of ruining our friendship? You jealous *asshole.*"

"Nora!"

I didn't get to squeeze in another word after that because he had crushed his lips against mine. I was glad I was already sitting down. Otherwise I would have collapsed into a mess on the floor. His free hand was placed against my neck, gently holding me in place. The warmth of his palm and the caress of his fingers sent heat flowing through me. In comparison to his tender touch, his kiss was rough and passionate. It was wild, beautiful and dangerous, but something about it made me feel so protected.

Colours danced behind my closed eyelids as I melted into his lips and enjoyed the taste of his kiss. It was sweet and fresh, like honey and spearmint. My head was spinning, heart racing and before I could process it further, he drew away from me like he had just been electrified and placed his hands back on the steering wheel, avoiding my eyes.

He sat there, breathlessly. "Sorry," he muttered angrily, gripping the wheel so tightly his knuckles turned white.

I didn't move. I didn't say anything either. I was thankful for the darkness because I felt a blush creep up my neck and branch colour through my cheeks. I tried to control my breathing.

We sat in silence for a moment, before Ryder spoke.

"You were right," he said, now breathing steadily as he looked out the windshield. "I *was* jealous."

"I..." My voice trailed off.

"Just... Christ, Nora. I missed you. We were hardly hanging out anymore. With all the training I had and you always disappearing with Dan, I felt so alone. Not to mention my parents were fighting non-stop vith the affair. Home wasn't home anymore. I tried to distract myself vith sport." He let out a humourless laugh. "I remember how I used to sit on your front doorstep every afternoon after practice and wait for you to come home. Eventually, your parents noticed and they felt sorry for me and that pity, that *embarrassment...* I was sick of that feeling."

I swallowed, feeling guiltier and guiltier with every single word.

"It didn't make it any better that I had the biggest crush on you," he continued. "That night on the beach, when Will said I was addicted... He wasn't talking about drugs or alcohol. He was talking about you. I was addicted to *you.* And yeah, Dan getting all your attention, especially when I needed you most, made me feel like crap. I did some really stupid things... I confronted him before the footy game and threatened him to dump you. I didn't think he'd do it... But the next day, when I found out he did, I freaked out. I didn't want you to know I was the reason he did it so I ditched you too. I was angry and hurt and scared that you'd hate me, so I left before you could."

Everything fell into place and I finally understood. Dan's strange behaviour as the game progressed. The way he kept his attention alert and how he would freak out if I touched his arm. Then the way he avoided me the next day and couldn't meet my eyes, even just in class. Not to mention the way he dumped me through a friend.

"I thought it was just some stupid little crush and throughout the years, I convinced myself that this was all your fault. I wouldn't have lost you if you hadn't been so selfish. I wouldn't have been influenced to do half the crap I did if you had just been there for me. I *hated* you all this time..." he explained, then took a breath. "But there's a thin line between love and hate... and honestly, this whole handcuff thing has driven me crazy but it's also been the best thing I could have ever asked for. Because it made me realise that I didn't hate you for so long... I've just *loved* you for so long."

I stared at him with wide eyes. I wasn't sure if the kiss had made me hallucinate or he really was saying what I was hearing. My lips parted to answer, but no words came out. Instead, they just opened and closed like a startled goldfish as I tried to form a coherent response.

"When I realised Caine likes you too, I just freaked. I know we haven't been the best with each other but we've been getting better and I didn't want to lose you again…" He sneaked a glance at me, then looked back at the driveway. "Feel free to interrupt me at any time."

But I didn't say anything. Instead, I placed my free hand against his cheek and brought him closer to press my lips against his again. And that one little action spoke a thousand words that only Ryder and I could understand.

Twenty One

Ryder and I talked most of that night, fingers entwined, foreheads pressed together as we shared secrets and memories. Eventually, we got tired and he fell asleep on the floor. We weren't one of those dramatically passionate films where the guy romantically falls asleep with the girl. We were two normal teenagers and even though the thought did cross my mind as we shared secrets and promises through the evening, it didn't seem appropriate to act like some long-term couple, especially when only a few hours ago we had just shared our first kiss.

In the morning, we went by our normal routine, nothing special about it. We awkwardly went through our bathroom time together, fussed over which cereal was better and struggled to get into the car without too much butt getting in each other's faces. There was the usual wrestle over which radio station to pick and the argument over which bands were the best as we listened to the reporters ramble over the day's news. Everything was just about the way it had been for the past six days.

But Ryder and I shared a secret, something I could see in the twinkle of his eyes and the corner of his lips as he smiled. Something only we could translate through small actions and expressions and I liked that. I liked that we weren't rushing it and that it wasn't forced.

When we pulled up at the student parking lot, we noticed that the school wasn't surrounded with its usual sea of students. Exchanging confused glances with Ryder, we searched the grounds for any sign of life. But it was silent, deserted and hostile. Not even the flags were raised to greet us.

I nearly jumped half a metre into the air when there was a tap on the window. Turning, I saw Caine standing there, looking tired and frustrated, books in hand and backpack slung lazily over one shoulder. I rolled down the window and he ducked into view.

"Christ. You would have thought staff would have a more effective way of announcing that there's no school today," Caine said, clearly annoyed. "Private investigators have been hired to dig up further information about the fire yesterday. Apparently it was no accident."

"How did everyone else get the message?" Ryder asked.

Caine shrugged. He looked tired. Bags had started to form under his droopy eyes, like he hadn't slept in a year. A shadow of stubble had formed on his chin and his dark hair was a mess- and not the styled mess either.

"Apparently there was some announcement on the radio this morning at seven, but I was dead to the world. Damn community service had me up all night," Caine answered, scrubbing a hand down his face. "Hey, mind giving me a lift? Didn't drive here this morning."

Ryder nodded towards the back seat and Caine opened the door, threw his things onto the floor and climbed in. There was something about him that was off. He smelt of ash and wood, earthy. I turned and looked at him as Ryder reversed out of the parking slot. Caine just looked irritated and exhausted. He was silent as he stared out the window.

"You look beat," I said, turning back to the front but looking at him through the rear view mirror. "What were you assigned to last night anyway?"

Caine caught my gaze through the reflection of the mirror and ighed. "Crisis hotline. I didn't even know we had one of those things." Ie shook his head. "Some dude called last night, panicking about ,omething, The kid was a damn mess."

"Sounds rough."

He groaned. "He talked way too much for a guy."

"Kind of like how you are now?" Ryder teased.

Caine shot him the finger, but they both exchanged smiles. It ;eemed as if the previous day's conflict had dissolved and I was glad. Caine decided he needed caffeine so we made a breakfast stop for the >est hash browns and coffee the city could offer. And since we had our >ooks, we decided to go to the library to do a bit of studying done.

It seemed that quite a few people had the same idea we had. We ;aw students from school clustering around in study groups or by themselves. People had laptops and earphones, others with stacks of books and pieces of paper scattered everywhere. A lot of the people I recognised as the top students of school. People with the best grades or the most stubborn parents *demanding* the best grades. Then there were the occasional juniors just hanging around for the free Wi-Fi.

Ryder, Caine and I found a large table at the back of the library, enough that the three of us could scatter our things without being too cramped. We all had different subjects to study, so we pulled out various textbooks and exercise questions. Caine was focusing on his business assignment about management and finance, Ryder was studying for a law exam and I was reading through my notes for an English presentation. That left barely any talking.

As I was highlighting important facts and key points, trying to summarise a million pages into about two, Caine swiftly slid a note into the corner of my folder. He was sitting across from me, with Ryder next to me. I looked over at Ryder who was engaged in his studies, earphones in to block out distractions. Then I looked up at Caine who just stared at me. At first I thought he was staring at me to pass the note over to his friend, but when he made no further indication, I just assumed it was mine.

The note was a messily torn piece of lined paper from the corner of his notebook. Written in a messy guy-scrawl in black pen was:

I have something to ask you.

I looked up at him, but he was already back to his books, silently mumbling things to himself as he transferred his summary notes onto a fresh piece of paper. Picking up a coloured pen, I wrote back:

What's this about?

I folded up the same piece of paper and tossed it over to his books. He kept the pen he was using in his hand and unfolded the note, reading it quickly, then bending his head down to scribble down a reply. His hair fell into his eyes and his hand ran like lightning across a fresh piece of paper.

I had absolutely no idea what he could be asking about. I dreaded it would be about his business assignment because I had absolutely no idea about entrepreneurship, management and organisation. Unless he wanted a quick Googled answer I searched up on Yahoo answers or a dodgy response copied and pasted straight off Wiki, then I knew I'd hardly be much of any use to him.

However, as Caine was frantically writing something down, I noticed something. He had rolled up the sleeves of his senior hoodie and out poked a piece of white fabric. At first, I thought it was just a T-shirt he was wearing underneath, but as he shifted, I realised it wasn't. It was a piece of dirty fabric wrapped around his forearm and tied up to secure it...like a bandage. A really hastily wrapped bandage. As I examined it further, I saw a patch of dried blood on it.

Quickly, I tore off a piece of my notebook and wrote:

That injury on your arm looks like it hurt. What happened?

I crumpled it up and with my poor aim, blindly threw it in the direction he was at. It didn't exactly land by him, it kind of bounced off his forehead and landed on the papers in front of him. He looked down at it in confusion and didn't move for a moment. Then he found me staring at him intently and smoothed out the wrinkles on the paper. Once he read what I had written, he looked extremely uncomfortable as he tugged the sleeve of his hoodie down.

He took more than a moment to respond, but eventually, he abandoned the piece of paper he was previously writing on and ripped out a fresh piece. Then he tossed it towards my side of the table.

Nothing.

I frowned, but he just shrugged and grabbed the piece of paper to add something. When he flicked it back, it read:

Doesn't matter. Don't worry, okay?

I shook my head and wrote:

That is a serious injury. Looks like someone slashed you with a knife.

He tensed as he read my reply and it took him a while to respond. I waited patiently for a reply and even tried to do some of my work while I waited, but I was way too out of it to concentrate on anything but that cut on his forearm. It didn't look very accidental either. It couldn't have possibly been Caine himself that made the slice. From where it was positioned, there was no rational excuse. I mean, if it was a finger or even hand cut, then I guess there could have been the reasonable explanation that he had accidentally cut himself while cutting the vegetables for dinner. But with a cut that serious and on his *forearm,* there just *had* to be someone who had done this to him.

When I got his reply, it said:

I went out into the woods near my house last night. There's some pretty sharp crap out there. Ha. Should have been more careful.

I raised an eyebrow. Although it did explain why he smelled like the woods, no tree could scratch into his skin *that* deep. Not wanting to push him any further on the subject, I folded the note into my pocket and said nothing more. I pretended to become absorbed into my studies, but my mind kept flicking back to Caine's injury. I stared blankly at my Shakespeare notes completely distracted.

Then Caine slid another piece of folded paper into my notebook.

Can I ask that question now?

I just nodded. Caine gazed down at a pre-written note in his hands. It was small and already crumpled and damp-looking as if his

hands were all sweaty. He took a deep breath and placed it in front o
me.

*Before I ask my real question, can I ask...are you and Ryder
together?*

I stared at his question for a long time as a million thoughts ran
through my mind and I got a headache. Eventually, I picked up the same
coloured pen and wrote the truth.

No.

I could feel him looking at me. Reading me.Studying me. A
second later, another note appeared.

Do you...do you like him?

I took a deep breath.

Yes.

Caine stared at my answer for far longer than I stared at his. It
was only a word but he seemed to study it, as if there was a hidden
meaning behind those three letters. At first, he showed no sign of
emotion, then there was a glint of... disappointment. But it quickly bled
to something that looked a lot more like anger. Caine packed up his
books and shoved them into his bag, crumpling pieces of paper as he
zipped it up and swung it over his shoulder.

He took one look at me, then turned and walked away, crushing
my answer in his fist and tossing it into the trash. I felt horrible.

"Caine," I called out, but he was already lost in the aisles of
books.

A person to the side of the room hushed me and I sunk into my
chair, feeling like I had just murdered a puppy. Ryder pulled out one of
his earphones, oblivious to what the past twenty minutes had just been
about.

"What just happened? Where's Caine?"

"He left," I answered, looking where he had just walked off,
hoping he'd come back.

"Nora."

When I turned to Ryder, he had a note in his hands and he slid it
over to me. I recognised the black ink of Caine's pen and the messy

andwriting. Then, after a moment, I realised it was the essay-long question he had been writing before I interrupted him about his arm. He must have dropped it on his way out.

So, I have this confession. Before we properly met, I would have never considered you as anything more than just a girl. But now that I've kind of gotten to know you, I've seen you in a whole different way. I've seen beauty and talent and greatness and I really want to see more. I'm not so great with romance so this already kind of sucks, but I'll just get down to the point and ask: Will you go out with me?

I rejected him before he could even ask.

Twenty Two

The day proceeded with mostly silence. Ryder didn't say much after he read the note from Caine. He kind of just sat there, staring at the carpet and tapping his pen against the table absentmindedly. Eventually, it became too much and we decided that our concentration was broken and that we should just head home. It was midday then and when we arrived at my house and we were greeted with a seriously insane Eve.

It was one thing coming home to a pregnant, hormonal sister. But it was a whole other thing coming home to see your pregnant, hormonal sister dancing on top of the dining table while *Single Ladies* blasted from the television. She clutched a celery stick in one hand as she awkwardly shuffled around, looking extremely uncomfortable with the huge mountain of belly poking out as she danced.

Patrick stuck his head out from the kitchen. "I seriously hope our baby inherits my tranquillity," he said to us, a grin plastered on his face before lovingly looking back at his girlfriend. "Why are you two home so early?"

"School wasn't on today," I explained, picking out a slice of
ucumber from the salad, to which Patrick scowled at me and told me to
vash my hands. He had become a serious hygiene spaz since Eve's
oregnancy. "We went to the library to study for a bit."

"Well, you're just in time for lunch," Patrick answered, sliding a
olate piled with thick beef patties to us. "Help set the table, yeah?"

"Okay," I said, grabbing the fresh bag of buns while Ryder
grabbed the stack of meat and the tomato sauce. "How did she even get
up there?" I nodded towards my sister.

"Beats me. Never underestimate a pregnant woman."

I shrugged at Ryder and together, we walked into the dining
room. Patrick drizzled some ranch dressing over the greens and soon
joined us at the table, where Eve was jabbing Ryder in the chest with her
stick of celery, announcing that she wouldn't get off the table until he
sung a line from the Beyoncé song.

Ryder sighed and then into the celery microphone he sung
unenthusiastically, "All the single ladies, all the single ladies, now put
your hands up."

After her final hip wriggle, Patrick took her hand and together,
they struggled to get her off the table. How she got up there in the first
place was a complete mystery and how she had so much energy was
beyond my comprehension. She was pregnant and I had heard, in the
embarrassing moment of the sex talk from my parents, that pregnancy
sucked and you hurt and got fat in weird places and you developed
foreign habits and tastes. But with the way my sister was acting, it was as
if her baby bump was nothing more than a cushion under her shirt.

"Don't you get back pains and whatever?" I asked as Patrick
took some bottles of fizzy and glasses of ice back to the table.

Eve shrugged, blowing a piece of hair that had fallen from her
clip. "Usually. I'm just in an incredibly happy mood today."

"Why?" Ryder raised an eyebrow. My sister exchanged a quick,
secretive smile with her boyfriend, then looked back at us. "We went to
the doctor's today and found out the sex of the baby."

My eyes widened. Ryder congratulated them. Then I blurted, "So is it a boy or a girl?"

Eve kept a knowing smile on her face, then took a butter knife to slather mayonnaise on her bread. Patrick didn't answer either. He just distributed some salad across the table, looking insanely proud.

"You'll find out on Saturday," my sister said after she made her burger and took a bite. "Like everybody else."

"Why Saturday?" I asked.

"We're having our baby shower then," Patrick announced.

"Since guests don't know the sex of the baby yet, they're just going to bring neutral colours, like orange."

"Are you seriously considering dressing your baby in orange?" I questioned, watching as Ryder helped himself to lunch and built a tower of a burger.

"What's wrong with orange?" Eve asked, crinkling her nose up. "I like orange."

"I don't know. Just, you don't really want to see your baby dressed as a tangerine, do you? Or as bright as a road cone? Do you seriously want to embarrass the kid when it looks back at its baby photos and sees that its parents dressed them up as a goldfish?"

Eve rubbed her belly, in that motherly way. "I think my baby would make an adorable goldfish."

Patrick leaned over and kissed her bump. "It'd be a pretty cute road cone too."

I rolled my eyes but we continued to make our lunches. I had just finished making my sandwich when there was a knock on the door. Before Patrick could scrape back his chair to answer it, Mel and her cheerful head of red curls bounced into the room. She was always comfortable with coming over.

"Oh, burgers," she said, dropping down into the spare seat. "Mind if I steal one?"

Patrick motioned towards the bread. "Help yourself."

"So," Mel said, squirting tomato sauce into her sandwich. "Heard anymore news about the fire?"

"What fire?" Eve asked, looking startled.

It occurred to me that I hadn't actually told them about the real reason we weren't at school. Patrick looked concerned, Eve looked freaked. But Mel answered confidently, either happy to be gossiping or not noticing how worried my sister or her boyfriend was.

"Oh, this fire at school. Burned down about a classroom or two, but it didn't grow much more after that. No one was harmed. But I heard the fire wasn't an accident," Mel explained. "Apparently there have been police and private investigators swarming the area. But I'm pretty sure school is back on tomorrow..." Mel babbled on, but paused, and looked at us. "Hey, isn't it Wednesday tomorrow? Wednesday is your one week mark. Wednesday is when the chief officer gets back from holiday and you guys get to be set free!"

I had been so preoccupied with other things that I had completely forgotten that the due date for us to be set free was less than twenty four hours away. My stomach twisted in all sorts of directions. Happiness to finally remove the discomfort weighing on my wrist, relief to finally use the bathroom by myself and excitement to finally be, well, *alone*. But I had developed an attachment to not only the handcuffs but to Ryder too. And our friendship had grown, our relationship strengthened and I felt a wave of worry wash over me. What if once we were set free, everything will change?

What if Ryder goes out and meets a girl and realises that what we had was just an act of boredom? That he had only kissed and confessed because he needed entertainment. A million thoughts ran through my mind. It wasn't like that kiss was a contract. It's not like we were actually together now either. Whatever he did when the handcuffs came off was his business and his only.

But I still couldn't help feeling sick.

My lunch suddenly didn't look very appetising. I looked down at my half eaten burger and salad and pushed my plate away. Ryder didn't seem to be very hungry either. He just stared at his food, deep in thought.

It had been an intense few hours. From absolute happiness, to heartbreak and now a mixture of a million other emotions. I was a hurricane of confusion. An unidentifiable concoction. An unsorted mess.

A complete and utter disaster.

What on earth was I going to do?

Twenty Three

That night wasn't much different from the entire day. Ryder and I still kept talking to a minimum and Eve was still being her pregnant self. She decided she wanted to be the next Katy Perry, so Patrick, like the patient and loving boyfriend he is, drove down to the supermarket to buy two giant lollipops so she could turn it into a candy bra. I think Patrick did it more for his pleasure rather than hers, which was completely disturbing.

So while they were late-night shopping after dinner, Ryder and I stayed up in my room. He had the laptop running, typing up an essay with one hand, while I held up a book and concentrated on trying to understand the words on the page. But all I could think about was how awkward we were being.

At some point, I placed a scrap piece of paper in the section I was up to and placed the book on the bed. Ryder didn't seem to notice my shuffling around. He was way too preoccupied with his writing. Although the new stage in our relationship was still foreign territory to me, I tried to brush away my uncertainties and before I could back out, I placed my hand against his.

Ryder froze against the keys, keeping his eyes on the screen. He stayed like that for several seconds, unmoving and silent. As we sat there awkwardly, the tension in the room thickened, until it was hard to breathe. I started to panic, a million questions rushing through my mind. What if my hand was sweaty or it felt weird against his?

I tried mustering up all the confidence I had and dismissed any more negativity. Before I could even reconsider, I gently squeezed his hand. If anything, it made Ryder seem more uncomfortable. He sat there, looking slightly pained. I knew he wasn't particularly enjoying it, but once my hand had taken a firmer grip on his, I couldn't let go. It was as if I had glued myself to him and there was no turning back.

Trying not to show how nervous I was, I swallowed and with a soft voice I said, "Are you okay?"

Ryder coughed awkwardly and nodded. "Yeah."

Again, we sat there in silence, my hand just casually resting on his. My fingers thinking on their own accord and just kept squeezing his. I knew it was weird and Ryder especially thought it was creepy, me just squeezing his fingers like he had turned into a stress ball, but I couldn't stop.

"Can I have my hand back now?" Ryder muttered after a while, kind of shy and awkward.

"Oh, right!" I answered uncomfortably. "Sorry."

"It's okay," he replied, wiping his hand on his track pants and keeping his eyes on anything but me. "Squeezing kinda hurt." *And it was kinda sweaty too.* But Ryder had the decency not to say it.

We proceeded with the awkward silence. Ryder returned to tapping furiously at the laptop, brow furrowed like he was an athlete concentrating before they competed. I didn't have anything to do, so I pulled out my notebook and a few coloured pens. I threw the pens on the space between us and flicked to a fresh page. Might as well do some study.

I started brainstorming some ideas for my advanced English Shakespeare speech. I gotten down two pathetic dot points in various colours to look like I had put in more effort than I actually had, but it

idn't work. Sighing, I reached out to pick up another pen right at the
ame time Ryder reached down to collect his. Our fingers touched for
·arely a second, but we both shot back like we had been shot by
ightning.

"You just touched me," I blurted.

Ryder, for the first time all night, turned and looked at me. "God,
Nora, I touched your hand. I didn't grab your boob. Stop overreacting."

"*Excuse me?*" I argued, picking up my pen and jabbing him in
is boob. "I'm not the one who's suddenly developed a phobia for
·hysical contact!"

"You have clammy hands," he replied calmly.

"I do *not* have clammy hands." *Oh my God, I have clammy
·ands.*

Ryder just gave me a look, and then returned to his work. Again,
·ve sat in silence, a gentle, yet unpleasant tugging against my wrist as he
·tarted typing with both hands. When we first got handcuffed together,
·loing things was a hassle. The handcuffs would always bite into my skin
·nd rub uncomfortably against my wrist. Now that we had spent a week
·ogether, the pain and discomfort was minimised to a few manageable
·ugs. And although I had just about gotten used to the feeling, the way
·ve were acting made me lose my calm and suddenly, his movements
·were irritating. Suddenly *everything* was irritating and I blurted out the
·thing that was bothering me the most.

"Why are we being so awkward?" I asked, a slight anger tainting
·my words. "We're like two awkward fifteen-year-olds on a first date."

Ryder stopped typing, but didn't look at me. "I think you know
·why."

"If I knew why, I wouldn't have asked," I snapped, trying to
·control my temper but his tranquillity was just making it worse.

He sighed, using his free hand to pinch the bridge of his nose as
·he squeezed his eyes shut. "I shouldn't have kissed you."

His words caught me off guard. All anger drained and I was
·filled with hurt. All I wanted to do was get away. I stared at the links of

the handcuffs in desperation, hoping that if I concentrated enough, they would just break and I could run for it. I kept my gaze down.

"What do you mean?" My voice shattered and it didn't sound as unaffected as I would have liked.

Ryder placed his hand against mine, but I moved it from his grasp as if he had just injected me with poisonous venom. I tried to get as far away from his hand as possible, but it was hard when I was chained to it. His fingers hovered in mid-air for a moment, before he let them drop. I could still feel the way his fingers wrapped around mine; gentle touch with rough hands. I could still feel the warmth of his palm and the way my small hand could disappear into his, so protected and safe. Shaking my head, I forced myself to distance from those thoughts.

"A lot is going on right now, Nora," he said, frowning. His voice was gentle but his words hurt like daggers. "There's all this crap with Chris and then there was the fire the other day. Not to mention Caine who's seriously troubled and I haven't been the best friend to him. I just think that the kiss was bad timing."

I knew we weren't technically together, but it still felt like we were breaking up. I tried putting on a brave face but even staring at the handcuffs made me sick. Not having the courage to look up at him, I kept my gaze down, staying silent and letting a strand of hair hide away my eyes. I could feel tears welling up and my vision started getting blurry, but I bit my lip and tried to fight them back.

"I've been thinking about this a lot, ever since Caine stormed off. I felt so hopeless sitting there instead of going after him. He's all macho for show but really, when he's hurt, he crumbles. And with the handcuffs and you-"

My head snapped up. "What? I was restraining you from comforting your friend, is that what you're trying to say?" I demanded. "All this is my fault?"

He didn't answer. Instead, he said, "Are you crying?"

I wiped furiously at my eyes and looked away. "No. That's ridiculous."

Ryder used his free hand and placed his fingers under my chin, bringing my face back to his. He looked at me with concern, those faded blue eyes glittering with worry. He gently stroked his thumb down my jaw and I tried not to let any more tears escape. I was embarrassed and angry and not to mention hurt. I clenched my teeth and tried to gather myself.

"The handcuffs have been restraining the both of us from lots of things. It's been interfering with my practice and school. I've been distracted from things like my family and friends. Don't try to deny it, but you know the same applies for you. You hardly see Mel anymore, it's hard to study and your sister is just weeks away from giving birth. Plus your parents come home Friday from their holiday. It's just been really hectic and we haven't been giving our full attention to anything," Ryder explained, holding my chin in place as he whispered.

I kept quiet.

"When the handcuffs get taken off, I think it'll be a great opportunity. I want to focus on my other priorities," he said so quietly I almost didn't hear.

My heart shattered, mostly because I agreed, but part of me also kind of wanted for us to fight for each other. Sure, the kiss was unexpected and wild but that's what made it mean so much. I guess deep down I knew it was bad timing but I wanted to treasure the moment a little longer than just a night before other things brought us back to the cruelties of reality.

I let a tear slip after that and I had no regrets of letting it escape. It was just one tear, but it brought out so much passionate hurt and anger it was as if my heart had bled out the emotions into something physical so the whole world could understand. It ran down my face in a wild, hot mess.

Ryder leaned in and caught the tear in a kiss, letting it die on his lips. It was such a bittersweet feeling. His lips felt like both fire and ice against my skin. "I'm sorry."

I wrenched free from his grasp and looked away. "I'm tired."

It was still early but Ryder didn't say anything. He just got off my bed and got down to his space on the floor, flicking the lampshade off on his way down. "Good night, Nora."

When the darkness took me into its embrace and promised me the protection of shadows, I finally set free the tears.

Twenty Four

We fell into routine the next morning, silent but cooperative. There was the same struggle to get out of bed without ripping each other's hands off. Then there was the awkward bathroom situations, consisting of an uncomfortable shower each, the difficult task of dressing (one sleeveless dress for me, one half ripped up shirt for Ryder) and as always, the peeing business. Ryder did his usual aim, fire, shake without complaint. I, on the other hand, struggled to pee without making it tense. I made Ryder sing a nursery rhyme, just in case something awkward happened, like a god forbidden fart.

When that was over, we went downstairs, made breakfast and listened to Eve read a Dr. Seuss book to her stomach. Throughout the entire morning, my mind had been screaming: This is the last time you'll do this handcuffed. It made me feel both relieved and kind of heartbroken. Although they were a pain in the ass, I couldn't help but feel a sense of gratitude towards them. Without the handcuffs, Ryder and

I would have never reunited. And even though it was over, it was beautiful while it lasted.

We pulled into a parking space in the student lot and Ryder killed the engine. He sat there for a moment before turning to look at me. "Nora, I-"

But he stopped short, hearing a knocking on the passenger side window. Leaning over, he fiddled with the automatic window controllers until the glass slid down. A man with chin-length silver hair tied back at the nape of his neck bent down and shot us a smile. His eyes were a faint emerald and although the shade was pale, they still glittered like precious gemstones. Within the corners of his eyes, deep wrinkles lined his faded skin as he noticed the handcuffs and smiled wider.

"Hi, can we help you?" Ryder asked.

"Ah, just the kids I was looking for," he said, reverting his gaze from Ryder to me. "I'm Hunter Evens, chief officer of the local police department."

Like the welcoming principal she was, Mrs. Westfield had organised a variety of different finger cakes and biscuits along a table at the back of her office. Some coffee equipment was also set up; real mugs, rather than foam and metal spoons in replacement of plastic. With the way she set it up, it was if we were gathering for a tea party, rather than further elaborating our handcuff situation.

"Cheesecake?" Mrs. Westfield gracefully offered him some from a platter, but Hunter politely dismissed with a flick of his thin hand.

"Lactose intolerant," he explained, settling with his black coffee.

I never would have expected Hunter to be the chief officer. If anything, he could have just been a grandparent or even a substitute teacher. I mean, the guy had a freaking *ponytail* for crying out loud *and* he was wearing a sweater vest matched with a pair of beige chinos. He just seemed like a wealthy elderly man who would be better suited at a country club rather than a high school.

"Now," he said, after taking a slip of his beverage, "how exactly
did this happen?" Hunter gestured towards our cuffed hands.

"We were picked for a public demonstration during one of our
career presentations. It was meant to emphasise the strength of these new
handcuffs, but then the key got lost and some kid shoved half his rock
collection into the keyholes. That's where we are now," Ryder said in
one breath. "But down to what's important: How are we going to get set
free?"

Hunter placed his coffee down on the table and walked up to us,
kneeling on the floor and gently placing his slender, pale fingers under
the thick chain of links that bound Ryder and I together.

"Expensive, these things are," he said, running the smooth metal
beneath his fingertips. "The most innovative and specialised piece of
equipment designed especially for the contemporary police force."

"Handcuffs?" Ryder scoffed, just as unimpressed with them as
he was on the first day we encountered them.

"Don't be fooled by the simplicity, Mr. Collins," Hunter
answered, letting the handcuffs slip from his grip. "You're wearing one
of the most modernised pieces of equipment that could essentially
improve consistency in the police department. The one you're wearing
now is the only copy we own, that's why we've been so hesitant to just
cut them off."

Obviously Hunter had been doing his homework, considering he
knew our names prior to us even introducing ourselves.

"So, basically, you let three members of our local police force
bring in the *only pair* of high technology handcuffs into a *high school*
and let them demonstrate on *two students*?" I asked, raising an eyebrow.

Mrs. Westfield scolded me for approaching a highly appreciated
officer with such a disrespectful attitude, while Hunter gave me this
snobby look. The kind of look the girl behind the counter gives someone
when they ask for an item of clothing in the next size up. Or the look the
checkout person at the supermarket gives me when I fiddle around in my
purse looking for a stray ten cents so I can pay for my pack of biscuits.

The same look I get when I look at a shirt and try to fold it the same way but it still ends up looking like I just ate it and spat it back onto the table.

"Obviously, it was never intended to conclude in this kind of situation. All people make mistakes, Miss Montgomery. It was meant to be an opportunity for promotion. To really emphasise our area of expertise and get people inspired to join our workforce. Evidently, we may have done the exact opposite," the chief police continued, standing up from his position on the floor and leaning back on Mrs. Westfield's desk.

I watched as our principal craned her neck behind him to see what was going on. She struggled for a few brief seconds, but when she decided she couldn't grow a longer neck to get a better view, she stood and walked calmly over to us. She smoothed her navy, polyester skirt and crossed her arms.

"How do you suggest we approach this?" she asked, in her most business-like tone.

Hunter examined the handcuffs for a while longer. "I suppose we'll have to just cut them off. It would seem even more highly unprofessional if we remain them handcuffed. Our reputation is already in the downfall. It's a shame we don't have a replica. These handcuffs would have had a huge impact on the contemporary police department and I bet it would have been recorded as a significant historical event."

I was starting to think Hunter had a fetish for the handcuffs.

"I'd just like to examine the material that has been blocking the compartment where the key is meant to go," he answered.

Then, that's when something seriously magical happened. Now, it required a lot of awkward arm positions and wrist twisting, which made me wish I was double joined to reduce the pain shooting through my limb. When the keyhole was facing the floor, Hunter tapped it three times with his long, slender finger and a majority of the pieces of rock and gravel just fell out and dropped onto his palm.

But, to Hunter, it was as if the handcuffs had crapped out Jack's magic beans. He studied them with great intensity like he had never seen a rock in his life. When he was done staring at them, he placed them onto

Mrs. Westfield's desk then did the exact same miraculous thing to Ryder's side of the handcuffs. Again, it just fell out. I stared at him amazed. This could only have one reasonable explanation:

Hunter was secretly either a) Jesus, b) Santa Claus or c) Obama. Because all those people were seriously powerful.

Hunter looked up at us. "That seemed easy," he said, seeming a little surprised himself as he reached into the pocket of his trousers and produced a little silver key. Patiently, he placed the key carefully into the hole and turned slowly, as if careful all this easiness was going to backfire.

But it didn't. With a satisfying click, the handcuffs cracked open and instantly the new sensation of freedom was bliss. I rolled my wrist, listening to the cracks of the bones and felt my muscles relax from their tension. It was kind of like taking off a cast that had been plastered on for months. Minus the awkward growth of hair, the air exposure was refreshing. I couldn't help but stretch and wave and do all sorts of simple things that had been such a hassle being handcuffed.

When I had recovered from my excitement, I looked over at Ryder who had been released and was rubbing his wrist. He examined it, as if he expected it to look different. As soon as he was done, he dropped his hand, got to his feet and scooped up his bag.

"Thank you, sir."

His tone was polite, but his face was expressionless. They shook hands in an extremely business-like manner and Mrs. Westfield announced our dismissal to class. Ryder was already heading for the door and I wanted to catch up with him so I quickly picked up my books. I was ready to scamper out of the room but thought it would be much more appropriate if I showed my gratitude beforehand.

So I walked up to Hunter and said, "Thank you."

I didn't know what else to do. Ryder had shaken his hand but he had that formal, business element to his attitude. Something I didn't possess. Besides, ever since Ryder called my hands clammy, I had been afraid to touch *everyone's* hand. I considered hugging the old man, but that would have been inappropriate, so, like the socially awkward person I am, I just curtsied.

Yeah. That's right. I full on *curtsied* like he was the queen of something. And before I could process the weird expressions on their faces, I ran for the door. Once I was outside and the chilly air could cool my cheeks, I searched for Ryder. I walked down hallways and passed classrooms, climbed stairs and went out into the quadrangle.

But I couldn't find him.

Twenty Five

I saw little of Ryder after that. The classes we had together, he always seemed to be absent and whenever the whole school had lunch, he was always with his group of friends. It was as if the past week had never happened. Ryder was back, basking in his shower of popularity, his shirts no longer mangled and looking much more in place with his blazer full of badges.

Whenever our eyes caught for the briefest of moments, he always looked away and never turned back. I was too afraid to approach his group without getting death glares and I never found him loitering around school by himself. I never saw much of Caine either.

As the days rolled by and Saturday came, it was time for Eve's baby shower. Our parents hadn't come home yet. They were supposed to arrive Friday night but their flight got delayed so they'd be arriving in the afternoon, hopefully in time to see Eve slice the cake.

It was good to be able to wear something that covered my shoulders. From wearing nothing but sleeveless shirts and jeans, it was good to finally have minimal exposure. Late Saturday morning was nice weather for winter. The sun was shining and there was hardly any breeze. Dressed in a knit sweater dress with a pair of boots, I was in charge of guarding the gift table, arranging the presents and directing people to the refreshments table.

Patrick and Eve were circling the crowd, greeting guests, laughing at pointless things and letting people rub Eve's belly like it was a magic ball and it had the answers to all of life's questions. At some point, she waddled over, cradling four mini quiches, and poked her nose into one of the gift bags. Literally.

She inhaled deeply, then straightened. "Do you think anyone bought me ham?"

I raised an eyebrow. "Eve, the point of your baby shower is to receive presents for your *baby*, not your stomach."

"Someone could have bought a ham for my baby," she replied, stuffing the crumbly pastry in her mouth.

I sighed and busied myself with stacking a few of the gifts to make room for the ones coming in. Eve must have noticed something was wrong because she placed the quiches down and reached over and squeezed my arm.

"Thanks for helping out, Nora," she said, her touch warm and comforting. "You've been really down since the handcuffs got taken off."

I smiled weakly. "Yeah," I replied lamely.

Eve grinned mischievously. "Which is why I invited the Collins."

I nearly choked on my breathing. "You invited *the Collins*," I repeated.

Imagining June Collins at my sister's baby shower was a nightmare: dressed in her shiny pumps and navy business suit, parading the place like a general, rather than a guest. I shuddered at the thought and started absentmindedly shifting a few gifts around the table. But then I thought of Ryder by her side, with his cool attitude and messy hair. My stomach flipped.

I wasn't sure if I was happy or scared about the possibility.

Eve said nothing more as she picked up her food and walked way to a cluster of women who gushed and gossiped. Patrick was busy ssociating with a few of his friends who were mostly speaking in huckles, grunts and sips of their beverages. Everyone seemed be having good time.

As another guest handed me a perfectly wrapped cellophane gift, with a matching bow, a white taxi pulled up at the curb. And then, two walking tomatoes stepped out of the vehicle.

Those two walking tomatoes were my parents.

Dad was dressed in one of his awful, Hawaiian print shirts and wrapped around his hips was one of those horrible bum bags. He waved at us from the car, before walking towards the boot and pulling out the luggage. My mother, wearing one of her I'm-a-tourist T-shirts and wedge thongs took one look at us and came hurdling over.

Eve instantly left the group of girls and wobbled over to our mum. They exchanged an awkward hug, my sister's belly bump getting in the way, but they didn't seem affected. They still squeezed and laughed and gushed over how soon Eve was to giving birth. Then after their little moment of affection, Eve asked if Mum bought her a ham. It was a negative.

"Nora!" my mother screeched, arms open as she rushed past people and wrapped me up in a tight hug.

Circling my arms around her small frame, I squeezed tight. Inhaling the familiar scent of her citrus shampoo and body wash made me realise how much I had missed her. I lingered a little longer than necessary before finally breaking apart.

Mum brushed a piece of blonde hair away from my face and smiled at me. "I've been so worried about you."

"Me?" I questioned.

"Yes. Your sister is so hormonal, being so close to her due date. And good God, what is this obsession with ham?"

I laughed. "Patrick has been the responsible one. He's been taking care of us."

Mum smiled knowingly. "Should have known. He's a good man Where is he anyway?"

She took my hand, squeezed it and then disappeared into the crowd to find him. As soon as she left, dad appeared, face red as he rolled the luggage up the driveway. I walked over to help and he caught my eye, grinning and letting go of the bags to greet me with an embrace. But loosening his grip on the handles of the baggage caused them to start rolling down the hill. Dad swiftly reached out just in time to catch one of them but the other was already on its way down the slope. Quickly, I raced after it and grabbed hold of it before it went tumbling down towards the road.

He grinned as I walked back up the driveway and slung his arm across my shoulders. "What would I do without you?"

"I don't know," I teased. "Hardly anything."

He laughed and kissed the top of my head. Together, we made our way into the house, Dad talking about the extravagant prices of everything in California but how beautiful the beaches were. I listened to stories of adventures and got little snippets of historical information my parents discovered.

"What about you, kiddo?" Dad asked, running a hand through his thin, greying hair.

I thought back to Ryder. My parents had an adventure while they were gone, but so had I. Getting chained to Ryder, the kiss, the fire, getting a ride to the police station in the middle of the night, community service, the mystery of Caine's cuts.

Instead, I said, "Oh, you know, the usual."

When the cake finally came out, the group erupted in excited whispers. This was the moment everyone was waiting for. The secret everyone was dying to know: the sex of Eve and Patrick's baby. It was a massive looking cake, something that looked like it belonged in a wedding catalogue rather than a baby shower in the front garden.

It was three rectangular pieces of cake, piled upon each other to make a tower. Little grey pearls decorated the edges of the cake, along with cute little graphics outlined in white icing fit for an infant. There were images of a cradle, a bottle, a dummy and little booties too. Sprinkled over the entire design was a light dusting of silver powder. The cake was absolutely stunning.

"Before we cut the cake, we'd just like to thank everyone for coming today," Patrick said, arms wrapped around his girlfriend. "We appreciate all the gifts and support we have received on the journey to raising our first child."

"Oh! And if anyone bought me a ham, please see me when you get your slice of cake. I have an extra big piece for you." Eve winked at the crowd and a few people chuckled.

But I don't think they knew she was serious.

The crowd held their breath as Eve took the knife from the table and gently sunk it into the cake. Patrick stood behind her, arms around her stomach, fingers gently and absentmindedly stroking her bump. My sister took her time in cutting the cake, creating so much tension that the girl next to me was twitching in anticipation.

When she finally cut out a little section of the bottom slab of cake, she held it up on a little plastic plate. Inside the small casing of white fondant, grey pearls and swirls of icing was a light blue sponge.

Eve was having a baby boy.

The crowd cheered and a few of our closest friends and family ran up to congratulate Eve and Patrick. They shook hands, hugged and talked over this huge announcement. I stayed behind and watched, thinking about how happy they looked and decided that having a nephew would be my next new adventure.

Across the crowd, I saw a checked blue shirt over a graphic T-shirt and dark, messy hair. When the figure turned around, I saw his eyes. Ryder's eyes, the palest of blue, like the colour of rare tinted diamond, glittering with glory. Quickly, I made my way through the crowd, pushing through guests and snaking my way through towards him.

But when I broke out into the clearing where I thought he was he wasn't there.

"Looking for someone?"

I turned and saw my mother standing there, watching me with curious, hazel eyes. I looked back to where I thought I saw Ryder and shook my head. Mum didn't believe me, I could tell by the way she looked at me, but she said nothing. She wrapped her arm around my shoulders and steered me back towards my sister.

"Congratulations," I said, once we approached.

Eve reached out and squeezed my hand. "Thank you, Nora. For everything. You've always been here for me... for us." She rubbed her belly and looked up at her boyfriend who kissed her nose. "So, as the first and only future aunt of our child, I think you should be one of the first to hear what we have decided for the name... Hammy."

"H-Hammy?" I repeated, not sure that I heard it right.

My mother just stood there, staring at Eve in intense silence. "Like... Short for Hamish or Hamlet or..."

Eve just shook her head. "No. Just Hammy. Not short for anything. I mean, it's perfect, isn't it? My addiction to ham is just a sign that I should be naming my children after my cravings. Pregnancy is the new prophecy."

A few of Eve's friends joined us then and soon enough, my sister drifted off into their conversation. While she was engaged in her little interaction, Patrick turned to us.

"We are *not* naming our son Hammy. Don't worry," Patrick reassured us, eyes shifting towards Eve to make sure she wouldn't overhear and get upset. "She's just going through that really hormonal stage. I'm sure once we have the baby she'll come to her senses and she won't name our first child after food."

"There are worse things he could be named after," I pointed out.

Patrick cringed. "One day, I'll tell my son the story about his mother wanting to name him after ham."

We laughed.

Twenty Six

After a majority of the guests had gone and most of the mess was cleaned, I got a call from Officer Brandy about a community service shift. I had been assigned for a late afternoon hour of sorting donated clothes at the Church fund raiser. Since I didn't exactly have a car, my transportation was again reliant on my parents. And because I had to tell them my exact location, I was forced to confess my run-in with the law to my dad. It wasn't like he was going to accept the fact that I was going to spend my afternoon at Church. We weren't exactly a very religious family.

"So, explain to me why you're spending your afternoon at a Church," Dad said. He turned and looked at me briefly. "You didn't turn into one of those nuns, did you? Is that even legal at seventeen?"

"Dad, no," I answered. "Because if you really want that kind of commitment at your age, try giving all that dedication to your studies in the HSC this year, yeah?" he babbled on.

"Dad," I said, trying to interrupt.

"But on the other hand, my youngest daughter being a nun doesn't sound too bad. Nuns aren't allowed to, you know...get down with the dirty. Snake and the bush.Birds and the bees. Penetrated by-"

"Oh, God, Dad, please stop," I quickly interjected, feeling completely disturbed and embarrassed at my dad's use of the word 'penetrated'.

He laughed at my reaction. "Just saying. I'm going to be grandfather soon. It's going all too quickly." He smiled weakly. "Personally, I don't think Eve is ready to have a baby. She wants to name her child after that hyperactive squirrel on *Over the Hedge*. Remember that movie?"

"I remember." "Seems like only yesterday we all watched that as a family. Now you're all graduating and having babies named Hammy and..."

I looked at him. "You're not going to go all Oprah on me, are you?" I teased.

Dad puffed out his chest. "Dads don't cry." He shot me a playful grin, then added, "Now, remind me about the church stuff."

"Community service," I answered. "Kind of got in trouble with the police."

I sunk into my seat. It was supposed to be the casual teenager slouch that so many of us had mastered, but rather than nonchalance being the reason, it was embarrassment. I kept my eyes out the window and watched the houses fly by; roofs painted in neutral tones of creams, browns and greys.

Although any normal teenager would be worried about getting in trouble, I wasn't. I was more afraid of the disappointment. Despite Eve's seriously disturbing cravings and weird habits, she was a brilliant student. One of those girls that kept her grades up, was in the leadership team, played sports and socialised, all while keeping her hair absolutely perfect. She was the type of student that made others gape in awe, wondering how she could balance life so effortlessly, while the rest of the normal high school community was having trouble handing in

omework on time and running out of excuses to why they miss the
thletics carnival every year.

My sister had left a trail of memorable achievements, which,
while I was happy for her, it also laid down a whole lot of expectations
or me to follow in her footsteps. So far, the only legacy I had left for
emembrance was being handcuffed to the all-star Ryder Collins.
Someone, who was now avoiding me like Herpes.

"What kind of trouble did you and Mel get into?" Dad asked,
after a brief pause.

It was funny how he thought I had dragged *Mel* into this. The
only untamed thing about Mel was her hair and eating habits. Prior to
Ryder, the wildest thing we had ever done was skip the first five minutes
of first period on a serious hunt for a tampon. I mean, we were both
twelve and Mel had just gotten her period and her mum is a total
abelling freak so she wrote Mel's name on every individual coloured
tampon covering just in case she 'lost them'. And one must have fallen
out of her pocket on the rush to homeroom so we were on a treasure hunt
for a missing tampon.

"Ryder Collins, actually."

Dad frowned, almost like he was trying to remember who the
hell Ryder Collins was. But when it finally clicked, he looked at me with
a confused expression. "I thought you weren't friends."

"We aren't," I muttered, playing with my fingers. It was a true
answer.

"Then?"

We were about a block from the church. We were so close, yet
so far.

"Just the wrong place, wrong time, wrong people-"

"Nora, you're not doing drugs or anything?" Dad asked, looking
like he might have a heart attack.

"No!" I quickly assured him.

"Good," he answered, pulling up at the curb.

Just as I was about to jump out of the car, he leaned in to the
centre console and locked the doors. With my hand desperately tugging

on the handle, as if it would just magically open if I repeatedly tried, looked longingly at the stalls surrounding the church.

"Tell me exactly what happened, Nora Montgomery."

I turned to face him and sighed. "Just some kids at school got into a fight on the beach one night after the street fair. I just happened to be around."

Dad let out a low whistle. "What was the fight about?"

I looked sheepishly at the toe of my shoe and grumbled, "Me." I was pathetic and sounded a lot more stupid out loud than in my head. "Not *over* me," I quickly added. "Just about me."

"What about you?" Dad could get the cop questioning going quite well.

I sighed. "Just a nasty comment that went around school." I knew Dad was going to press further so I added, "Something not worth repeating. Ryder defended me. So did Caine." Seeing his blank expression, I added, "Ryder's friend."

He examined the situation further and nodded, then unlocked the doors. He was letting this go way too easily, so I knew he was going to do more, but my part had been satisfied.

"I'll pick you up in an hour."

I climbed out of the car, but before closing the door, I poked my head through and said, "Don't do anything idiotic, Dad."

He gave me a grin, ignoring my comment. "Have fun."

There were tonnes of clothes that had been donated. Piles of boxes covered the grassy area, from baby clothes to grandma clothes. So once I got assigned a table, I started unpacking boxes that were labelled: $10. I organised the clothes in sizes and seasons along the tables. Most of it drew minimum interest but there were a few printed dresses that were so vintage, they were kind of cute.

I had my head down for most of the time, concentrating as I rearranged the clothes and folded them up neatly so it would provide more room on the table, that I hardly realised another box come in.

"Hi, yeah, these are some more donations. But this looks like an extremely feminine pile... Great. Could you please direct me to the men's section?"

I looked up to see Caine. He looked kind of flustered, the wind blowing his hair into a messy tuff. His face looked pale, his cheeks tinted pink from the cold and his eyes, once they caught mine, looked afraid. Like I had just pulled out a gun from my skirt and demanded him to hand over his tatter tots.

"Hey," I whispered. It wasn't meant to come out so soft and weak, but I couldn't help it.

"Nora," he said, looking around frantically. "Uh, what are you doing here?"

"Community service," I answered. "You bringing in donations?"

"Yeah," he answered, shoving his hands in his pockets. "Just some old stuff I grew out of."

I placed my hand in the box and pulled out a *Thomas the Tank Engine* T-shirt. "Yeah," I agreed. "You probably outgrew this a long time ago."

He cracked a smile, but it vanished just as quickly as it appeared.

"How's Ryder?" I couldn't help but ask.

His face fell and he suddenly looked even more uncomfortable. I realised I should have asked how *he* was first, before bringing up his best friend and instantly I regretted the words that had spilled from my mouth.

"I- I'm sorry... How are you? Really?"

He shrugged and let out a sigh. "It's been crazy, Nora. There's a lot of stuff going on right now, especially for Ryder."

"Is there anything I can do to help?" I asked.

Caine looked at me with kind eyes. "I think it's best if you just keep doing what you're doing and stay away."

That wasn't the kind of response I was expecting, but nodded like it didn't affect me. "Okay."

He turned to leave, but hesitated and instantly, my stomach fluttered, expecting more news about Ryder. I knew it was selfish, especially because Caine was such a great guy once you got to know him, but this was probably the last time I'd have any contact with any of them.

"Ryder... He's not doing too well. He really does have stuff to deal with right now, stuff that isn't related to you. But through all the crap he has right now... you're still his top priority. Just stay away from him right now, because I know for a fact that he will eventually come back to you."

He gave me a small smile then turned and walked down the street. And although he told me to leave Ryder alone, I was surprised to find that he called me that exact night.

Twenty Seven

The phone rang after dinner, with perfect timing too. I was in my room, staring at triangles and wondering how it would ever help me in the future. Trigonometry homework and I had an unwritten agreement. I'd make the shapes look beautiful by decorating them with highlighters in return for them not giving me a headache. So, getting a call was a great break from my intense procrastination session.

Walking down the stairs and into the kitchen, I found my sister sitting by the counter with a tub of ice-cream and a giant spoon. Patrick was sitting at the dinner table, glasses on as he went through some papers. When Eve spotted me, she vaguely flicked her spoon in the general direction of where I supposed the phone was.

"Why haven't you guys moved out yet?" I asked, searching for the phone.

Patrick, eyes still on his papers, replied, "We decided to stay until the baby is born. Eve is so close to her due date and the hospital is much closer from here."

I raised an eyebrow. "You guys are staying for the food, aren' you?"

Patrick looked up from a stack of papers and smiled sheepishly "Yes. Eve insisted and I've learned never to mess with a pregnan woman."

I had to agree with that, so I returned to searching for the phone. It wasn't by the receiver or the counters. I couldn't find it by the spice rack or the fruit bowl. It wasn't where the knife block was located or where the tea set sat. I started getting anxious wondering who had called and my patience was being tested.

"Eve," I groaned, searching high and low. "Where did you put the phone?"

My sister, who was happily digging through the tub of cookie dough flavoured goodness, looked up and frowned at me. She sat there for a moment, licking her spoon clean before she lit up like a firefly in remembrance.

"The freezer," she said, matter-of-factly.

Opening the freezer, sure enough, I saw the phone there. Scooping it up in my hands, I brushed away the crystals of ice that had made its way around the device. Quickly, I retreated back to my room and closed the door, my heart racing with adrenaline, curious to find out who was calling.

The phone was cold, pressed up against my ear. "Hello?"

There was a clatter in the background before a voice replied hesitantly, "Nora?"

I knew that voice anywhere. The velvet of his words, the warmth in his tone. Ryder Collins was on the other line. I was suddenly extremely uneasy. It was the first time we had spoken since the handcuffs were removed and I didn't want to make any mistakes that would drive him away. I had to sit down to stop from shaking with nerves.

"Yes?" My voice was all breathless and hoarse.

"Um…hi," Ryder answered awkwardly.

"Hey." My reply was barely over a whisper. I was being bsolutely pathetic, so I took a deep breath and told myself to man up. Was there something you wanted to talk to me about?"

"Oh, uh, yeah-" There was a rattling sound, as if something had ⟩een dropped and in the distance, Ryder swore. "Um, sorry, I dropped he phone. So, anyway, I kinda of-" Something else dropped again, but his time, it wasn't the phone. Ryder made an irritated groan and the ⟩ounds of his shuffles echoed through the room. "*Christ*. Okay, uh-"

"Ryder, stop fidgeting..." I was surprised to hear my voice come ⟩ut so clear and soothing and even more surprised to find that Ryder ⟩tayed still.

After a brief moment, he started talking again. This time, much nore in control. "I'm sorry...just kind of nervous I guess."

I couldn't help the smile that escaped. Knowing that cool and ⟩ollected Ryder Collins got nervous was a secret that hardly anyone was aware of. And I felt privileged, both of knowing he got nervous and that for this particular situation, it was because of me.

"I totally understand..."

"Oh, God, he *told* you?" Ryder answered, nerves coming back and panic rising in his voice. He swallowed.

I dropped the smile. He wasn't nervous because of me. "Who told me what?"

He coughed and didn't say anything.

"*Who* told me *what*?" I repeated.

It took Ryder a while, but eventually, he muttered, "I ran into your dad at the supermarket today."

Oh, God. Now it was my turn to panic. A trickle of sweat ran down my brow so I shakily swiped it off with the back of my sleeve. The phone was suddenly *burning* against my ear. What did my dad say? What did he *do*? Well, now it explained a lot of things: Dad's cheerful mood at dinner and Ryder's agitation.

"What happened?" I really didn't want to know the answer, but I figured that *not* knowing the answer would be even worse.

"Well... He kind of cornered me by the meat section and threatened me with a giant leg of ham..." Ryder sounded absolutely humiliated as he confessed and I usually would have thought it was cute if my own cheeks weren't burning with embarrassment.

"He...threatened you...with a ham..." I repeated slowly, feeling the heat surge all the way to the tips of my ears. Just imagining my father, a giant leg of ham in his arms, with his horrible leathery tan threatening a teenage boy in the supermarket, made me want to crawl into a hole and live there forever.

"I am *so* sorry," I quickly apologised. "Whatever he said, I did *not* say anything that would drive him into doing that kind of thing. He acted upon his own accord."

Ryder shuffled uncomfortably on the other line. "I know. Because, well, before he whipped out the ham like a freaking ninja, he actually thanked me... for taking care of you the other night at the beach."

"Then... what did he threaten you for?" I questioned. "He threatened me into saying yes for dinner tomorrow night," Ryder replied, discomfort dripping from his tone. "You...You're coming over for dinner tomorrow night?" I asked, instantly thinking about what to wear and how to do my hair. "What time will you be over?"

"Actually..." Ryder started, shame clinging to every word. "Your dad invited me to dinner with him... Just him."

I didn't say anything. Neither did he.

"Is that weird? Because I'm really freaking creeped about having dinner plans with your dad. Not only do I have a date with a *dude* but he's kind of an... *old* dude and I hardly even know him. So is this even appropriate?"

I honestly had nothing to say.

"Am I supposed to dress casually or do I have to impress him with a suit and tie? What do you think he wants to talk about? Do you think he's going to bring a ham? Oh God, your family is addicted to ham!" Ryder babbled on, sounding uneasy and generally a little unwell.

When I proceeded to sit in silence, he whispered, "Can you
lease come over?"

His voice was barely over a whisper, vulnerable, yet holding
nto every ounce of strength he could muster. What Caine said was true.
tyder eventually did come around. I mean, it took my dad's threats, a
inner date and a ham to get him to, but I was grateful he finally did.
And now that he was ready, I was finally going to get some answers.

"I'll be there in ten."

Twenty Eight

I had never really snuck out before, so once I hung up, I just sat there, completely clueless. How was I going to get from my house to his? What was I supposed to do if I got caught? What was my back-up story and who would cover for me while I was gone? How long would I be gone for? It was only eight thirty but how long would it take for someone to realise I was missing?

Delinquents had so much to think about.

Eventually, I decided from all my experience watching TV series and movies, I'd just use that knowledge to my advantage. I was dressed in all black with a little flashlight key ring hooked onto a loop on my jeans as I went around my room, turning off lights and locking doors. From there, I painfully opened my window, cringing as the movement made it squeak and cry in reluctance. Deciding I'd get caught if I opened it any more, I stuck my head and arms out and awkwardly reached for the closest branch.

Now, I don't know why movies always conveniently have eriously easily accessible and climbable trees outside their windows. I on't know why people in movies make it so falsely inaccurate that it's a iece of cake sneaking out. Because honestly, it just gives you false ope. I figured this out as I ungracefully wriggled out my window and stretched for the branch that seemed to be *just* in my range of reach.

In movies, this would be where my epic ninja skills kick in and I start climbing the branches like a freaking fruit bat. But unfortunately, eality was in my favour that night so I kind of just clung as tightly as I could to the branch and let my feet fall from the ledge of the window. I swung back and forth, quite dangerously, to a point where I decided I was going to die. Then once I regained my balance, I painfully made my way towards the trunk; years of primary school monkey bar practice had finally paid off.

Although the bark bit into my palms, threatened to cut my skin and bless me with blisters, I tried to ignore the pain and made my way to the safety of the trunk. It was at good timing too, because the branch I was clinging to was making creaking noises that didn't sound very reassuring. Uncomfortably wrapping my legs around the trunk, I started making my way down.

Cartoons make it seem like trees are just giant stripper's poles and that you easily slide down to safety. But really, it's a process filled with a lot of uncomfortable movements, painful sliding and intense grabbing. You pretty much have to grope the tree for dear life and hope that you don't lose your grip.

I was about a metre or so from the ground when my neighbour, Mrs. Elton, spotted me. She was taking out the rubbish, sorting through to separate a few recyclables that had gotten mixed up in the wrong bag but noticing me basically hugging a tree with all limbs, dressed in nothing but black, must have given her the wrong impression.

It took her two seconds to sprint towards the garden hose, turn it on full blast and spray me. The water attack surprised me so much, that I let go of the tree and painfully landed on the grass with a thump. I placed

my hands in front of my face, trying to block as much water as possible
as I spluttered and tried to explain.

"Burglar!" Mrs. Elton cried for about the fourth time.

"No! You have the wrong idea!" I tried to explain as quietly as
possible but it was hard over her raging tone. "I live here!"

The water hesitantly scooted in the other direction, long enough
for my neighbour to see me clearly. She seemed flustered when she
realised it was me and quickly went over to turn the hose off. But by
then, shadows were moving in the upstairs master bedroom and I knew I
had to bolt. There was no way I was going to climb back up that stupid
tree just to save my ass from getting caught. I was already out, so I was
going all the way.

Without saying any more to Mrs. Elton, I made a run for it.

I reached Ryder's house fifteen minutes late. After waiting that
long, he probably didn't want to see me but I had gone through all that
effort, so I decided to give it a shot. I didn't want to knock on the front
door. Both his car and his mother's were parked in the driveway and I
really didn't want to make my night worse by having to indulge in a
conversation with *her*.

Ryder's room was on the second floor and there was no way I
was going to do any sort of climbing to reach it. Instead, I pulled my
phone out from my jacket pocket, wiped the water from it, checked that
it worked and texted him that I was outside.

I waited about twenty seconds before the front door opened and
there he was, dressed in sweatpants and an old T-shirt. He looked at me
and gave me a weary smile.

"She's not home. There's a work party tonight and she knew
she'd probably drink. She took a taxi." Ryder stepped back and held the
door open. "Coming?"

I made my way over, wet fabric clinging to me and
uncomfortably rubbing against my skin. When I stepped into the pool of
porch light, Ryder raised a single eyebrow at me.

"What happened to you?" he asked.

"Don't ask," I muttered, not wanting to recount my unfortunate series of events and stepped into his house.

I quietly followed him into his room. It was warm in his house and bright. It glowed with a welcoming golden hue, making the space feel smaller and less intimidating. Inside his room, it was neat. Study rearranged on his desk, clothes folded on his computer chair, trophies lined up, bed made up. And sitting on the corner of his desk was an assortment of cookies and milk.

Ryder noticed my stare at the food. "You can take some. I got them for us." Then he added, "They're packaged so don't expect anything special..."

He didn't have to say anymore because I was already crossing the room, fingers wrapping around a chocolate chip cookie and dipping it into a glass of milk. Ryder was rummaging through some things behind me and when I turned around, he was there.

We were close, so close that I could see the bags under his eyes, the lack of colour in his cheeks, the way his lips could only force a half smile. There had been a lot going on. But despite all that, he wasn't thinking of himself because in his hands were some clothes.

"I got you a change of clothes," he said, holding them out. "You look cold. Get changed and I'll put your wet clothes in the drier."

I swallowed the remains of my cookie and nodded. "Okay," I whispered.

After I took the clothes from him, he stayed in his place, leaving me sandwiched between his desk and his chest. We were so close, I could feel the warmth of his body radiating onto mine. His eyes held mine as his hand raised and cupped the side of my cheek. His fingers were gentle, holding me with care as they slid down my jaw, his thumb brushing over my cheek. His touch was warm and innocent and made me crave more. He smiled slightly and dropped his hand, walking to the other side of the room.

Feeling lightheaded, I exited his room and got dressed. I changed in the bathroom, peeling off my wet garments and replacing them with

Ryder's. He gave me a pair of track pants and a fleece jumper. The
were warm and they smelled of him.

When I returned, he was sitting backwards on his desk chair. H
noticed my arrival and motioned to his bed. Feeling awkward,
tentatively sat on the edge and folded my hands in my lap.

"I'm sorry I haven't been around much."

The way he opened the conversation was not what I wa
expecting.

"It's okay," I answered anyway.

He ran a hand through his dark hair and sighed. It gave me three
perfect seconds to admire how his shirt clung nicely, shape of his bicep
and shoulders.

"It's just been really hectic," he explained, looking at the floor.

I nodded and waited for him to continue.

"My dad's back in town," he blurted suddenly.

Of all the things I was expecting to say, his dad's return had
never crossed my mind. Now I understood why Ryder was so tense.
Although he never liked to admit it, his father was someone who affected
him much more than he liked. Although he had mentally convinced
himself to separate himself from his dad, emotionally, he struggled with
clarity.

"When?" I questioned.

"The last night we were handcuffed together. I got a text from
my mum and-" He took a shaky breath. "It's just got me really stressed
out."

"Have you seen him yet?"

He shook his head and looked up at me. "I don't want to, Nora. I
don't want that bastard coming within a five-foot radius of me or anyone
I care about."

"You can't just ignore the problem and will it to go away."

"He's done enough damage to my family. If he lays a single
finger on my mum, or you-- Christ, I'll *kill* him. I'll--"

Ryder looked like he was going to kill *someone* if he didn't calm
down. The wild, passionate fire burned behind his eyes and his fists were

:lenched, ready to punch through something. Hesitantly, I placed my 'ingertips under his chin and gently drew his face toward mine.

"Ryder."

Maybe it was the way I said his name with such gentleness. Maybe it was the way I looked at him with pleading eyes. Maybe it was he way my thumb gently brushed across his jaw. Whatever I did, he seemed to calm down. My hand found its way to his cheek and he gently eaned into my palm, closing his eyes as his own hand covered mine.

It took him a couple of seconds to regain his composure, but when he finally opened his eyes, they were back to completely tranquil and calm. "Sorry... I'm sorry," he whispered, taking the hand on his cheek and kissing across my knuckles.

"We'll figure this out."

We were close, breath mixing, lingering, and drawing us closer until lips were pressed together. It was a soft kiss, gentle and sweet, allowing us to appreciate the beauty of the moment. It wasn't rushed or desperate; just wonderful. Ryder took his time, slowly moving his way over my lips, across my jaw, and all the way to the end of my shoulder. His hand gently found its way up the hem of my shirt and pressed his warm palm against the bare skin of my side. His touch was careful, delicate. He kissed my forehead, the apples of my cheeks, under my eyes and across my nose until he placed his lips back against mine for a long, gentle kiss.

"I like the sound of that..." he muttered, breathlessly.

"Of what?" I mumbled.

"Of us."

Twenty Nine

Sneaking back inside the house at six in the morning was just as difficult as sneaking out, especially because I was practically seeing double and couldn't walk straight from a complete lack of sleep due to the addictiveness of Ryder Collins' lips. His silky voice mumbling secrets as his lips travelled to kiss across my face had enough adrenaline to keep us awake until now, where I was brain-dead from happiness and fatigue.

I was pretty sure Dad had figured out my absence and I was way too tired to give a crap for any punishment, so groggily, I made my way towards the front door. Yawning, I raised my knuckles to knock but to my surprise, Eve stood there, in bunny pajamas and matching slippers with a bowl of cereal in her hands. She looked smug as I shuffled silently into the house and clicked the door shut.

"Was Dad mad?" I asked, rubbing my eyes.

Eve shook her head. "They don't know."

"Then how…" I trailed off, dropping onto the lounge chair and curling up like a child.

"I was seventeen not too long ago too, you know," she answered, dropping down next to me as she shoved more cereal into her mouth. You did give Mrs. Elton a heart attack though. Your pathetic little attempt to sneak out only attracted attention. I honestly can't believe we're related sometimes. I need to teach you a thing or two about sneaking out."

I groaned sleepily. "So how do you know if everyone else doesn't?"

"Mrs. Elton, bless her soul, was so embarrassed about the little incident that happened last night that she totally covered for you. Besides, she knows us Montgomery girls sneak out all the time. How do you think I got past her all the time?" She sighed dreamily. "Nights sneaking out with Patrick, making out in his car-"

"I think I just threw up a little."

"What makes *me* want to throw up is that you're wearing half his clothes."

I had wriggled back into my pants before I left but I liked how comfortable Ryder's jumper was so I kept it with me.. I smiled dreamily. And just as I was about to drift to sleep, Eve smacked me on the butt. Hard.

"Ouch," I complained, looking up at her through tired, squinted eyes.

"You need to get out of that jumper and hop back into bed before dad sees you wearing that."

I knew she was right, which annoyed me, but I obeyed and sleepily lifted myself from the lounge and shuffled towards my room, trying to keep my eyes open. Once I was locked in my room, I hid under the covers and fell asleep.

~♥♥~

I slept for a blissful ten hours and woke up on Sunday afternoon, feeling hungry. Peeling off Ryder's jumper, I went to the bathroom and took a quick shower to reluctantly scrub his smell from my skin to ensure

Dad didn't notice I smelled different. When I had changed, I went
downstairs, only to hear Eve's maniac laughter ringing through the
house.

"Eve?" I called. "Patrick?"

But when I entered the kitchen, there was Ryder, looking
extremely uncomfortable as my sister laughed hysterically at him.
Patrick, who was extremely talented in ignoring her weirdness, was
preparing her – probably third - afternoon snack.

"Do it again!" she chanted like an excited little girl.

Ryder looked around the room awkwardly until he saw me. He
took the chance of scraping his chair back and scrambling away from my
older sister. He looked good that morning, with his dark messy hair and
checked button down that made his shoulders look broader and figure
look more defined.

"Hey," he said and in one quick motion gently brushed his lips
against my forehead. It was so quick and easily concealed that no one
would have noticed the little action of affection. "I was wondering if
you'd like to come over."

"No," Eve waited, taking hold of Ryder's forearm, to which
Ryder stiffened. "Nora, you *have* to see what he can do. Please, Nora.
Make your boyfriend do it."

I blushed. "Do what?"

"Look! Just do it!" Eve insisted.

Ryder, who looked seriously pained at that point, looked over at
my sister in defeat. She grinned happily and lifted up her shirt. For a
second, I thought she was going to flash everyone but she stopped once
her belly was on full display and Ryder hesitantly pressed his palm to her
stomach.

Eve burst out in a fit of giggles.

I, on the other hand, just stared at them confused, like I didn't
understand some kind of inside joke. Eve's laughter slowly settled and
she looked at me with watery eyes.

"Oh, isn't it hilarious, Nora?" she asked me. I blinked. When I didn't respond, she rushed to her boyfriend and playfully poked him in the ribs. "Isn't it funny, Patrick?"

"Very funny, baby." He wrapped his arm around her and kissed her nose.

"I don't get it," I awkwardly piped up.

Eve placed a hand on Patrick's chest and smiled. "Whenever Ryder touches my stomach, he kicks."

"Who? Ryder?"

"No!" she answered. "The baby."

That made a lot more sense. Eve then went on about how funny it was and Patrick joked that his son was already protecting his mother. Taking this as a grand opportunity to run for it, I took Ryder's hand and led him to the front door. There, sat his sleek, black car. I smiled, remembering the car.

Once we were inside, Ryder reached over and gave me a *real* kiss. It was soft and gentle and he tasted of spearmint and I enjoyed it. The car smelled just like Ryder too, of aftershave and soap. Then he leaned back, gave me a heart stopping smile and started reversing out of my driveway.

"Your sister scares me," Ryder said, once we were on the road.

"She scares everybody." I waved a dismissive hand.

He nodded. "I wanted to come over as a surprise but you weren't awake yet and so your sister started talking to me like I was one of her girlfriends at a tea party. I officially know how regularly she pees since she got pregnant, her weird cravings and her mum-and-bub bonding routines."

I absorbed nothing but the first part. "You came over to surprise me?"

"Yeah..." He looked uncomfortable as colour spread across his cheeks so I dropped it and smiled to myself.

"So what are we going to do today?" I asked as we rounded to Ryder's street.

But when we stopped at the front of his house, I saw a silver car
sitting out the front, which definitely wasn't Ryder's or his mother's. As
I was contemplating who the mystery person could be, the driver's door
opened and out stepped Caine, lips pursed and jaw set.

"There are actually some things we need to talk about."

Thirty

When I walked into the Collins' house, I wasn't sure what I was expecting. My stomach twisted into a knot as I silently followed them into the kitchen. Ryder offered us something to eat but I declined. I didn't think I could hold it down. Then the room fell in this extremely awkward silence which made me more uncomfortable than I already was.

He did, however, pour us glasses of Coke, which I happily took between my hands and started rubbing the glass against my face, the cool condensation seeping into my skin and cooling down my cheeks. At that point, I didn't matter how ridiculous I looked, I just needed to calm down.

Once I was done with the face and glass rubbing, I brought the rim of the cup to my lips and chugged down the cold, sweet liquid in four gulps. It made my throat fizz up from drinking too fast and when I slammed the glass down, I was breathless. It took me a moment or two to recover but when I was better, I was ready for this confrontation.

"What's this all about?" I asked, nerves dominating curiosity.

Ryder didn't say anything. He stood there and stared at the kitchen table. Caine didn't say anything either. He just pulled off his

jumper, revealing a T-shirt and a bandage that looked like it was in dire
need of a change. He sucked in a breath as he examined the blood that
was seeping through the cloth.

"You're not afraid of blood, right?"

I shook my head, but felt sick anyway. Caine started peeling the
bandage off and it looked absolutely awful. A deep looking gash sliced
through his forearm, dried blood and yellowing puss surrounding the
injury. I felt something rise in the back of my throat but I swallowed it
and kept staring. It was horrible, but I couldn't tear my eyes away, like a
traumatic car accident.

Caine laughed humourlessly. "I knew it was infected."

Ryder was already looking under the kitchen sink for the first aid
kit. "I told you. You should have gotten it checked out, man."

"It would have just led to questions and police. We're already
too deep in with that stupid fight down at the beach the other night."

"Again," I repeated, feeling left out of the conversation. "What is
this all about?"

Caine and Ryder exchanged glances. If this discussion was going
to give me answers about why Caine has a giant cut in his forearm, I kind
of wanted the whole conversation to progress a little faster. Eventually,
Ryder sighed and opened the first aid kit, in search for some cotton
swabs and some disinfectant. He kept his eyes anywhere but on me.

"The fire at school," Ryder explained, "happened to be
deliberate."

"And it's a lot more serious than a few burned school supplies,"
Caine added. "A year seven girl is in hospital. She's hearing impaired, so
she didn't hear the announcement, or the alarm. She wasn't paying
attention to the lights either."

"Will she be okay?" My voice was barely over a whisper.

Caine shrugged. "Honestly, no one knows. I heard she's got
some really bad burns. But the point is, her parents are pissed and
obviously, they want to lock these assholes in jail."

"Problem is... They think those assholes are us," Ryder finished,
scrubbing a hand down his face.

I wasn't sure how to process all of this, so I just sat there, looking back and forth between the two like a game of tennis. Ryder was busying himself with rummaging through the first aid kid, even though everything needed was already sitting out on the bench. Caine was concentrating on cleaning up his wound and putting on a fresh bandage.

"Caine and I have been pulled out for questioning these past few days," Ryder explained, finally shutting the first aid kid. "Apparently being handcuffed isn't evidence enough that I had nothing to do with it."

"We *do* know who it was though," Caine responded, using his free hand and teeth to tie a secure knot to keep the bandage in place. "Chris Baker. He has a kid brother and he's the one who called the crisis hotline the night of the fire. Guess Chris overheard the conversation, realising his brother freaked and that I was on the other line. Then those assholes waited for me in the woods by my house on my way home and some dick slashed me with a knife. It hurt like a bitch. It *still* hurts like a bitch."

Ryder then took my hands in his across the table. His hands were warm and rough and completely enclosed around mine. With our fingers laced, he brushed his thumb down mine and gave me the faintest ghost of a smile. I returned the small curve of my lips.

"I didn't want to drag you into this," he said softly. "But I didn't want any more secrets between us. Not after last night."

Caine's eyebrows shot up at that.

"Don't be a pervert," I muttered to Caine.

He held up his hands in a defensive gesture.

Ryder and I laughed and let go of each other, just as the phone rang. The three of us exchanged worried glances. Could it be the police? Some kind of specialised detective? Possibly even Ryder's dad? Ryder looked pained, kind of like a child who was constipated and even Caine looked kind of green.

It rang once, twice, three times.

"Maybe we should answer it," I suggested.

No one moved. No one said a word.

"It's just a phone call, right?" Ryder said, staring distantly at the phone. "Maybe it's just another round of community service or something."

I stood from the stool I was sitting on and headed towards the phone. We were being ridiculous. I decided the worst case scenario was that it was the police who wanted to call us in for questioning. Evidently, they couldn't accuse any of us without any legitimate evidence. We were all innocent victims; unaffected but nevertheless lives threatened.

"I'll answer. How's that?" I said.

Ryder looked a little relieved and slightly ashamed that I was the manliest in the room. And on the last minute, his hand placed over mine and together, our fingers curled around the phone.

"There's no longer a you and I. There's an us."

I smiled at Ryder and together, we brought the phone between our ears. It was rather uncomfortable, our heads squished together in a competition to hear who was on the other line but just as I was about to suggest we go on speaker phone, a voice spoke, quite uncertainly.

"Hello?" It was Patrick. "Ryder? Nora? I'm not quite sure I have the right number, but it was listed under Eve's phone. Listen, I need you to come and get us."

In the background, there was high pitched scream of pure agonising pain. At first, I didn't understand, but then it occurred to me: Eve was having her baby.

"Oh my God," I cried, snatching the phone from Ryder. "Her water-"

"Is all over the front seat of my car. We were on our way to buy tacos and then her water broke and I was in a hurry reversed of the drive through and hit that spiky thing and Nora, you've got to get here now because we are not giving birth in my car."

It was the first time I had heard Patrick lose his cool. But somehow, through all the panic, I could hear the sound of his happiness, his excitement, his fright and pride of being a father. Eve started wailing in the background.

"Patrick! Patrick! I can feel it... Oh, God, I can feel it. If you
on't want your son to be born in a Sedan, then bring me to the god
amned hospital!"

"Where are you?" I asked.

"Corner of Greenwich and Paisley."

He hung up after that and before I could tell Ryder, he took my
and and together, we raced into the car. I was having mixed emotions
nd worry and joy, and even though we raced through three continuous
treetlights, I couldn't help but nervously smile. Eve was going to be a
nother of a beautiful baby boy and I was going to be his aunt.

Thirty One

"I'm really starting to regret this," Caine spoke up from the front. "Please make sure there are no pleasant surprises in the backseat later."

As a last minute decision, Caine followed us outside and jumped into his car, motioning for us to follow. He had a coherent reason too. Ryder's little sports car was unsuitable for a pregnant woman to be seated in the back. So, instead, we used Caine's car, which, from the look on his face, told us that he was starting to regret the offer. Every few minutes, his eyes would skitter from the road and onto the rear view mirror where he'd check Eve wasn't doing anything she wasn't supposed to.

"God damn it!" Eve yelled in pain. "Drive faster!"

Her screams were glass shattering, thick with agony. But Patrick seemed to distract her at times by whispering soothing things into her ear and letting her squeeze his hand. Most of the time, she looked angry at him, like she wanted to slap him with her fist but there was the rare millisecond moments where the *real* emotions of being a mother shone on her flustered, sweaty face.

Caine hit the pedal and we went soaring through intersections and streetlights, barely escaping collisions and getting a lot of shouts and honks. We broke about twenty-seven road rules, went over half a dozen legal speed limits and made a lot of dangerous swerves, all while Eve was shouting painfully at us to hurry.

When we got to the hospital, Eve was ushered into a wheelchair and was instantly pushed into the birthing wing. That left the three of us in the waiting room. Caine returned to his car to check for anything unwanted, Ryder went to look for food and I went outside to call my parents. When they answered, they instantly thought something was wrong. My voice was loud and my words were rushed, turning my speech into a flurry of gibberish.

"Eve," I wheezed, after the seventh time. Her name was the only coherent word I could pronounce and after a moment it clicked.

"Oh, you mean- Oh, my! We'll be there soon."

When she hung up, I walked back into the waiting room and sunk into a chair. My legs jittered in discomfort and my chest squeezed to a point where I had to gasp for breath. A nurse even came over to ask if I was alright, but I could only nod and press my head between my legs. I closed my eyes and tried to slow both my heart beats and my breathing.

I wasn't the one having the baby. But yet, I felt sick to the stomach, head spinning, palms sweating and body shaking. Horrible thoughts filled my head, of breathing complications, the child being sick, Eve having to go into surgery because of internal bleeding.

Before I could think of anything else, Ryder's arms wrapped around me and he pulled me to his chest, holding me close as he kissed my forehead. "Don't worry, Nora. Everything is okay."

"You said 'is'. Not 'will be'."

He smiled. "Because everything *is* okay. Right now, right here, everything is fine. And everything from here, is going to be okay."

Ryder leaned in and kissed a tear that had rolled down my cheek and made its way down my jaw. Then he held me, protectively, lovingly, reassuringly. He didn't have to say anything to make me feel better. Just his hand running down my back, warm and gentle held enough comfort to make the sickening feeling disappear.

Caine was sitting on the other side of the room, a magazine in his hands. He looked up from the pages and caught my eye. The cover of the tabloid covered from the nose down, but his eyes were all I needed to see to understand the sadness that lingered behind his expression. I was the one to break the eye contact. I buried my face against Ryder's side.

My parents arrived at the hospital ten minutes later. Mum looked excited, beaming proudly as she strode into the room while Dad followed, looking red-faced and a little uncomfortable. I supposed if I were a man with my daughter having a child, I'd be feeling awkward too.

"How long have you kids been here?" Mum asked, dropping into a chair. "How is your sister?"

Ryder checked his watch. "Nearly twenty minutes."

I shrugged. "She seemed like a normal pregnant woman before she went in. Pained and hormonal."

Mum nodded in understanding and politely crossed her legs. I didn't move from Ryder's embrace and my parents didn't seem to notice. I guess they were concentrating on Eve. Dad was still standing, arms crossed as he stared at nothing in particular, deep in thought. After a moment, he spoke.

"I'll go see if I can get some coffee," he announced. "Do you kids want anything to eat? I think there are vending machines around here somewhere."

Caine slapped the magazine back onto the table with the other assortment of reading material and fished out a few coins from his pockets. Quickly, he counted them on his palm and handed them to my dad, to which he politely rejected.

"No, no." Dad shook his head. "I'll pay, son."

Something about that made Caine uncomfortable, but he didn't argue. "Well, at least let me help carry the stuff back here."

Dad nodded in agreement and turned to Ryder and I. He raised an eyebrow at our position but didn't say anything on the subject. Instead, he asked if we'd like anything. Ryder pulled out some money

nd with an effort, managed to get Dad to sternly take it and told him to
.et something for us to share.

When they returned, with Smith's chips, lollies in white paper
ags, some coffee and a couple of bottles of water, we each picked up
omething and ate. I wasn't hungry, but putting something in my mouth
.nd chewing was a distraction and it made time pass a lot faster. I had
inally straightened and sat cross legged in my chair, scooping sugary red
:louds from a little paper bag and eating them while I listened to the soft
:runch of Ryder's chewing as he ate from a bag of barbeque flavoured
:hips.

Hours had passed before a nurse came out. I was starting to feel
.ick from eating so much sugar but the clench in my stomach was more
:rom excitement. The nurse announced that Eve was exhausted but
:amily could visit for a few minutes and see the new baby boy.

Ryder gently squeezed my fingers before I followed the nurse
.nto Eve's room. Inside, there she was, looking tired and sweaty, clumps
3f damp hair curling on her forehead but despite her fatigue, she looked
proud and happy, her child cradled in her arms.

"Oh, he's beautiful," my mother cooed, reaching out for the
baby.

Eve gently passed him on and rested back in Patrick's arms.
"We've decided to name him Hamish… Little baby ham."

"You *still* want to name him after ham?" I asked, but I couldn't
help the grin that spread across my face.

She nodded and Patrick took her hand. "Our son is named after a
processed meat," Patrick teased, but you could see the pride in his face
when he said the words 'our son'.

Mum passed Hamish to me. He was wrapped in the softest, blue
blanket and when she passed him over, I felt an overwhelming sense of
discomfort and happiness. The foreign feeling of holding a baby and the
unease of how I should place him in my arms was mixed with the pride
and joy I had for holding my nephew for the first time.

"He's so gorgeous." I instantly melted, when his sleepy eyes
squinted up at me.

Eve sniffled happily and said, "When we get home... we'r
having a ham party."

I silently wondered when my sister's weird pregnancy side
effects would clear and dreaded they would never fade. But the though
was quickly dismissed as I passed the baby to my dad, who looked teary
eyed as he pursed his lips tightly and held his grandchild.

"Dad, you aren't crying, are you?" Eve teased, but her eyes
watered as well.

"No," Dad answered firmly, even though his eyes wavered with
water. "No."

Eve just smiled. "Nora, we'd like you to be the godmother
Without you, this week, I don't think I would have made it. Through all
the hormonal moments, the cravings, the outbursts and complete
scenarios of weirdness, you stuck to me... almost as if we were secretly
handcuffed."

Eve winked. I smiled. Tears were shed throughout the room and
beaming smiles were shared until the nurse came in and announced Eve
needed some time to rest but really, I think she was about to be trained
for her first breastfeeding lesson- just like in the movies.

So we left as a proud, happy family.

Ryder and I helped Eve and Patrick pack up the car so they could
explore the new world of parenthood in their own home. Eve, who was
still as weird as she was when she was pregnant, had stopped her
obsession with eating food and was now addicted to something else:
dressing her baby as food. Hamish was in her arms, dressed in an orange
carrot suit with a little bonnet of green on his head.

Patrick didn't seem to mind though. He hauled a bag into the
boot of the car and on his way to the driver's side, kissed his son on the
top of his head. We all exchanged hugs and stayed out on the front lawn
until their car drove away. My mum dabbed a tissue under her eyes and
smiled slightly.

She sniffled. "Are you kids hungry? I'll make some snacks."

My parents disappeared into the house and that left Ryder and I out on the front lawn. "These last few weeks have been... eventful."

"I know," I agreed.

Ryder ran his fingers through his hair. "We still have a lot coming."

"I know."

"It's going to be crazy, Nora."

"I know."

Ryder turned and gave me a lopsided grin, capturing me in his arms. "Stop saying that."

I let out a laugh, but sobered. "We're in this together."

"That was such a High School Musical line," he answered.

"Should I start dancing and singing?" I asked.

"No," he replied, circling his arms around my waist and pressing my back against his chest. He rested his chin against the top of my head and we stood like that, looking out onto the street in a calm silence. I knew he was right, we had a lot coming...

...but I had gone through a whole week of handcuffs, kisses and awkward situations and I was confident that I could tackle anything more that was to come.

Thirty Two

Ryder

After graduation, you're confronted with a million possibilities, a thousand responsibilities and only a hundred abilities. It's intimidating knowing that high school eliminates a selection of those skills, a number circled in red pen estimating your overall success in the future if you decide to pursue a certain career. It's a natural characteristic for the human race to enjoy something they're good at and despise anything they're not.

My final examinations would determine which universities I could attend, which courses I could study and which career path I could choose. Two weeks ago, I had a clear understanding of what I wanted my future to contain: graduating from university with a law degree.

Then, a pair of handcuffs made my clear thoughts of my future veer off the road, into a cloud of confusion. Well, a pair of handcuffs and Nora Montgomery, former ex-best friend with golden hair and caramel

yes who was beautiful and awkward and could never form a coherent
entence when her emotions took over. Two weeks ago, I had a million
nd one reasons to hate the girl and now, I have a billion and one reasons
⊃ love her.

"What are you thinking about?" she asked, gently nudging my
oot with hers.

"Nothing," I answered and gave her a reassuring smile.

"You seem worried." Nora pulled a pained expression, a face
hat made her nose crinkle and eyebrows draw together. It was something
he did when she was concerned.

It was weird how a couple of weeks back, I didn't know her
nkles slightly rolled in when she walked. Or that she chewed her lip
vhen when she was concentrating. Two weeks ago, I never realised she
lidn't have to smile for her dimples to show or that her nose twitched
ifter she sneezed. But now, it was like I was aware of everything.

"There's nothing to be worried about," I replied, stretching out
ɔn the hammock in her backyard.

But there was a lot to worry about: the dinner with her dad, the
arrival of my own father, the fact that I would be doing my final
examinations in a couple of months' time and that the police were
tracking my every move. I felt like I was wearing a house-arrest tracker,
where one wrong step would cause them to come running for me.

Nora raised her eyebrows but said nothing and settled into the
spot next to me. Although I had told her there was nothing to be worried
about, she still seemed tense. Instantly, I felt guilty for lying, but I didn't
want her to stress over my problems.

"Hey," I said, picking up her hand and lacing her fingers through
mine. "How about after training tomorrow, we hang out. Just me and
you."

She seemed to perk up at the idea as I kissed the back of her
hand and settled back, gently rocking us. "Sounds good."

"Then it's settled," I said, looking up at the sky.

Since it was still winter, it got dark pretty fast. The sky was
starting to transcend into the darkest shade of blue, the stars faded, but

still out there. I placed my other hand under my head and stared upwards.
It was a quiet night, mostly because Eve and Patrick had left and there
wasn't a constant rummaging for food in the kitchen. Instead, there wa
only the faint sound of a knife hitting a chopping board- Mr.
Montgomery making dinner, I presumed.

Nora must have noticed the faint sound of slicing because she
turned her head to look at me. "Are you staying for dinner?"

I returned the gaze. Although her dad had acted reasonably civil
at the hospital, I wasn't expecting the same treatment. "Not tonight," I
said, sitting up and letting go of her hand. "I should actually get home."

"Oh," she answered, "alright."

Disappointment laced her tone, but I needed to leave. So, with a
quick kiss on her forehead, I exited the Montgomery house.

When I returned, a dark SUV sat in the driveway. At first, I
didn't make much of it. I figured it would be a few of Mum's associates
over for a long night of planning and organising, but the more I looked at
the vehicle, the more familiar it grew. When I realised why, a shiver
crawled its way up my spine, tormentingly slow, making my whole body
convulse in remembrance.

There was a knock on my window before I had time to figure out
what to do. My head spun towards the intruder, trying extremely hard not
to control my temper as I rolled down the window and his familiar face
came into view.

"Ryder."

He looked the same, just a little more stubble on his chin that I
remembered as a kid. I scowled, a sudden impulse to let the rumble
forming in the back of my throat let loose and growl out defensively. I
had strong urge to go completely feral just like a wild animal, but
instead, I kept my hands on the wheel and tightened my grip until my
knuckles turned white.

"What are you doing here?" I said, as calmly as I could, keeping my eyes anywhere but on him.

"Ryder, I'm your dad. Don't I have special rights to see my son whenever I please. C'mon, mate, we're family." I heard him lean down, placing his arms against the door and poking his head in.

I wanted to reach over to the console and wind up the window while he was still wedged between it, but instead, I tightened my grip on the wheel and gritted my teeth.

"You walked out on us," I answered. "You're not family. You've got nothing to do with us. Leave."

"I brought presents," he stretched out the words and sung them slightly.

I slammed my hands against the steering wheel and turned to face him. "You think I'm that easy that you can just buy back any little respect I ever had for you? Take your damn presents and shove them up your fu-"

"Ryder," he cut me off before I had the chance to finish. "You got some damn nerve using that filthy language with me."

"How?" I was yelling by that point. "You did the exact thing to Mum before you left. You made her feel like crap. It was bad enough that you packed up and left, but you didn't have to say the things you did."

Before he could say anything more, I reached over and flicked the button, watching the window roll up. He seemed to struggle against the window, as if he could stop it from moving, but when it got dangerously close to slicing off his fingers, he removed his hands and swore. It wasn't enough to stop him though. He scratched against my window, squinting to see me through the dark tint. When I was sure he could see me, I flipped him the finger and opened my door, causing him to stumble backwards.

Without a look back, I stormed my way to the house, unlocked it and shut the door before he had time to follow. As I fully entered inside, Mum rounded the corner with a freaking cricket bat. *A cricket bat.* And she wasn't going to hesitate to aim it at my head, but when she realised who I was, her expression faded from worry, to relief, then to anger.

"Ryder," she snapped. "I almost killed you."

"Hey to you too," I answered teasingly, throwing my things onto the floor. "Jack is outside stalking us."

I started addressing my dad as Jack ever since she started death staring me whenever I called him anything that suggested fatherly sentiment. Mum pressed her back against the wall and quickly peeked behind the curtains. When she ducked her back, she closed her eyes and spoke. "Is she…"

Her voice was barely over a whisper and she didn't need to finish her sentence.

"I don't know," I answered honestly, watching her hold back tears.

She was asking about the girl he had run off with.

There was a moment of vulnerability that had crept its way over my mother's face, like a crack in the mask of emotionlessness she tried to convince everyone of. She looked tired, clutching the cricket bat tightly before she let it slip from her fingers and fall to the floor. Slowly, she slunk onto the carpet.

Mum had grown a reputation of being a strong and determined business woman who never got too emotionally attached and most of the time, she was able to keep her cool exterior, but whether she liked to admit it or not, Jack was her weakness. Slowly, I walked over, dropped beside her and circled my arms around her. She sunk into the embrace, placing her chin against my shoulder.

"I never wanted to see that man again," she whispered.

"I'll take care of it," I reassured her, even though I had no idea how the hell I was going to do it. "Have you eaten yet?"

She shook her head against me.

"I'll make some pasta."

I gently slid away from my mother and helped her to her feet. On our way to the kitchen, she glanced back toward the window, staring into

he darkness outside. I had to gently drag her away and force her to sit at
he table, and draw the curtains to dampen her temptation.

While I cooked, Mum stared at nothing in particular. A fly
probably could have wormed its way into her mouth and she wouldn't
have taken any notice of it. Her eyes were almost glassy as she kept her
attention ahead.

As I was waiting for the pasta to cook, I reached into the fridge
and poured her a glass of lemonade. When I was younger, she was the
kind of mum who would make homemade lemonade in glass pitchers
and serve it during barbeques in the summer and to my friends when they
came over to use the pool. She stopped making it when Jack left and
started bringing store-bought lemonade, even though no one in the house
drank it. When my father announced he was coming back to town, I
decided to recreate her famous beverage. It brought back happy
memories.

I set the glass down in front of her.

She looked down at it at first and it took her a moment to
respond, but she finally said, "Thank you."

Mum raised the glass to her lips and took a small drink. When
she lowered the glass, she sucked in her cheeks.

"I didn't do it right, did I?" I already knew the answer.

"It's a little sour," she admitted, peering down into the contents.

I bit back a laugh. "Want more sugar?"

"I'll be fine. Thanks, honey."

I placed the small jar of sugar on the table anyway and returned
to my cooking. As I was draining the pasta, my back pocket vibrated. I
placed the pot into the sink and checked my phone for the message. It
was from Nora. Eve and Patrick had stopped by with the new baby. She
claimed her sister was using her child to score free meals at home.

Along with the message, she sent a photo. It was one of her and
her nephew, sitting on the couch together. Hamish was dressed up as
some sort of green vegetable and Nora was kissing his forehead.

Aren't we cute? she texted.

Extremely. Do you want to know what would make it even cuter?

What?

Me. You kiss Hamish's forehead. I'll kiss yours.

You should have stayed for dinner then.

I should have.

But I couldn't have left my mum. I glanced over at her. She had gone back to staring. While I grabbed the plates with one hand, I used the other to talk to Nora.

What is Hamish even meant to be dressed as? A cucumber?

Oh, God. Don't ever let Eve hear you say that. She got super pissed when I said he was an adorable asparagus. He's meant to be a celery stick.

I don't see it.

Trust me, neither do I.

Once dinner was plated up, I headed toward the table. My mother picked up her fork, but didn't make a move to start eating. I sent one last message to Nora, explaining I was about to have dinner and placed my phone back into my pocket.

"So, who's got you smiling like you just won the lottery?"

I didn't realise I was smiling so much. She looked at me expectantly, waiting for me to answer. She seemed genuinely curious, and even better, *distracted*. So, I didn't try to redirect the conversation like I usually would with relationships.

"Is it Montgomery?" Mum pressed before I had a chance to answer.

"Yes."

"Never seen you light up like that. All I did was say her name."

I took a forkful of pasta and shoved it into my mouth, hoping to stop the constant, yet unconscious, smiling she kept referring to. My mother was never particularly welcome toward Nora while we were handcuffed and I wondered how she felt about her.

"What do you think of her?" I asked, taking the pitcher of lemonade and pouring myself a glass. As soon as I took a swig, I nearly choked. Mum was being awfully polite when she said it was *a little* sour. I almost couldn't stomach it.

"Are you asking me permission to propose to her?"

My eyes widened and I placed the glass down. "That's a little early, don't you think?"

Then she did the unexpected. She laughed. *My mother laughed.* And it wasn't her usual polite, but unamused laugh. It wasn't her harsh, unimpressed laugh. It was genuine. It made the corners of her eyes crinkle. It made me remember the mum I used to have. It reminded me just how beautiful she was.

"Nora Montgomery is the only girl who would give me a run for my money in terms of remaining the number one woman in your life. I've seen the way you look at her," she said. "I used to get looked at that way."

Silence fell between us. I stabbed shells of pasta while Mum started drinking from her glass. Despite her claims that it was sour and ignoring the fact that I had taken the sugar jar out, she still drank it like it was water.

"When you were five years old, you came home from your first day at school and the first thing you did was ask me if you could marry a girl in your class. You didn't even know her name yet."

I felt my cheeks heat.

"When you were seven, she was at our house and fell out of the tree. She broke her arm. She didn't cry though. You did. You were so worried about her."

My cheeks went from heated to flamed.

"You had no idea what happiness was yet. But that girl made you feel it before you could understand."

I hoped that meant her approval. "Does that mean you like her?"

My mother just smiled.

Thirty Three

I peered out the window the next morning with a cup of coffee
and a breakfast burrito to see that Jack's car still parked out the front.
The temptation to throw my food at his car surged within me, but
instead, I placed the rest of it in my mouth and re-entered the kitchen.

"He's still there," I announced, dropping into a chair.

Mum absentmindedly reached into the fridge and pulled out the
juice. It seemed like a normal thing, only, she poured it into her coffee.
Before she overflowed the cup, I reached out and took her hands. She
glanced up at me like she was confused, then a tired look washed over
her face and aged her features ten years in three seconds.

"I don't think I can go to work today," she said, pressing her
fingers to her temples. "But I can't stay in here while *that man* is stalking
us. I really think I should call the police, Ryder."

"No," I answered, a little too quickly.

I was already in enough trouble with the law and adding Jack
into my record would only support their accusation of arson. Although
Mum knew I was questioned by the police, she didn't know what it was
about and with Jack returning to town, I didn't want to mess with her

urther. It had only been a few hours since he had come back and she
lready looked like a train wreck. After our dinner, she wandered into her
oom and didn't come back out until midnight. She started walking
round the house, muttering incoherently.

"I'll deal with it," I assured her. "I promise."

She gave me a weak smile as I reached over and kissed her
cheek, then grabbed my bag and exited the house. The door to the
driver's side of Jack's car was open, music drifting from the stereo.
When he noticed me approaching, he got out of the car and blocked my
way.

"Ryder, all I want to do is talk. How about I take both you and
your mum out to dinner tonight?"

"I'm busy tonight."

"Tomorrow night?"

"No." I gritted my teeth.

He sighed dramatically. "Then what suits your schedule, Paris
Hilton?"

"No day. Not ever." I answered. "You had your chance to talk
years ago. We don't want you here. You need to leave."

"You're blowing this way out of proportion." He crossed his
arms across his chest and stood his ground.

"You're *stalking* us." I could help the rise of tone in my voice.

"You're my *family*."

Jesus Christ. I glared at him and tried to restrain myself from
slamming my first into the hood of his car. Instead, I pulled out my
phone from my pocket and held it up.

"I have the police on speed dial," I threatened, although it was a
complete lie. "Just because I'm eighteen doesn't mean I can't get your
sorry ass in jail."

He looked from the phone to me and back again, a satisfied
smirk tugging at the corners of his mouth. "You can't get rid of me that
easily."

I laughed humourlessly. "Then I'll just have to call Janice."

Jack seemed to falter at the mentioning of his mother's name Janice was the scariest grandmother you could ever encounter and she was extremely religious too. She didn't believe in divorce, especially because of adultery. Jack still hadn't announced the news to his mother and my mum was too ashamed to face her, but he knew Janice would blow up because of this.

He pursed his lips in obvious irritation. "We'll talk later," was all he said as he climbed back into his car and reversed out of the driveway.

Getting into my own car, I pressed on the pedal and got the hell out of there. Due to wanting to escape all the havoc at home, I was early for school, so as I neared the intersection, I made a last second decision, flicked my blinkers on and turned towards Nora's street. I hardly reached her house before I slammed on the brakes. Nora was at the corner of her block, eating a muffin as she waited for the bus.

Slowly, I reversed back towards her, rolled down my window and went, "Need a lift?"

She looked kind of surprised and gave me that wide-eyed Bambi look. Then, she wiped her mouth with the back of her hand, picked up her bag and headed towards me, leaning down to peer through.

"I don't know," she said sceptically. "The way you drove up to me was totally psycho."

I ran a hand through my hair and gave her a weak smile. "I'm sorry. A lot went on last night."

I picked up my stuff, threw it in the backseat and waited. Nora raised an eyebrow and opened the passenger side door, sliding into the seat next to me. When she had her seatbelt on, I pulled away from the curb. We didn't say anything. I focused on driving the legal speed limit while Nora picked at her muffin. Usually, the silence between us was easy, but she squirmed uncomfortably in her seat.

"Want a bite?" she blurted.

I quickly redirected my eyes from the road, to the muffin that was now under my nose. I tried shifting away so I could focus back on driving, but Nora's hand followed me.

"It's banana and pecan," she pressed.

"No," I said, dodging a face full of cake, "thanks."

She withdrew and stared down at her half eaten muffin that sat in her lap. Keeping my eyes on the road, I reached over, found her sticky fingers and laced them through mine. Her hand was warm and soft and covered in muffin remains, but it still felt great in mine.

"My dad's back," I explained as I stopped at a red light.

"No," she whispered in disbelief. "How's your mum?"

"Shaken," I answered.

The conversation continued once the light turned green. Nora was careful to stay within the boundaries and never pressed on the issue. One of the things I liked about her was that we shared a history. I didn't have to explain or worry about judgement because she just understood. And it was those friendship characteristics that made her such a great girlfriend.

Girlfriend.

I glanced at Nora for the briefest of seconds and watched as she pulled a piece of hair behind her ear and quietly looked out the window. I stared at her awkward sitting position –knees together, feet apart, toes pointing towards each other- and found myself smiling. She really hadn't changed since we were friends.

I found myself thinking about us as a couple: being able to kiss her whenever I wanted, being able to pull her against my chest when she cried, holding her hand as we entered school. But most importantly, being able to introduce my best friend as my girlfriend.

As I pulled into a parking slot and turned off the ignition, Nora made a move to get out, but I gently tightened my grip against her fingers which caused her to turn around. She looked at me questioningly, hazel eyes confused as they swirled with mixed emotions. But before I could chicken out, I leaned in and pressed my lips against hers. Nora tasted like sweet, like strawberries and sugar and I found myself placing my hand against the small of her back, drawing her closer. The kiss was soft and more on the shy side like two awkward teenagers saying goodnight.

When I pulled away, she looked flustered, a blush creeping across her cheeks. Her fingers absentmindedly reached up to hover close to her lips. "You...I..."

"Are we still on for this afternoon?" I asked nervously.

"Yes," she whispered.

"Good," I answered, leaning in and smiling. "Because I have something to ask you."

Will you be my girlfriend?

"Collins!" Caine caught me in a head lock and ruffled my hair. "Ready for training this afternoon?"

"We're going to dominate Peyton High," I answered, breaking away from his reach and causing an eruption of cheers from the class.

Wolf whistles and hearty slaps of encouragement aside, I made my way to my seat. Tyler was leaning against his desk and grinned when I approached. He was on the footy team with us.

"Collins, I saw you and Montgomery this morning," he said, smirking.

"Yeah, that's right. I got to walk the most beautiful girl to class."

Caine dropped into the desk in front of me and looked ready to join the conversation, but when he realised the topic of discussion, he sunk into his seat and sat there uncomfortably. Caine and I were still on the awkward side of liking the same girl. Most of the time, we could dismiss it completely, but other times Caine didn't refrain from becoming as awkward as a hermit crab. Seeing Caine lose his cool made me lose mine.

As class started, we all bent our heads, pretending to be concentrating so we wouldn't get called out to answer random questions that none of us had studied. Rather than concentrating on the equations on the board, I picked up my pen and scribbled a note.

We're cool, right?

I tore the piece out and crumpled it up, aiming it at the back of his head. Caine turned around, a scowl on his face, which attracted the attention of our seriously pissed-looking teacher. She slapped the text book in her hands closed and dropped it onto the table.

"Gentlemen," she said, pursing her lips. "Problem?"

In unison, we chorused, "Nope."

Then we bent our heads and got back to work. I watched as Caine reached behind him and felt around for the paper. When he finally got it, I waited for a response. It came a few minutes later.

Yeah, man. Of course.

I wasn't entirely convinced, but it would have to wait until practice.

Thirty Four

"I'm thinking about asking Nora out this afternoon," I said to Caine as I took my sweat-stained training shirt off.

"To where?" Caine muttered as he intoxicated half of the locker room with his deodorant.

I coughed in his direction and held my hands out in attempt to get him to stop spraying. "Dude, Tony over there is an asthmatic. Dial it down, yeah?"

He sighed slightly but threw the can back into his locker.

"I'm asking her to be my girlfriend," I continued, pulling a new shirt on, keeping my gaze away.

I took Caine's silence as a negative response to my news. I didn't expect him to go all feminine on me and start squealing or something, but a grin or a stupid, cocky remark would have been okay with me. Even an encouraging smack on the back or a joke would have passed. But Caine kept quiet and from the corner of my eye, I could see he wasn't moving.

"Are you sure?" he asked slowly.

"We've been through a lot, you know? And I made a mistake by not asking earlier." I slunk onto the bench and thought about the handcuffs. "I mean, after graduation, we might go to different universities. I want to take my chance while I can."

If I even get into university, I thought meekly. I had tried to block out the thought of the local police department stalking me as much as Jack was, but it was hard when we were so close to graduation and teachers started talking about our final exams and future employment. After this whole arson thing, I'd be happy to even get a job.

Caine seemed to take this into consideration. And eventually, he sighed and slammed his locker closed. "I'm all supportive for Rora."

"What?"

"You know," he said, "like Brangelina and Kimye."

I raised an eyebrow. "Are you really going to come up with a relationship name for us?"

"Yep." He winked and grinned, but quickly sobered. "Look, we've been through enough crap. Wouldn't say I'm heartbroken – because that's so chick flick Friday - but I do confess I'm bruised, bro. I still like her, but we really should have called dibs," he joked. "No worries. Best man won."

I smiled. "Thanks, Caine."

Caine grabbed his things and swung it over his shoulder and grinned. "Don't get all sentimental about it. I gave you the best mate blessing. I didn't propose to you or anything."

I held my hands up in defence. "It's okay, I know me and you taking it slow," I teased. "We're way too early in our relationship, but I do expect us to get married before graduation."

He grinned and grabbed my neck with his arm and held me in a headlock, pressing his knuckles into my hair. Laughing, we exited the locker rooms and parted ways. It felt great getting something off my already full plate and knowing my best mate had my back again got me in a much better mood.

"Collins!" Coach Dunphey yelled from across the field as he was collecting cones.

I jogged up to him. "Yes, sir."

He dropped his meaty hand against my shoulder. "Glad to see you back on the team without the-" he paused "-extra accessories, also referred to as Montgomery."

"Got to admit, Coach, that she did make me look better." I grinned triumphantly.

Coach seemed to take my teasing into consideration. "Could be an asset to the team too. She can divert attention easily and could potentially distract the other team."

I raised an eyebrow. "I'm going to overlook the fact that you said that about my girl and leave now."

Good God. It felt great saying that, talking about Nora like she was already mine. I wanted to do it again.

"Your girl, hey, Collins?" He elbowed me.

"All in good time, Coach," I answered, that goofy grin still on my face.

"Good to have you back on the team," he said, slapping me on the back. "Now get the hell out of here and bring your A-Game for Saturday night! We're going to kick Peyton High's asses!"

"Make them beg for mercy," I agreed.

He gave me a knowing smile and with one final pat, left. As I turned and jogged off the field, I searched the crowd for Nora. Mostly, it was just the footy team and some people waiting for their rides to arrive but I finally found her. She was up on the hill with Mel sharing a bag of something as they huddled over their homework. When I approached them, Nora looked up and smiled.

"Hey," she said. It was a windy day, causing her hair to fly wildly around her. She looked beautiful.

"Jelly baby?" Mel asked, holding up the bag.

"No, I'm alright," I answered and watched as she shrugged and grabbed a handful. *Christ,* that girl could eat a lot and not seem to gain any weight.

Nora stood, brushing pieces of grass from her uniform and collected her things. Usually, I was comfortable with girls and I was pretty confident, but with Nora, she made me re-question everything. Was I supposed to kiss her in front of her friend? Kiss her cheek? Forehead? Was I supposed to hug the crap out of her or take hold of her hand? Was I supposed to play it cool in front of Mel or just go for it?

"So," Nora said, interrupting my thoughts. "Ready to go?"

I nodded and started climbing up the hill as a shortcut to the student car park but stopped short. Mel didn't seem to have moved from her position and I felt guilty just letting her stay there by herself. Although it would have changed my plans with Nora, I turned.

"Need a lift?" I asked, smiling at her.

Mel looked up at me with wide eyes, half a purple jelly baby between her teeth. Quickly, she shoved the whole thing in her mouth and shook her head. "No, thanks though."

She seemed to blush slightly as she turned away and busied herself with her homework. I didn't want to pressure her or anything so I turned back to Nora who was waiting at the top of the hill and followed her back to my car. Once unlocked, I opened the door for her to slide in, then threw my things into the backseat.

Throughout the entire day, I had been brainstorming ideas for that particular afternoon. Food seemed like a good idea. Food was pretty much my *only* idea.

"Are you hungry?" I asked.

She turned and looked at me with her knees drawn to her chest, teeth chattering. "Yeah."

I reached over and turned up the heating. Nora shivered as the car slowly heated up and that only made me want to reach over and wrap her up in my arms. Distracted by thoughts of holding her, I was completely unprepared for the sudden jerk of my car. When I drew my attention back to the vehicle, I noticed I had run out of petrol just as my car spluttered pathetically and stopped in the middle of the street.

"Crap," I muttered, trying to start the engine again so I could swerve towards the curb, but it was a goner.

It wasn't a part of my half-planned out plan. I groaned and checked my rear view mirrors for incoming traffic, but we seemed to be

away from most of the after-school rush. A street sign was up ahead and
I leaned in to get a closer look, squinting to make out the letters: Harvey
Avenue. The closest servo was at least two streets away.

"We're stuck, aren't we?" Nora asked, looking up at me.

"No," I scoffed, frowning.

She raised an eyebrow.

"Yeah," I confessed in defeat.

She let out a soft sigh and dug around in her bag. "I'll call
someone to pick us up."

Honestly, I didn't want to give up, but maybe it was fate's way
of trying to tell me that it just couldn't work out. As I was about to agree,
I caught sight of an everlasting span of green grass. It was a park and
something about it made my confidence rise back up. Before Nora could
punch in any numbers, I stopped her.

"Wait," I said, reaching out to hold her hand.

I didn't have to say anything more because she understood: I
just wanted to hang out. I needed it, especially after my day and she just
seemed to *understand.* She sunk into her chair, curled her fingers
between mine and together, we shared a silence as brilliant as music.

~♥♥♥~

After pushing my car towards the curb, we sat there with the
radio on and listened to music while we talked, her hand rested in mine
and whenever she shifted, the sweet smell of *Nora* just drifted over and
tempted me to kiss her. But instead, I let my eyes linger on her a little
longer than necessary in return for restraining from kissing her until I
asked her out.

Eventually, we were getting stiff sitting in the same position so
we decided to go for a walk in the park. Since it was winter, it was
already dark. The full moon was out and the stars were shining in a
never-ending blanket of blue. It seemed to drop a good seven degrees
too, causing Nora to shiver as soon as she was out of the car. But luckily,

had stored my school hoodie in the boot of my car so I helped her into
t, took her hand and together, we walked through the park.

We stuck to the path so we wouldn't get lost because all we were
elying on was the weak illumination of street poles and moonlight to
;uide us through. As we walked along the winding road, the gravel
)eneath our shoes crunched and the wind howled around us. Nora
hivered and I took the opportunity to draw her closer, wrapping my
irms around her protectively and enjoying the warmth of her against me.

This is it, I thought. *I'm finally going to ask her out.*

But as I opened my mouth to speak, Nora had run away and was
1eading towards the swings situated in a large pit of sand. She turned
1alf way and waved me over. I couldn't help but grin at her easily
imused personality. The smallest things could make her happy.

She sat in one of the swings and I took the other. At first, we
1idn't swing. We just sat there, gently swaying back and forth, looking at
the shadows drifting through the dark park. At some point, Nora spoke.

"Ryder," she said, fingers trailing along the metal links of the
swing, "what do you want to do after graduation?"

The question surprised me. For my mum and her work mates, it
was the same rehearsed line of "university, achievement, family". When
it came to my friends, it was the nonchalantly arrogant answer of "wealth
and success". And when I asked myself the question, all I was left with
was a question mark.

"I don't know," I answered honestly.

"Hm," she hummed and wrapped her fingers around the chains.

"What about you?"

"Same," she agreed. "Would have thought we'd have it all
figured out by now, huh? Being so close to graduation and all."

I had a feeling the conversation was going to get really intensely
deep, where we'd reflect ourselves and start getting all comprehensive
about the meaning of life. But instead, Nora tipped her head back and
looked up at the sky, admiring the silvery clouds that seemed to glow in
the sky. When she lowered her gaze back to me, they bubbled with
excitement as she kicked off the ground and started swinging.

"I bet I can land further than you," she challenged, already moving her legs to get as much height as possible.

I pushed off the ground, a grin on my face. "I am the champion of this. You're going down, Montgomery!"

That caused her to throw her head back and laugh. I gave her a wink and proceeded to kiss the stars with how high I was getting. As Nora swung, her blonde hair flew back, causing it to look like flickering golden flames. She looked beautiful in the moonlight.

"On three!" she announced, her voice rising in excitement.

"One."

"Two."

"Three!"

As we reached the peaks of our height, we let go, hearts hammering, pulses racing, palms sweating as we lunged into the air. There was that perfect three seconds of feeling like flying before we landed in the sand. Rolling around from the force, I knocked heads with Nora, but rather than causing her pain, she got lost in a fit of giggles.

"I think I won," I said, joining in with her laughter.

She placed a hand on her stomach as she tried to contain herself. "In your dreams, Collins! I clearly smashed you."

I couldn't help but laugh harder. "The evidence is pretty clear. I won by a mile."

She shook her head in denial and flipped onto her side to look at me. The glow from the moon caused her features to illuminate under the light, emphasising every light and shade of her face. Her hair seemed to have more colour, a more untamed wildness that I hadn't noticed before. And before I could think, I had my arms around her and giving her the most gentle of kisses. She tasted sweet and salty, like strawberries and sand. Her hands made their way to my neck as I pulled her closer, letting my fingers trail up and down her sides. When we broke apart, we were breathless, hearts pounding as we looked at each other.

"Nora," I whispered, even though I didn't have to. The moment just felt too delicate for me to raise my voice. "I lied."

"What?" She looked at me, frowning.

"I lied. I do know what I want after graduation."

She tilted her head curiously. "What do you want?"

"You."

There we were, tangled in each other's arms, covered in sand, lying completely content under the stars. The wait for her response seemed to take forever and before I could brush off my stupid question with a joke, she smiled and leaned in, kissing me again, this time, with more passion. It was wild and unexplored, adventurous and exciting. But before I could enjoy it further, she leaned back, pressing her forehead against mine.

"I guess we share the same interests, because I want you in mine," she mumbled, lips still brushing against mine. "But you know, today you've given me a ride to school, your footy jersey *and* asked me out. This should be classified as a high school marriage. We're basically engaged now."

I laughed. "How about being my girlfriend for now and we'll discuss that later?"

"Agreed." In that moment, there was nothing more beautiful than the smile on her face.

I smiled to myself. My mind lingered upon having her in my future and I suddenly realised graduation didn't seem so unclear. I had one part of my puzzle: Nora Montgomery.

Thirty Five

Math was one of the very few classes I shared with Caine. I hadn't seen him prior to that period but as soon as I walked into the classroom, he jumped me from behind the door. He caught my head in his arm and dug his knuckles into my hair.

"Ryder, my main man."

I laughed. "Caine."

He let go of me and we made our way to our seats. "So, update on Rora?"

"Seriously, stop with that," I answered, but I couldn't help the smile on my face.

"Well, did she say yes or not?"

Tyler was sitting in front of us and he tipped his chair back to listen. "Are we talking about Rora?"

"Seriously?"

Tyler shrugged and bumped knuckles with Caine.

"See? Rora is a thing now," Caine insisted. "So, is she your girl or not?"

"Yeah, she's my girl." The way it rolled off my tongue felt great.

"Nice." Tyler nodded in approval.

Caine placed his hand on the back of Tyler's head and gently pushed him away so that his chair went tipped back onto four legs.

Okay, junior, do your work now. I've got to talk to Collins about something."

Tyler frowned. Between the three of us, he was the only one who was still seventeen. The guys liked to make fun of him for it.

"Why can't I listen in?"

"Grown up stuff, champ. Turn eighteen first."

Tyler flipped him the finger but smiled and turned around.

"What's going on?" I asked, quietly, just in case Tyler decided he wanted to eavesdrop.

"I had community service yesterday. Officer Brandy may have tipped that they're going to visit today."

"God," I groaned. "When?"

"Sometime this afternoon."

The police department had been hot on our trails, trying to dig up information we didn't have. All our questionings had been identical. The same things are asked, a snarky comment or two escape, patience is tested, and everyone leaves the room in a bad mood. After my night with Nora, I wasn't ready for my mood to be ruined. Not now. Not today.

When class finally started, we were given an exercise to complete. My mind was somewhere else though and my eyes kept moving toward the window.

"No need to take it out on your pencil," Caine whispered from beside me, nodding at my curled fist.

I instantly eased my grip, but I was still distracted. "Don't tell me you're not pissed about this too."

"Didn't say I wasn't. But they'll come. We've done this before. It's not like this is the first time."

"That's why I'm so pissed."

We didn't say anything after that. I took one last look out the window before I turned back to my textbook. I decided I should finish as many of the questions as I could so that I wouldn't have as much homework when I got home. But as soon as I granted myself permission to focus on my work, there was a knock on the door.

My stomach tightened as our teacher crossed the room and opened the door. She didn't have to reveal who was there for me to know it was for us. She returned a moment later with two slips of pink paper and handed one each to Caine and I.

Officer Brandy is here to see you. Please come to the front office to sign out before leaving the school grounds.

Caine and I exchanged a look.

~♥♥♥~

I was staring directly where my reflection was supposed to be but my attention was drawn beyond the mirror, to what sat behind it. They were watching me, I could feel it. They were trying to grill me into answers I didn't have. Typical.

As soon as we got the notes, we packed up our things and headed to the office. We were greeted by two police officers to escort us downtown for more questioning. We had been having regular visits since the handcuffs were removed and every time they found new evidence, they called us down.

The door opened and Officer Brandy walked in with Officer Pam, causing my eyes to tear away from the mirror. Pam was a middle-aged woman with red hair and a bitchy attitude. I watched as they both took the seats in front of me, stacks of papers smacking onto the desk.

Pam adjusted her glasses. "Ryder."

"Pam."

"*Officer* Pam," she corrected. When I didn't answer, she continued. "How have you been since our last visit?"

"Delightful." It was much more sarcastic than I had intended. "And yourself?"

The whole questioning thing was getting really old. An anonymous tip-off had gotten me there. Had the police not considered that the *real* arsonist wrote the letter to redirect attention from him/herself? Chris Baker and his asshole friends had caused us to get a

ecord in the first place. But a stupid testosterone-filled fight on the
beach seemed like nothing compared to the crap I had landed in.

She leaned forward, obviously exasperated with my attitude.
'You're skating on thin ice, kid. If you know any information about the
fire, you need to tell us."

"I don't know anything."

It was mildly the truth. I knew Chris was involved, but really,
what evidence did I have? Caine had the advantage of telling them what
he knew about the phone call at the crisis hotline, but unless he had a
recording of the conversation, his word was worthless. Making
accusations without anything to back them up would only pull me deeper
into the mess.

Pam sighed and threw her hands up in annoyance. Officer
Brandy straightened his tie, wiped the back of his hand across his
forehead and looked at me with a red face.

"Your previous record isn't easing up your position as a suspect.
We can easily change your status to a witness. You're a good kid,
Ryder," he said.

"I was *handcuffed* to Nora Montgomery. I was eating lunch with
two other friends. They're witnesses of my whereabouts," I answered,
the same line as usual.

"Maybe we should bring Nora in for some questioning," Pam
suggested to Brandy.

"No!"

But it was the wrong thing to say. Pam raised an eyebrow. It
must have looked really damn suspicious when I replied with a shocking
tone outrageously quickly. Instantly, I wanted to swallow my tongue, but
instead, I squared my shoulders, leaned back and tried to save myself.

"Please don't bring her into this. She knows nothing about it," I
said.

Pam had both eyebrows up by then. "Was that a hint of a
confession?"

I scowled. "No. Stop twisting my words."

"I'd change the tone of voice, Ryder. Wasn't very respectful," Pam answered, pursing her thin lips.

I refrained from letting out an annoyed growl and clenched my fists under the table. When I had regained my composure, I looked up and met Pam's eyes. She held my stare with confidence as she spoke.

"We'll let you go for now. But this isn't the last you've seen of us," she said in her icy tone before standing and striding towards the door.

Officer Brandy gave me a sympathetic smile and followed her out the door while I picked up my things from the table and shoved them back into my bag. Every single time I walked into the questioning room, they insisted on checking my bag for any weapons or illegal substances, which was unnecessary since they always seemed to pull me out during school and the only bad thing they would find was week-old lunch.

Outside, Caine was already there, zipping up his bag. Checking the clock on the far wall of the room, I noticed it was just past three. School had just ended. Tearing my gaze away from the clock, I focused back on my friend. As I approached Caine, he looked just as stressed as I felt.

"This is bull," I muttered.

"Tell me about it," he grumbled back as we left the police department.

We seemed to share the silent tension, directed at the same people as we headed towards our cars. We didn't get in our vehicles right away. We just kind of death stared pieces of gravel on the road before Caine spoke up.

"You want to get a burger? This police crap is making me hungry," he said, spinning his keys between his fingers.

A double-decker Angus sounded brilliant but just as I was about to agree, I remembered something. "Can't," I said, scowling. "I've got something on."

"A date with Nora?" Caine smirked, leaning against the side of his car.

I let out a humourless laugh. "More like with her dad."

"Since when were you dating your girlfriend's dad? Shouldn't Nora know you're cheating on her?" Caine laughed.

I hung my head. "Kill me, yeah?"

But he just slapped my shoulder, giving me a sympathetic pat and getting into his car. "I'll remember you, Ryder Collins. See you tomorrow if you're alive."

With one last smirk, he tore out of the car park.

~♥♥♥~

As soon as I got home, I jumped into the shower, then quickly changed. Jack hadn't arrived yet, but I knew he'd eventually come back to stalk my family. My mother was making herself some cereal when I came downstairs. She looked extremely tired.

"Where are you going?" she asked, looking at my attire.

"Dinner," I answered.

"With who?"

"Mr. Montgomery." I didn't realise how weird it sounded until I heard myself say it.

"And why are you having dinner with Nora's father?" she asked.

"Because his daughter is now my girlfriend."

I loved announcing it to people, but my stomach clenched as I waited for my mother's response. At first, she just stood there, putting things away. I didn't think she had heard me, so I decided to repeat myself. But before I could open my mouth, she spoke.

"I'm surprised you didn't ask her sooner," was all she said before picking up her cereal and exiting the room.

I followed. "Is that a sign of approval?" I called after her.

She smirked at me from the stairs. "Be sure to impress her father. Have fun."

I smiled and shook my head, grabbing my keys on the way out of the house and waiting outside for him to call. Mr. Montgomery hadn't really mentioned any details about our dinner plans except for the time and a date.

I had never been on a date with another dude before and I wasn't sure how I felt about having my first with my girlfriend's dad. I felt awkward and freaked all at once, especially when I was about to get into my car and drive over but found him sitting in his Dad-mobile - one of those large family cars used for holidays at the lake and for lots of passengers.

At first, I thought he was just there to lead me to wherever, but then he opened the passenger side door and waited for me to go inside. So, awkwardly, I made my way over and climbed in. When I shut the door, Mr. Montgomery didn't even wait for me to buckle up. Instead, he stepped on the pedal and we were on our way.

Before his arrival, Nora had called and given me some pointers. 1) I should dress formally, and 2) Do not speak of ham so my previous encounter with him will not reoccur. But when Nora said formally, I thought she meant an ironed shirt. But seeing Mr. Montgomery in a business suit made me feel seriously underdressed in my trousers and black jacket. The only thing formal about my choice of clothing was the graphic print of a tie on my T-shirt.

This was going to be one hell of a date.

Thirty Six

The place Mr. Montgomery took me wasn't too fancy. It wasn't exactly a five-star place with waiters offering champagne but it was classy enough to make me feel uncomfortable. Nora's dad was an organised man and had already booked in advanced for a reservation. The table was in one of the far corners of the restaurant and as we made our way over, we received the longest of stares.

I couldn't blame them though. I agreed that we were an unlikely couple.

As soon as we sat down, he got right to business. "Are you dating my daughter?"

"Yes."

He grunted in disapproval. "How long has this been going on for?"

"Since yesterday," I answered, then quickly added, "Sir."

Mr. Montgomery picked up the laminated menu from the centre of the table and quickly scanned through it before setting it down. He was looking at me like I was about to be dinner, and although I should have taken it seriously – especially when he attacked me with a ham only

a few days ago - I couldn't look past the fact that during his holiday, he
spent way too much time under the sun, making his skin look leathery
and sun burned.

"My daughter tells me you defended her after a small incident
that occurred on the beach," he explained, looking at me. "Is that true?"

"Yes."

Before he could say anything more, a waiter walked over to take
our beverage order. Mr. Montgomery recited his without hesitation and it
was obvious he was a regular customer. On the other hand, I struggled to
find the cheapest drink, but finally formed a sentence that was
understandable and the waiter walked off with his scribbled notepad.

Mr. Montgomery leaned back in his chair and studied me. "I
don't like you."

I blinked. I honestly had no response to it. What else was I
supposed to do? Snap back a stupid and immature remark like, "Well, I
don't like your mum" or "I don't care, dude"? It wasn't like it was a huge
surprise anyway. I suspected the dinner wasn't going to be a bonding
session.

"But the fact that you protected Nora is enough to get me to
warm up to the idea of you getting intimate with my daughter," he
continued as a staff member dropped our drinks onto the table.

I tried to ignore the use of "intimate" in his sentence and instead,
picked up my glass and took a refreshing drink.

"But if you *ever* dare to hurt my little girl, I will personally hunt
you down and the rest is predictable," Mr Montgomery warned, giving
me threatening glare.

"Understandable," I agreed. "But I would never hurt your
daughter."

He seemed pleased with my reaction and the way I handled the
situation. With Mr. Montgomery, I didn't feel the need to announce my
feelings for his daughter. Not only would that be weird and extremely
awkward, but I felt like he respected that aspect of my relationship would
be better shared with Nora and just Nora.

"So, tell me about yourself," he said, picking up his glass and taking a long, generous swig. "I know almost everything about twelve-year-old Ryder, but I'm clueless when it comes to eighteen-year-old Ryder."

I hated questions like the one he had asked. I always blanked out and couldn't remember anything remotely interesting about myself. The only things that came to mind were: Ryder, eighteen, male. And although I had to hesitate and think of something to respond with, I eventually had something to say about myself.

"I've played footy since the start of high school, I was involved in the organisation of a lot of community events and I'm currently studying for my finals," I answered, hoping three things would suffice.

With his glass in hand, he stirred the liquid and nodded as he considered my answer. "And after graduation?"

"University."

"Studying?" he pressed.

"I don't know," I answered honestly.

"Unprepared," he replied, scowling in my direction. "You've got to toughen up, son. There's a whole wide world out there filled with mistakes and broken promises."

Jesus. That was encouraging.

"Thanks," I said bluntly. "But I just want to focus on high school right now."

"What could possibly be more important than your future?" Mr. Montgomery challenged as he sat back and looked at me, smugly waiting for my answer.

"The present," I retorted. "I have enough on my plate right now. So I could concentrate on today, rather than the rest of my life."

Nora's dad just raised the glass to his lips and drank while he thought. When he lowered the cup, he smiled. It was slight and hardly there at all, but the small twitch of his lips was enough to reassure his approval. But quickly, he sobered and the seriousness on his face returned.

"What's 'on your plate right now'"? he asked, a slight tone of concern creeping into his voice.

"My dad."

I don't know why I confessed about the family drama, especially to Nora's dad, who had only shown mixed emotions about me as he challenged me through questions and comebacks. But admittedly, I needed to get some of it off my chest. Nora was great to talk to but there were certain limitations. A quick conversation that could last for ten minutes would expand to double the length. For most times, I just wanted to lift things off my shoulder, have someone listen and comment once in a while, then let it be done. Caine was usually my wingman, but I hadn't found the opportunity to tell him anything with everything going on, especially with the police.

With the mentioning of my father, Mr. Montgomery placed his glass down and looked me over with genuine worry. I didn't have to elaborate on the two words because news travelled fast and the story of my dad's scandalous affair had been the talk of town for years.

"How are you holding up?" he asked.

I shrugged and peered into my glass.

From the corner of my eye, I could see him scrub a hand down his face. "Listen, Ryder, I'm sorry I've been rough on you. Just looking out for my little girl, you know? Seems like yesterday my oldest was just a baby and now she has her *own* baby. Being a dad isn't easy. But that's not an excuse for what yours did. You're in that time of your life where you need fatherly guidance and I confess I'm not the best in the world, but if you need anything, don't hesitate to call."

I looked up from the fizzy contents of my glass. I wasn't sure I heard right. "What?"

He smiled. "I'll look out for you."

Then he sat back and for the rest of dinner, there was minimum talk. It was uncomfortable and comfortable all at once. Mr. Montgomery had no hesitation to insult me, but it was more teasing rather than hurtful. For my first and hopefully *only* man-date with Nora's dad...it was surprisingly okay.

~♥♥♥~

When Mr. Montgomery dropped me off, I was glad to see that Jack's car wasn't parked out front. It would have an awkward situation, especially because I would have found out what Nora's dad's definition of 'looking out' for me consisted of. I mean, he was a plumber for crap's sake. Bum cracks and all.

The light outside was still on, a weak light illuminating from the bulb, suggesting a replacement. It took the normal sixty seconds of fumbling through my keys, thinking crap-I-have-way-too-many-of-these-things before I finally got the door opened.

Mum was sitting at the counter, dressing gown on with a mug of something between her palms. Steam gently drifted up from the cup, suggesting it to be freshly made and hot but she seemed oblivious to any burning sensation. Instead, she looked down at the table. At first, I thought she was just doing more of her absentminded staring, but when I neared, I saw what she was looking at.

Her wedding ring.

"I thought you threw it," I said, as I entered.

"I did." She laughed humourlessly. "I threw it at him when I confronted him about the affair."

"Why is it out?" I leaned across the table to look at her.

She kept her gaze down. "I found it… I guess I wasn't paying attention to where I had thrown it that night. Since I didn't go to work, I did some cleaning and found it."

I gently slid it away from sight and put it in my back pocket. She seemed to stare at the place where the ring had been, as if she were still trying to picture it there. A twisting sensation formed in my stomach as I watched her slowly crumble. But before she could break out the waterworks, I placed my arms around her and she sunk into the hug.

Ever since she had mastered the mask of emotionless, we rarely ever hugged. She used to tell me that carelessness expressed strength. But it was times where my mother was at her weakest, that I thought she was at her strongest. That it took a crap load of guts to show how really damaged she felt.

"Thank you, Ryder," she whispered against my shoulder. "You were always the better half of both your father and I."

Then after a few shaky breaths, she leaned back and smiled, getting up from her chair. "I'm exhausted, but I need to take out the rubbish."

As she started heading towards the bin, I stopped her and placed my hands against hers. "I'll do it. Go to bed." She seemed to consider, a moment of hesitation lingered but she finally let her shoulders sag and sighed. "Remember to double lock the doors."

I nodded.

Before she reached the stairs, she turned. "Thank you."

From the look in her eyes, I could tell she was thanking me for more than just taking out the rubbish. As I tied up the bag, I walked out the front door towards the bins, threw them in and wheeled them towards the front of the house for emptying the following morning.

The night was cold, causing my breath to materialise in front of me. I shoved my numb fingers into my pockets and made my way over back into the house. But before I made it to the door, a pair of headlights blared from behind me, followed by the screech of tires and the crash of a collision.

When I turned to see what the hell was going on, I saw the bins on their sides, rubbish scattered across the lawn and the road. As I looked towards the vehicle, I was blinded by the headlights. Placing a hand to shield the brightness, I tried to make out the figure behind the wheel. But I didn't have to guess for very long. The lights were switched off and as my vision cleared, I could see who the driver was.

Chris Baker.

Thirty Seven

"Oi, Collins!" Chris leaned out and smirked.

"Having trouble keeping your car on the road, aye, mate," I said, nodding towards the rubbish scattered across my lawn.

I was pissed, there was no doubt about that. But I'd rather eat dog food than admit that to Chris. Although I could keep a calm expression, my fists balled up by my sides, ready to take a swing. That animalistic instinct washed over me again and knew that if it came down to a fight, I'd have no mercy.

"You seem tense," he noted. "But your bitch, Montgomery, isn't handcuffed to your wrist anymore, huh? Guess she can't calm you down."

Chris could insult me however much he wanted. I could handle anything he threw at me. But when he added Nora in, I completely snapped. With my fists clenched by my sides, I stalked up to his car, flung back my fist and threw it through his opened window, aiming for his jaw.

But he knew he had flicked a switch and was obviously waiting for my aggressive response, so he easily caught my punch with his hand

and laughed. He shook his head at me, like any attempt to hurt him was already thought out and he knew exactly how to avoid my moves.

"Collins, if you want to start a punch-up, then don't hit like a girl."

I scowled and ripped my fist from his grip, giving him an explicit response and flipping him the finger. Retaliating with violence was what he wanted, especially right there at the front of my house, where people could witness and report back to the police. It would only be more evidence to support what crap I had already gotten in with the law.

"You really want a fight? Harrison Oval, midnight," he suggested, then, with a smug look, gave me a look over. "And I'd recommend brushing up on your moves if you want the slightest chance."

Then he pressed the pedal, his car roaring back to life, wheels squealing against the grass and kicking up mud as he drove away. I glared in the direction the vehicle had disappeared for a solid ten minutes since it had departed as I tried to regain my composure. My heart was racing with adrenaline, thinking of all kinds of torment I could give to Chris Baker. But with each violent philosophy, my head throbbed harder until I could hardly comprehend, nor hardly remember what the hell I was doing outside.

Eventually, my fingers uncurled and I turned, marching back into the house. I took the stairs two at a time and found myself in the bathroom, rummaging through the medical cabinet for a Panadol. When I finally found the little box of pills, I took two, swallowed them and washed my face with cold water.

When I looked up into the mirror, the face that stared back at me looked different. Obviously the same person, but significant changes had happened within the past twenty-four hours. I found myself backtracking to the previous day with my biggest worries being my stalker father and asking out Nora.

I found myself scowling in the mirror, suddenly regretting how I didn't savour those few hours with her. How all troubles seemed to drain

nd I finally felt in control. So, staring at the guy with tired eyes and an
unshaven face, I promised myself that I would now appreciate the good
times.

Exhausted, I exited the bathroom and headed to bed. With the
lights off, I threw myself down and closed my eyes. But it was one of
those nights where I was so tired that I couldn't sleep, so I stayed as still
as a statue, concentrating so hard on falling into unconsciousness, that I
couldn't.

So, instead, I placed my hands behind my head and looked up at
the dark ceiling. The painkiller was starting to take effect and the
drumming in my temples was slowing to a steady, tolerable pulse. While
I had some time to sort out the crap in my head, I took the time to
organise my thoughts.

1)My dad was a jerk and I hoped he'd just go to hell. It was
stressing me out, not to mention that Mum was completely distraught
about it. Soon she'd be dressing in tracksuits, eating beef jerky and
quitting her job. The organised, determined June Collins would be no
more.

2)Nora's dad was better than I had anticipated. Although there
were insults, they weren't meant to offend. Or were they?

3)The police were tracking my every move and it really pissed
me off because I felt like it had gotten to a point where I couldn't even
use the bathroom without someone just bursting through and telling me I
was violating the law.

4)Chris Baker was a dick who needed his ass kicked. His
proposition was starting to sound really great and through all the other
crap I was going through, I couldn't expect things to get worse.

5)Caine and I hadn't seen much of each other. At school, we
disappeared, doing our separate things and after school, the only reason
we would meet up is for our questioning sessions with the police. For
some reason, I felt like I was betraying him, because my girlfriend – of
twenty-four freaking hours - seemed to know more than my best friend.
And it felt really weird because Caine was like my blood brother. He still

didn't know about my dad returning to town, nor about the encounter
with Chris.

Although I should have called Caine for back up, I didn't. This
was between Chris and I and I didn't want to drag him into any more
crap. Instead, I promised to catch him so I could explain everything.
Switching my position, I caught a glimpse of the glowing orange
numbers on my clock. It was quarter to twelve.

I should have just forgotten about the fight. I should have just
admitted I was too tired to make rational decisions. I should have just
had a good night's sleep.

But, of course, I didn't.

Harrison Oval was located on the outskirts of town. It was where
a lot of footy tournaments were held and after-parties were hosted -
mostly because of its remote location, and also because it was situated
near the hospital, just in case any accidents happened. From my house,
the oval was a fifteen-minute drive away, so by the time I arrived, it was
already twelve.

Pulling into the car park, I kept my headlights on and searched
the area for Chris. It was mostly dark and majority of the shadows
belonged to the night. Just when I thought Chris was being an asshole
and making crap up, an inky movement stirred in the distance. As the
shape approached, I realised it was him. He was squinting because of the
lights, but a smirk pulled at the corners of his lips.

"Didn't think you'd show," he said, from a few metres away.

I got out of my car and slammed the doors, keeping the lights on
so that I could see him. "I'm glad I disappointed you."

As I approached, we circled each other. It was nonchalant, both
of us not making any moves to attack, but keeping careful eyes on each
other. Chris kept his hands in the pockets of his leather jacket, a devious
grin plastered on his face.

"Why did you frame us?" I asked, since we were just dancing around the field. Might as well get some answers before the attack. "What benefit did you get out of it?"

But Chris just laughed. "What makes you think I was involved?"

"Because I'm not an idiot."

"Not a complete one anyway," he answered, tilting his head at me in consideration. "Fine, I confess I was involved. But I wasn't the mastermind of this scheme."

That caught me off guard. I tried searching his face for any clues of lying, but with the awkward lighting, all I could make out were hidden features that gave away nothing. All that was clear was the obnoxious smirk that was planted firmly in place.

"Who?" I asked.

Chris just scoffed.

"Who?" I demanded, voice growing louder.

But he just shook his head. "What makes you think I'll give you information, Collins? You'll have to pay. I prefer cash."

It was my turn to laugh. "Guess I'll just have to beat the crap out of you to get some answers."

I hardly finished my sentence before I lurched forward, breaking the distance between us and punching him right in the jaw. He stumbled back, surprised, and clutched his chin. He swiped the back of his hand across his lip and when he drew, observed the blood that glistened there. His head snapped towards me, a feral look in his eyes as he swung at me.

I was able to dodge his first swing, but his second got me in the gut, earning a splutter and a cough. But despite the choking sensation, I threw my fist at his nose, hearing the satisfying crunch of bones under my knuckles. When I withdrew my hand, blood was splattered across my fingers, but I didn't care. Instead, I kept forwarding.

Chris looked furious as he smashed his fist in my direction. But instead of avoiding the blow, I moved in the wrong direction, allowing better contact as his knuckles connected with my throat, causing the suffocating sensation to return. And while I was in a state of vulnerability, trying to regain my breath, Chris caught me in a headlock and squeezed my neck until I was gasping for air.

I was starting to struggle. My strong start was starting to fade and Chris was starting to advance on me. Grabbing his forearm that was wrapped around my neck, I used his weight against me and managed to throw him over me until he landed painfully on his back. I watched as he gritted his teeth from the blow but quickly recovered, shoving me backwards until I was on the ground with him.

We wrestled on the grass, throwing punches and shoving each other. Blood was flowing and it was all over me, but I wasn't sure if it was mine or his. Soon enough, we made our way back towards the car park, kicking gravel as we tried to take each other down.

I managed to get a pretty packed blow at Chris' shoulder, but he got me in the ribs as I bent on my knees in pain, trying to suck in a painful breath of air. While I was down, he kicked me to the ground. My hands dug into the gravel, bits of rock digging into my skin so hard I was sure it had ripped a layer of skin.

But that gave me enough willpower to get up and take another swing at Chris. It was a stronger hit, one that caused him to stumble. I took this as an advantage and pinned him to the hood of my car, grabbing his shirt with one hand and giving him another solid punch.

Chris rolled his head back, seeming unfocused, but when I got his attention again, he smiled psychotically. Even with his busted lip, he smiled as wide as he could, causing the split to become more opened.

"You're wasting your time with me," he said.

I was so distracted by his obnoxious grin that I didn't realise he had the upper hand. In one quick motion, he flipped us until my back was against the hood of my car and he had a fistful of my shirt. Just when I thought it couldn't get any worse, he pulled an army knife out of his pocket, flicked it opened and pressed the tip under my chin.

"It amazes me how you can be such a high school star," he said, glaring at me as he pressed the knife harder against my chin and gently scraped it across. It wasn't enough to draw blood, but it would definitely leave a mark.

"What I don't understand," he continued, "is how you haven't figured it out yet. You're a footy legend, a straight A student and a community hero. How can you not know by now?"

"Know what?" I dared to ask, but it was a bad move. Chris slipped the knife lower until it pressed against my throat.

"Who it is!" he exclaimed, obviously exasperated. "The facts are all laid out on the table, Ryder. I suggest you figure it out fast."

Then, there was the shattering sound of glass smashing. My eyes looked down to see Chris as he kicked one of my headlights. Before I could stop him, he kicked the other until we were swallowed by darkness. Then, the knife seemed to be off my throat. I reached my hands out, trying to search for where he was, but someone hit the back of my head and I blacked out.

Thirty Eight

I didn't have to open my eyes to know where I was. The strong aroma of disinfectant and cleaning products filled my nose in an intoxicating mixture. Being in a hospital meant that someone would be questioning my injuries and I was in no mood to explain. So, I kept my eyes shut and tried extremely hard not to flinch when someone's warm fingers brushed against my forehead.

"What happened to him?"

It was Nora. Her voice was as warm and sweet as honey, concern dripping from her tone. It was hard to tell what time it was without giving away my consciousness, but I already felt guilty knowing she was there with me, no matter the hour.

"I don't know. But he smells like Chris." Caine.

"No... he smells like chemicals," Nora corrected him.

"I meant the situation seems like it's directed at-" Caine paused, then sighed irritably. "Never mind. It's too early in the morning for my patience."

Nora seemed to stay quiet, her warm fingertips still sliding
across my forehead to brush the hair from my face. She was close, I
could tell. I could feel her breathing and smell her minty breath.

"This is getting way out of hand," she finally said and I felt her
fingers slide away.

"Tell me about it," he answered and I could picture him rubbing
his temples in sign of a migraine. "But we're neck-deep. It's too late to
back out now."

"Have you told the police about the phone call?" she questioned,
voice low.

Caine paused. "No. I have no evidence."

"Tell them anyway. Maybe they'll look into it and find
something," she suggested.

But Caine seemed to stand his ground. "No. Look, I know what
I'm doing."

Nora dropped it after that and I heard her shift in the chair beside
me. All conversations seemed to fade and the sound beat of the monitors
was soothing. The repetitive beep slowly calmed me into sleep.

Again, when I woke up, I didn't open my eyes. Instead, I stayed
alert to get to know my surroundings. At first, there wasn't much sound.
I figured Nora and Caine had either fallen asleep, went to get food, or
returned home to sleep. But then I heard the shuffling of feet at the foot
of my bed as a phone rang.

"Hello?"

The voice sounded quiet but it definitely belonged to Chris. I had
the urge to leap up and snap at him to leave, but I was intrigued by the
voice on the other line. So I kept as still as possible and listened.

"Yeah, it's me. I'm at the hospital."

He paused and waited for a response.

"I don't know if I can do this anymore."

It might have been the painkillers, but I swore I heard panic in his voice.

"This is getting way out of hand. Yes. Yes. I know. I said *I know.* Look, a lot of people contributed into this thing so maybe our tracks will be covered. I agree. How did we even get into this? Oh, yeah, that's right."

He gave an uncomfortable laugh.

"God, we must be desperate. Exam pressure must be getting to us. These exams are just a load of crap. Mm. Yeah. No. Collins won't say anything. Trust me - because he doesn't want to draw attention from the police! He won't confess anything. He won't. Dude, take a pill and calm down, *he won't tell.* Okay, okay. If he does, we'll redirect attention to that guy. *You know, the guy.* No! Not that guy. The other one.Nora's sister's boyfriend.Yeah, that one. What do you mean why? Because it was his lighter that was used!"

I suddenly felt sick. All this information just kept coming and I wasn't sure I could keep it down. At any point, I felt like I would just open my eyes just to lean over and throw up on the floor. But I wasn't going to be a wimp, so I swallowed.

"Wait, I have another call... Crap! It's her..." Chris sounded like *he* was going to throw up. "The bitch is on the other line. I'll call you back later."

Then I heard him exit the room before I could find out who *she* was.

The third time I woke up, I opened my eyes before I could concentrate on anymore conversations. The bright, artificial light was blinding and it took a moment to adjust my sight, but when I finally did, I found that I was alone.

And that I really needed a bathroom break.

So I climbed out, grabbed my drip and dragged it away. The bathroom took five long minutes of searching for. I admittedly took a

few wrong turns and bumped into some concerned doctors but I didn't
want to feel any less of a man than I already did. I mean, I was wearing a
gown. And there was no way I was going to bruise my pride by
confessing that I was lost and asking for directions.

Eventually, I found the toilet, did my stuff and walked straight
out. On my way back, I passed the children's wing – that's how *lost* I
was - and passed some sick kids. I felt extremely guilty as I walked past,
seeing them with tubes down all places, thin and pale looking. I made a
mental note to come back and hand out balloons.

As I reached the end of the corridor, I was about to round the
corner to go back to my hospital bed – if I could even find it again -
when I passed a room filled with cards, balloons and stuffed animals. It
seemed just like any sick kid's room, but then I saw my school emblem
sewed onto one of the bears, along with a dozen get-well messages and
signatures.

This wasn't just any normal kid. It was the one with the hearing
loss that got injured during the school fire.

The door was shut but the curtains were pushed back. I didn't
feel like I had any authority to enter so I lingered outside her window.
Bandages wrapped up her left arm, from her shoulder to her wrist and the
left side of her face, but despite her burns, she seemed happy. She sat in
her bed, with a food tray in front of her, scooping red jelly into her
mouth and then returning to shuffling a deck of cards.

Suddenly, she looked up. She had the biggest and brownest eyes
I had ever seen. The girl seemed to stare at me, emotionless…waiting.
Hesitating for me to react before she could show any emotion. I suppose
she was being cautious. I really wanted to ask if I could go inside, but as
I lifted my hand to point towards the door for permission, I chickened out
and instead, gave her a small wave. It took her a while to mimic the
action, but she finally did.

Then she went back to eating her jelly. Sighing, I turned and
made my way through the maze of the hospital until I found my hospital
bed. But I wasn't alone. Patrick was sitting in the chair, checking his
watch and patiently tapping his foot.

"Ryder," he said, when I approached. He grabbed the drip I was dragging and helped me until I was back in the bed like a helpless child.

Then he settled back in his chair. "Nora and Eve are getting snacks for you."

My stomach growled involuntary at the sound of food. I hadn't realised I was so hungry until that very moment. I nodded and settled back against the arrangement of pillows. There were a million thoughts running through my head because of the conversation I overheard earlier. But the more I thought about it, the more I started to question whether it was a dream or not.

"Do you know about the fire at school?" I blurted, before I knew it.

Patrick looked at me and nodded. "It's all over the local media."

"Where were you when it happened?" I asked slowly. "When the fire happened."

I tried to keep my voice as calm as possible. I didn't want to sound accusing because Patrick was a great guy and I didn't think he'd be involved and although Chris Baker was an unreliable source, he seemed to have more answers than me.

"At your school actually. I was doing a fill-in for one of the year eight music classes," he answered.

So he was there.

"Do you know who did it?"

"Sorry, kid," he answered. "The class I had was right before lunch, so I was getting ready to go home when all the commotion happened. I was in the car park by the time they made the announcement."

Nora and Eve came in at that moment with a tray stacked with hospital cafeteria food. The sweetest part of all was the kiss from Nora though. For the next half an hour, there was a lot of talking. I did most of the listening while I ate my food, but I couldn't concentrate a lot of the time.

I was too busy trying to figure out this mystery.

~♥♥♥~

Nora eventually had to leave for school. I spent most of the day sleeping, and when I wasn't, I was wandering around the hospital, passing the children's wing as I pretended to go to the bathroom. At one point, a nurse kept catching me and eventually approached me to tell me there was a bathroom located much closer to my room. In other words, she was politely telling me that I was disturbing the children and I should *go away.*

I didn't return to the bathroom after that incident. I went to sleep instead.

Nora arrived straight after school though, bag hung over her shoulder. She triumphantly held up two jelly cups, one green, one red. "I come bearing gifts."

She dropped onto the end of my bed, kicked her shoes off and sat cross-legged. She handed me the green cup and a plastic spoon before opening her own.

"You treat me well," I said, digging my spoon into the dessert.

"That's not all," she said, balancing her jelly on her knee as she reached over and picked up her bag. "I got study notes for you and your homework. But I knew you wouldn't really be pleased with the homework, so I ran to the store and picked up some chocolate."

"What kind of chocolate?" I asked, ignoring the fact that I had homework to do. Maybe if I didn't acknowledge the problem, it would go away.

"Macadamia, of course." She handed me the bar.

Instead of taking it from her hand, I reached out and gently took her wrist, pulling until she was tucked safely under my arm. "Best girlfriend ever."

"Brownie points for remembering," she said. "Bet you can't remember my favourite chocolate?"

I didn't hesitate. "Trick question. You don't really like chocolate. You like gummy lollies and caramel popcorn."

"Lucky guess," she muttered, but a smile crept its way onto her face.

I kissed the top of her head.

"You totally ruined my jelly by the way."

I looked over at the red mess now all over the floor and laughed, holding her tighter. "We can share mine."

"Okay," she answered, wriggling out of my arms. "But I really have to finish this essay. It was due last week and I don't think I can extend it any longer."

Nora crawled her way back to the end of the bed and started pulling out folders and pens. She stretched her legs onto the space she had recently vacated and started concentrating on her paper. I watched as she studied. Occasionally, she'd open her mouth without her eyes leaving her notebook and I'd reach over and give her a scoop of jelly. Sometimes, when I leaned over, I'd catch the corners of her lips in a kiss. She never looked up, but she always lit up like a firefly. It made me smile.

When she finished writing her essay, she wordlessly moved onto something else. I knew I should have mirrored her actions and started my own study, but I started getting sleepy. The jelly cup was now longgone and I had eaten a good amount of the chocolate. My stomach was full and I was happy.

"So, what have you been doing here all day?" Nora asked, typing furiously at her calculator.

"Wandering around," I answered honestly. "I found that girl's room."

"What girl?" she said distractedly as she chewed the end of her pen.

"The one who got injured during the fire."

"Rebecca?"

"How'd you know her name?" I asked.

"We had an assembly today. She was mentioned. I feel so awful about what happened to her."

I groaned. "Tell me about it. Whenever I pass her room, I feel so damn guilty."

Nora placed her pencil down and looked at me. "You didn't do anything wrong, Ryder."

"I know," I answered. "But I still feel like shit about it."

She smiled weakly and thought for a second. "How about we send her a little anonymous gift?"

I liked that idea. "What should it be?"

"Well, she's probably really bored in her room. How about we buy her a box set of DVDs to keep her entertained until she gets better. I'd imagine she's already got a crap tonne of flowers, bears, cards and balloons."

I stifled a yawn. "She does."

I was starting to get extremely tired. My eyelids were heavy, so I allowed them to close and sank back into the pillows. Nora noticed my fatigue.

"Sleep, okay?"

"No, I'm okay," I lied, trying to open my eyes, but they wouldn't.

"Ryder."

"Nora."

"Go to sleep."

"No."

"Please."

"Lay down with me."

I heard her shuffle around, felt the movement of her study being pushed away, then the familiar weight of her body as she situated herself into my arms. I pulled her close and blindly kissed her forehead.

"Talk to me until I fall asleep?" I asked, although it came out extremely slow and sleepy.

And she did. She whispered nonsense into my ear, told me secrets and stories, promises and memories. I can almost guarantee I fell asleep with a smile on my face.

Thirty Nine

The following day, I stayed home from school. Mum stayed the last night I was in hospital and took us back to our house the next morning. But although I was excused from study, that didn't mean I was off the hook for everything. I took the time of recovery to do a few things that needed to be completed. Like the grocery shopping.

Although Mum had gone into a stress overdrive and was now practically in a state of hibernation, I was still a growing guy who needed to be fed. My cuts and bruises still gave off a constant stinging, but with the medication the doctors had prescribed to me, the irritating sensation eventually settled to a throbbing.

Grocery shopping was a task I had inherited since I was fourteen when Mum discovered I was faster at navigating my way through the supermarket and getting things done. So, when I arrived, I grabbed a trolley and headed towards the breads section. Tossing a loaf into the pile, I started passing the other pastries and decided to get some cheese and bacon rolls. And as I headed towards where they were stacked, I ran into Eve.

"Ryder," she said, grinning as she shifted her baby from one side of her hip, to the other. Hamish was dressed in one of his food-related outfits again.

"Look," she said, grinning as she held up her son to my face, 'he's a peanut!"

I was starting to wonder where she was getting all these clothes from, but decided that it was best that I didn't know. Instead, I looked at Hamish, who was pulling a face that suggested he wanted to throw up on me and watched as he returned to his mother's side.

"How are you feeling?" she asked, adjusting Hamish's bonnet.

"I could use some sleep," I admitted, "but I've got stuff to do."

"Oh, honey." She shook her head in disapprovement. "You should go back home. Where's your list? I'll pick up your things and drive them back to yours."

"No, thank you," I politely declined. "I don't want to be any trouble. Besides, I won't be long. There isn't much I need to get."

Her face remained unconvinced, but when Hamish started crying, she seemed to reluctantly accept. "Take it easy, okay?"

I nodded in agreement and she seemed pleased. Just as I was about to walk away and return to my bacon rolls, Patrick appeared with a trolley. He gave me a smile as he neared, scooped up his son from his girlfriend and gently lowered him into his man pouch, where the baby sat comfortably supported.

Although I desperately needed to go back to bed, I knew that Patrick must have some sort of information about the fire, whether he was the culprit or not, I needed them. I never had the chance to ask while we were at the hospital because Nora walked in. So, while Eve went towards the fruit and vegetables, I lingered around Patrick.

"Hey," he greeted, giving me a gentle pat on the back, trying not to disturb his son. "How are you going?"

"Crap, to be honest," I answered, slowly pushing my trolley at the pace he was going.

"Yeah," he said, giving me a concerned look-over. "You look heaps tired."

"I am," I replied. "Had a lot on my mind last night."

"Anything I can help with?" Patrick asked, distractedly, as he grabbed a plastic bag and started filling it with apples.

"Actually, yeah," I said, coughing to clear my throat.

Patrick looked over at me to continue and I coughed again, just to waste time. He was a good guy and I shouldn't have doubted that. Why would he start a fire on purpose? What advantage would it give him? The only things that seemed to mean the most to him was music, Eve and Hamish.

Unless... they were the reasons he started it. Maybe he was financially insecure and needed money, but it got out of hand. Or maybe he was starting to feel the pressure and responsibilities that came with being a father. Just thinking about it in the middle of the supermarket was starting to give me a headache, so I parked my trolley out of the way, so other customers could squeeze by, took a deep breath and just started talking before I could back out.

"Do you smoke?" I blurted.

Patrick frowned at me and shook his head. "No. I'm really against the stuff. Not only will it affect my health, but it will destroy my family's too. They're way too important to me. Ryder, if you're thinking about any sort of drug, you shouldn't. You're so close to graduation and you have a lot of potential. Don't go down that road."

"You think I- what-" I started to splutter. "No. No. I'm not thinking about drugs."

He sighed in relief. "Good, because I know peer pressure can be tough sometimes. In high school, one of my best mates tried so hard to get me to smoke, he basically shoved half a used cigarette down my throat."

"Rough," I replied, then shook my head. We were veering off topic. "Look," I started, "the reason I'm asking is because the fire at school was started with a lighter."

He seemed to still, his actions frozen, just as he was about to drop another apple into the bag. It took a moment to respond but he finally, but ever so slowly, turned to face me, taking everything out of his hands so he could concentrate.

"Are you accusing me?"

"No," I said. "*Christ.* No."

He looked sceptical, so I continued.

"I've been questioned about it. Some ass tipped me off to the police even though I have nothing to do with it. I'm just trying to get as much information as possible to try and get the authorities off my back. I have a lot of crap going on right now and I don't need it."

Patrick's expression seemed to melt and he looked at me with sympathy. "I'm sorry... I can't help you, Ryder. Honestly, I don't know who did it and I don't have much information."

Much.

"Well, what do you know?" I asked.

He sighed and leaned in as he casually picked and dropped apples into his bag and shuffled over to weigh them. "I was one of the last people who had that lighter before it was used to start the fire."

"I thought you didn't smoke."

"I don't. I confiscated it from one of the kids who was in the class I had that day and gave him a lunchtime detention. He ran off before I could return it to him and give him a lecture. It was time for me to leave for the day, so I dropped it off at the principal's office," he said, being sure to keep his voice low.

"Whose lighter was it?" I whispered. "The kid probably snuck in and stole it back."

"That's what I thought," he confessed. "But I looked up the online records and the kid I confiscated the lighter from was present in the detention I gave him."

"This doesn't add up," I said, rubbing my head. It was starting to throb.

"You did nothing wrong, Ryder," Patrick said, dumping the apples into the trolley and giving me a serious expression, "but you need to drop it, okay? You're innocent and they have nothing against you, but the longer you linger around the scene of the crime, the more you're covering yourself with evidence."

"Patrick," Eve said, returning with a paper ticket, "would you mind lining up at the deli for me and getting me five hundred grams of triple smoked ham?"

Patrick leaned down and kissed Eve's forehead. "I'll go now. Take care, Ryder. Remember what I said."

Then he walked away.

I sighed. I felt like I had gotten somewhere, but at the same time, it was nowhere. After some complicated thinking of trying to connect the dots, I finally wheeled my trolley away and started grabbing the things I needed. All through getting the dairy section, the cereal aisle and the sweet shelves, I still tried to figure it all out, but when I finally thought I was getting somewhere, I'd always end up in the same confused place.

I guess I was thinking way too hard about all of it because I didn't realise I had run someone over until I heard a high pitched shriek. Snapping out of my own thoughts, I rushed over to help the woman up.

"I'm so sorry," I instantly blurted as I held her hand and pulled her to her feet. When she was fully standing, I realised it was Mrs. Westfield. The principal.

"Ryder Collins," she said, brushing her pencil skirt. "You've been so mischievous lately, both inside and outside of school." She pursed her lips and looked at me through her glasses. "Why aren't you at school?"

"I just got out of hospital," I answered.

"Surely, if you have enough strength to go shopping, you have enough to attend school," Mrs. Westfield answered.

Bitch.

"Why aren't *you* at school?" I answered instead.

She raised a thin eyebrow. "That is none of your concern, Mr. Collins. But since you were absent these past few days, I suppose you have missed the important announcement at the assembly."

I vaguely remembered Nora saying something about the assembly while I was in hospital, but I guess I was too drugged up to concentrate on what she was saying.

"I will be retiring at the end of the year," she said.

"What?" I asked in disbelief.

"Unfortunately, I'm being forced. My health has become such a condition that I will not be fit enough to run the school," she explained, adjusting her glasses. "However, it seems like perfect timing considering the fire." I stared at her. Was Mrs. Westfield the 'bitch' Chris was talking to on the phone the previous day? Was she disappointed she was losing her job and needed something to keep her there? There were so many filled holes, yet so many more questions related.

"Now, please excuse me, I have somewhere to be now," she said, looking at her watch. "Oh, and Ryder? Do be at school tomorrow."

"Yes, ma'am."

The hell I'd be at school. The scene of the crime needed to be investigated.

Forty

"Ryder," Nora mumbled against my lips.

"Mm," I muttered, but not because I was so engulfed in our kiss. It was more to do with the yellow tape surrounding the burned building that stood behind my girlfriend.

Nora gave me a small kiss before she leaned back a little and slid her hands down from my shoulders to adjust my tie and straighten the imaginary wrinkles on my uniform. It took some effort, but I finally tore my eyes away from the bricks covered in ash and looked down at her. She was always so patient and I felt guilty for not giving her my attention, especially since we hadn't spent much time together.

"Stop obsessing over this whole thing, Ryder," she whispered. "You've done nothing wrong so you don't have anything to worry about. Everything will eventually unfold."

I sighed. "I'm just so close."

"Yet so far," she finished, giving me a weak smile.

I reached down and threaded my fingers through hers. Rather than replying, I started walking her to her next class. We cut through the quad, the afternoon breeze warm against our skin, trying extremely hard o break through the winter cold and let spring develop. Even though the breeze was warm, allowing the temperature to rise slightly, Nora had left the house heavily clothed, thinking it'd be colder, but when realising it wasn't, was too stubborn to take off her eskimo jacket. So basically, my girlfriend was a walking marshmallow.

"Nora, take off your jacket," I said, poking the puffy material of her jacket.

She shook her head and swiped the back of her hand against her forehead. "I'm fine," she wheezed.

I paused in the middle of the quad and looked at her worriedly. "You're going to pass out if you get any warmer."

I placed the back of my hand against her cheek and felt her heat up. Then I leaned down and kissed her nose, while unzipping her jacket and pushing it off. Bundling the thick fabric in my arms, I took her hand in mine again and we headed back towards class.

"Apparently there's no school tomorrow."

A pair of girls from the year below us passed us, speaking loudly so it was almost impossible to not overhear their conversation.

"Why?" asked the blonde.

The brunette pushed back her hair and answered, "I heard the police made a discovery and the area needs to be closed for further investigation."

My ears perked up and Nora must have sensed it because she tightened her grip on my hand, stopped and jerked me back to meet her eyes. She folded her arms across her chest and gave me a stern look.

"I told you to stop," she said. "You're going to go to class, get through the rest of the day and then go home. Repeat it with me."

"I'm going to go to class, get through the rest of the day and then go home," I said in unison with Nora. Then quickly added in a low rush, "Right after I take a quick look."

The warning bell rang, signalling that we were late for class. The school grounds were just about empty, other than a random student racing through the area to avoid a lecture from an angry teacher.

I kissed her forehead. "Go to class."

"No," she answered, firmly. "The only way I'll go to class is if you go too."

"And if I don't?" I asked.

"I'm going with you."

There was no arguing with Nora at that point. She was stubborn and I knew that she'd stand her ground. So, I agreed for her to come with me. It just meant I'd have to be even more careful than planned because it was one thing for *me* to get in trouble, but something completely different if I got my girlfriend into my mess.

So, together, we turned back to the way we had arrived and walked towards the taped building. Looking up at the ash covered bricks, I thought there would have been a moment of hesitation, but as soon as my fingers touched the tape, I lifted it instantly and waited for Nora to duck under before I followed her. She swiftly bent and went through, then I followed.

Nora tiptoed towards the door, looking over her shoulders for anyone who might be watching and I followed, without the obvious signs of sneaking around. Before she would start creeping around like a mouse, I placed my hands on her waist so she'd settle and kept them there as she pulled her jumper over her hand, took the handle of the door and pulled it opened.

Before we stepped in, I mumbled into her hair, "If you hear someone coming, hide as quickly as possible and don't come out until it's safe, okay? If you get caught and the teacher has no idea who you are, act clueless and start talking gibberish. You can pass as a beautiful transfer student."

She craned her neck so she could see me. "What about you?"

"I'm already neck-deep into this. I don't exactly care where this leads to if I get caught," I admitted. "I'm just worried about you."

Nora gave me a reassuring smile. "We won't get caught."

Hopefully lingered at the end of her sentence, but it was unspoken.

Quietly, we slowly opened the door in case of any creaks or squeaks and once there was enough room to squeeze through, we sucked n and slipped through the gap we had created. Inside, the carpeted corridor was burned and the smell was suffocating. Nora and I – literally – crept through the opened classroom door, trying to touch as little as possible in attempt to reduce the traces of our whereabouts.

Inside the classroom, it was what you'd normally expect to see after a fire. There was burned furniture, crumbling by the corners and covered in ash. There were photographs of our school's graduating classes scattered across the floor, glass shards covering them. Book pages were burned, textbooks ruined and equipment destroyed.

"Ryder, I don't think we're going to find anything in here," Nora whispered from across the room.

From all the damage, I was starting to think the same. It would take a long time before we could find anything useful. But I must have been looking too hard because I hadn't realised that the whole room was a clue. Instantly, my head snapped towards one of the desks.

"What are you looking for?" Nora hissed.

But I was too lost in the moment. I had a theory. A downright outrageous one but it seemed to make sense from all the information I had gathered. Ducking my head under the desk, I started searching. At first, I was certain what I was looking for wouldn't be found, but then I saw it, hidden under some ash, taped to the bottom of the desk.

"Son of a bitch," I whispered to myself.

From how things were looking, my theory was a great one and it had evidence to back it up, but I didn't know whether my discovery was valid or not. I slowly stood up. Everything was still at that moment, not a sound, not a breath. And then the slow, steady pace of footsteps.

I placed my finger over Nora's lips, then gently lifted her towards safer ground. We were surrounded by glass and if she tried to escape, she'd make too much noise. She turned and looked at me frantically, wide hazel eyes darting back and forth in confusion. I gently moved my hand in the direction of the joint classroom and Nora silently ran towards the opened door to find a more suitable place to hide.

All I could do was crouch back under the desk I had been under and pray that no one would notice me there. The footsteps were coming closer, louder. My heart had found its way up to my ears and was now pounding frantically. My throat was dry from breathing through my mouth and when a shadow found its way through the opened door, I held my breath.

Now that the footsteps were closer, I could hear them better. Although the person's journey was fragmented from glass and broken bits of wood, when the shoes hit the floorboards, it was unmistakably a woman. I closed my eyes and tried to stay as still as possible.

"Ryder Collins."

I opened my eyes and looked up to see Mrs. Coleman staring down at me with her pointy shoes and hands on her hips. She gave me the same knowing smirk I had grown to know so well.

"Where's your companion?"

"I came alone," I answered, standing up and trying to fake nonchalance.

She raised an eyebrow and marched towards the opened door that led to the classroom next door. I held my breath again, feeling sick to the stomach. My insides clenched and squeezed and twisted in horror until Mrs. Coleman returned, holding Nora by the arm and tugging her out of the room.

"You kids have gotten in enough trouble already, haven't you?" she said.

We didn't answer.

"Quiet couple, are you? Well then, let's just discuss this in my office, shall we?"

Forty One

"**Why** were you in the building?" Mrs. Coleman asked. "You know the area is out of bounds to students."

"I'm aware," I replied. "How'd you know we were there?"

"This isn't a game of twenty questions, Mr. Collins," she replied, placing her elbows on the top of her desk and giving me a foul look. "But for your information, I was on second half lunch-duty. I had confiscated an inappropriate object from a junior student and was lecturing him when I saw you and Miss Montgomery sneak in. A foolish act on your behalf because you're both seniors but I seriously doubt you'll be able to graduate once I report this."

Nora seemed to be fidgeting in her seat, so under the table, I found her hand with mine. It seemed to calm her down, not completely, but it was an effort. Her leg stopped moving up and down but her face was still washed over with concern. I tried to give her a look of reassurance but all that did was make her worriedly chew on her bottom lip.

"I'm pretty sure the information I have is of enough value that I'll be forgiven," I answered, trying to muster up enough confidence to make my voice sound authoritative. "I have a theory."

Mrs. Coleman raised an eyebrow. "A theory?"

Her tone suggested interest.

"Of who started the fire," I answered.

She seemed intrigued and so did Nora. They both looked at me with wide, waiting eyes. But I had to be careful. What I knew could be said to different people at different times and each would produce a different response and conclusion. It was all about perfect timing to the right person. One wrong slip up and I'd be completely screwed.

"There are still some missing pieces, but I'm sure that the knowledge I have is enough for the police to figure out the rest."

I felt smug knowing all this information, but I knew I had to be careful. I was treading in deep water. The constant reminder made my head spin. There were so many things that could go wrong. As I tightened my grip on Nora's hand, I slipped my other hand into the pocket of my trousers.

"As an authoritative figure, I think it would be best if you tell me first." Mrs. Coleman took out a pad of sticky notes and grabbed a pen, ready to write everything down. "Which student should I put down to expel?"

It was sad to know she actually found pleasure in writing names down for expulsion. There seemed to be that wicked flicker in her eyes, like a wild animal ready to attack its prey.

"Not a student. A teacher."

Mrs. Coleman frowned. "I don't believe that's right, Mr. Collins. All staff members are highly respected people in this school and have been professionally selected to benefit the students' education. Unless you have some evidence, I'm afraid your theory is invalid."

"I have evidence," I answered. "I found it."

"Where?"

"The burned building," I replied. "Under the desk, was a key."

"A key has no relevance in the case of the fire," she corrected me, seemingly irritated at what she thought was nonsense.

"That's what I thought too," I confessed. "Until I discovered the shape and size of the key. It was small and silver. At first, I thought it was a diary key, but it was too thick for that. Then I thought it was a mailbox key, but the shape didn't seem to fit. Until I realised it was a key, the perfect shape and size for handcuffs."

Nora's eyes had grown to the size of golf balls and Mrs. Coleman's wasn't any better. She seemed to have dropped the pen back onto her desk, letting it roll across a few scattered papers until it hit a stack of books. She was way too intrigued in my discovery to take notes.

"Someone deliberately took it. Officer Brandy and Officer Garret and not even Drew had misplaced it. It was stolen by a staff member," I continued, brushing my thumb over Nora's pulse to find it racing.

"But why?" Mrs. Coleman asked. "What staff member would have any benefits in handcuffing two students together?"

"Mrs. Westfield was recommended she'd go into retirement because of her health. I didn't know about it until I ran into her at the supermarket yesterday. It was actually suggested for her to go into early withdrawal from her position two months prior to the handcuff demonstration. I remember a conversation between her and my mother at parent/teacher/student night."

The girls stayed silent.

"Obviously, her condition would have been broadcasted to the staff members but not the student body so employees were aware of possible future circumstances. When the police department visited the school, a teacher deliberately took the key, knowing a demonstration with the handcuffs was going to be done. Once the deed was completed and the students were chained, this started a huge media frenzy. Not only did the story promote the school to the district but it also encouraged a bad reputation to our principal, furthermore influencing her retirement."

"So, you're saying a teacher wants the position for principal so sabotaged the school in order to gain power and higher educational status?" Mrs. Coleman asked, sounding completely outraged with my theory.

"You know your scheme well," I answered, being sure to keep a monotone voice. "I must admit, it was a struggle to finally fit all the pieces together, so brownie points for making it mind boggling."

"Ryder Collins." Mrs. Coleman sounded furious. "Are you accusing me of this notorious crime?"

"It all adds up," I replied. "The classroom the fire was started in was yours. It was your desk that the key was hidden under. You were the one to recommend both Nora and I to be volunteers for the demonstration *and* you were the one to discover and announce the fire over the loudspeaker."

She narrowed her eyes at me. Nora squeezed my hand tighter.

"But that anonymous tip to the police that I was some kind of arsonist was a seriously weak move. What really confused me was that you targeted students to help with your scheme. At first it was bloody nonsense that they'd ever agree to help, until I realised they were all year twelve students: the weak ones. The pressure and stress of the final exams was getting to them, so you bribed them with bumping up their overall scores because you knew you were going to be one of the English markers."

No one said anything. For one second of dread, I thought I actually had gotten it all wrong, that I had just made a foolish mistake and it was in that moment when I was sure I was about to crap a brick. But it wasn't until Mrs. Coleman stretched and leaned back in her desk chair, arms crossed across her chest as she gave me an impressed, yet still confident in herself smirk.

"Admittedly, your little discovery was fascinating," she said. "I never thought anyone would figure it out, let alone a child."

I tried not to scowl when she referred to me as a child.

"I confess I am the mastermind behind the mystery, but really, your knowledge is essentially useless. Once you're expelled from this school, your word will be just childish, hormonal nonsense. You're a child. You both are. Ryder Collins - a boy who feeds off popularity because you feel you don't get enough parental attention. I know all about your family. Your father's affairs were quite scandalous. Nora

Montgomery - a blonde, nothing-better-than-average student who will end up just like her sister who is currently unemployed and mothering a bastard child-"

She never got to finish her sentence because Nora let go of my hand, stood and slapped her right across the face. It wasn't one of those little girly smacks to the cheek either. It was a full-fledged, whooper with a loud crack as if her hand has turned into a whip just for the particular purpose. She looked wild and determined, glaring at Mrs. Coleman with a passion that could ignite her and I stared at the magnificent scene of witnessing one of the best bitch slaps in history.

I couldn't have been more proud to call Nora my girlfriend.

After that exact moment, Officer Brandy burst through the door and wobbled over with his donut-filled belly. Officer Garret followed after him, cautiously pointing his gun at all directions before it landed on the teacher.

"Ma'am, you have the right to remain silent," Officer Brandy said as he casually walked over, took Mrs. Coleman's hands behind her back and chained her wrists together.

"How... Who..." Mrs. Coleman was in complete shock.

So, to relieve her from her confusion, I pulled out the phone in my pocket and showed her the still-ongoing call between the local police department and myself. I had started the call as soon as the conversation became interesting. I silently praised myself for developing the skill to use my phone without teachers noticing and mentally thanked Nora because it was thanks to texting her that I had gotten the dexterity.

Mrs. Coleman was then escorted towards the door and Officer Garret took charge and walked her out the building and towards the police cruiser. Officer Brandy stayed behind, hooking his thumbs in the loops of his uniform pants and looking at us with pride.

"I knew you were good kids," he said slapping me on the shoulder. "Ryder, you made a risky move throwing yourself into this like that. For future reference, you should be more careful."

"Future reference?" I asked.

"Yeah," he said, heading towards the door. "You'd make a terrific police officer."

With a final tip of his hat, he exited the room. As soon as he was gone, I pulled Nora into my arms and held her tightly to my chest. I inhaled her strawberry shampoo and the perfume that lingered on her jumper. I buried my nose in the crook of her neck and gently kissed her shoulder.

"It's over," she whispered.

"Nearly," I whispered.

Forty Two

"**Pretty** crafty moves you had in there, Collins," Officer Brandy said, grinning proudly.

"Thank you."

"Do you know what you want to study once you've graduated from high school?"

"I was going to go for becoming a lawyer, but things change."

He smiled. "Well, if you ever think you want to change, maybe you should consider being a policeman. We could need a guy like you on the team and I'd happily take you under my wing."

I had never considered becoming a policeman, but as soon as he suggested it, I found myself warming up to the idea. A pair of handcuffs had led to everything at that point, so perhaps it was a sign. Looking out for society and fighting crime appealed to me. Plus, Nora would love the uniform. I smiled at that.

"That actually sounds like a pretty good idea," I said.

Officer Brandy's moustache curled with his smile and he gave me a small salute before heading back toward his car. Mrs. Coleman was tucked away in the backseat and the whole school was surrounding the yard as we watched her get driven away. Whispers and stories floated their way through the student body, but none of them were even close to the truth.

"You did it."

Nora leapt onto my back and laughed, wrapping her arms around my neck.

"*We* did it," I corrected her.

She kissed the side of my face, smiling wider.

"Please keep it PG-13, because we have minors witnessing."

Nora jumped off my back and we both turned to greet Caine. He was grinning. As soon as he reached us, he gave us both high fives.

"Shit, Collins, I didn't know you were so smart," he said.

"I had my partner in crime." I placed my hand on Nora's waist and pulled her to my side.

She looked at Caine with a bewildered expression and shook her head. "I honestly did nothing. It was all this guy's doing."

Caine looked between Nora and I. "Literally,stop. I can't stomach this."

I laughed and kissed the top of Nora's head.

It felt good to have things back to normal.

Well, almost back to normal.

When I arrived home later that afternoon, Jack was sitting on the passenger's side of his car. His feet were up on the dashboard and he was doing the crossword puzzle in the newspaper. When he noticed me walking up the driveway, he tossed the paper into the backseat.

"Ryder, please talk to me."

I hesitated. With the victory of figuring out who the real arsonist was and clearing my name, I was feeling surprisingly generous. I turned and looked at him.

"Okay."

"It'll be ten minutes tops-" He hesitated. "Wait, what?"

"I said okay."

Jack looked torn between confusion and relief, like he wanted to take a second to register my sudden calm attitude, but he didn't want to waste the very little time I had granted him. My father climbed out of his car and circled the vehicle until he reached the driver's side. I slid into the passenger seat but kept the door opened, just in case I needed to make an escape.

"I know you hate me, Ryder," he said, keeping his eyes out the windscreen.

"I don't really keep it secret."

He laughed humourlessly. "Yeah. You don't."

Silence fell between us, neither of us really wanting to fill in the space. I let a few more seconds pass, let the distance stretch between us. I was ready to exit the car, when he started talking again.

"I realised I should have handled things better."

"Good on you for realising that now."

He frowned at my sarcasm. "I acknowledged my mistakes a long time ago."

"Then why didn't you act then?"

He took a deep breath and ran his hands across the steering wheel. "I was ashamed. I left things at such a horrible note with both of you."

"So why did you choose now to come back?" I pressed.

I wasn't sure what my father's intentions were. It wasn't exactly an apology, more of a half-formed explanation. I wondered how much more information he was going to share.

"Because you're growing up, Ryder. You'll be graduating, going to university. I realised I walked out on you at a time where you needed me most. I wasn't a very fatherly figure. You needed guidance-"

"I don't need a father to know how to become a gentleman."

"Your mother raised you well," he whispered, turning to smile at me.

I didn't return the gesture.

"How...how is she?" he asked tentatively.

"Better," I answered. "She's different now. But she's better without you."

I didn't want to describe the effects he still had on my mother, but I wasn't going to lie and say she was in a pristine condition either. So, I told the truth. She was strong, she was determined, she was a fighter. And she *was* doing better without him.

He nodded. Swallowed. "I'm sorry. For everything. I messed up."

"I know."

"Do you forgive me?"

"Maybe one day."

Jack nodded and seemed to understand. "Well, no matter what I did, I'm still your father. And I'll be here for you. My number is in the phonebook."

I started climbing out of his car. I gently closed the door and leaned in through the open window. "I think we'll be just fine without it. But thank you."

The conversation with Jack made me feel surprisingly liberated and I smiled to myself as I made my way back to my house. But before I could reach the door, he called once more.

"Ryder."

I turned and waited for him to talk.

"That girl…Montgomery?"

I was surprised he remembered her. "What about her?"

"Do you love her?"

I didn't hesitate. "Yes."

He smiled knowingly. "Don't ever do what I did."

"One step ahead of you. Bye, Jack."

I turned for good then and walked into my house. Once the door was shut, I leaned against it and waited until I heard his car back out of our driveway and onto the street. I slumped onto the floor and smiled. I suddenly felt a million kilograms lighter.

"Ryder, is that you?" my mother called.

"Yeah," I answered, getting up and finding her in the kitchen.

She was standing up on the table, barefoot, wearing cargo pants and a flannel shirt, changing the light bulb. Seeing her like that reminded me of her old self. I was immensely happy.

"He's gone," I announced.

Mum stopped what she was doing, hand freezing in mid-air. She slowly lowered her arm and looked at me as she made her way off the table. Her hands were shaking as she placed the dead light bulb into the box where the new one previously sat.

"What?"

"He's gone," I repeated.

The look on her face was a mixture of emotions. Fright and excitement and happiness. But above all, my mother looked relieved. She looked like she was about to crumble to the floor, so I gently bent down and held her upright.

"He's gone," she whispered.

I hugged her gently. "I promised I wouldn't let him hurt you again."

"You never made that promise."

"It didn't have to be spoken."

She hugged me tighter. "Thank you."

Epilogue

As soon as Mrs. Coleman was announced her sentence, life seemed to fall back into place. I was finally on good terms with the police again, essentially promoting my reputation at school and because all the pressure was lifted from my shoulders, I completely aced my final exams.

My dad, after months of trying to win my family back, finally left, allowing my mother to finally return to her strict self. As soon as the tires of his car squealed, confirming his final departure, she became the expressionless woman I had grown up to know and love. And although she showed minimum emotion to her work mates, her and I shared an emotional bond that was more powerful than physical embracement.

Nora and I had resumed our relationship, the way normal teenagers should, without the complications of police and accusations and would often meet up with Caine, who had met this 'amazing girl' but was keeping her identity anonymous. Although I urgently wanted to know who she was, I respected his decision, as long as he would eventually tell me. Although I doubted he would have the time between his sporting career and new girlfriend.

Even Mel had been seeing someone, a guy that could eat just as much as she could and shared the same passion for food. Her confidence seemed to spike ever since she met him and because of her exceeding excellence in English and gossiping skills, she was offered a full scholarship to the best journalism school in the country.

As for Nora, she was still undecided about which course to study for university, so she chose a Bachelor of Arts and hoped to discover herself more once school started again. We had both submitted our references during the year and had both been accepted into the schools of our choice. We wouldn't be attending the same university, but we'd only be forty-five minutes apart, which meant surprise dates and weekend trips would still be easy for us.

"Can you believe all this started with a pair of handcuffs?" Nora said as she lifted her head from my chest.

"I'm a Collins. We're attracted to trouble," I answered, grinning mischievously as I leaned in to kiss the corner of her lips but she tilted her head so instead, our lips met.

When she pulled back, she gently ran her fingers through my hair. "The complications of kissing a Collins," she whispered.

"Some good came out of it," I mumbled back, mesmerised by the beauty of her eyes.

"Yeah," she agreed. "I fell in love with my best friend, graduated from high school and got into university."

I fell in love with my best friend. The sentence stayed glued to my memory as I brushed back her hair and whispered the same statement into her ear and sealed the words with a gentle kiss below her ear. Wrapping my arms around her waist, I pulled her back against my chest.

"Not to mention, your best friend fell in love with you too."

The End

Can't get enough of Nora and Ryder? Read extra chapters from the author by signing up for her blog!

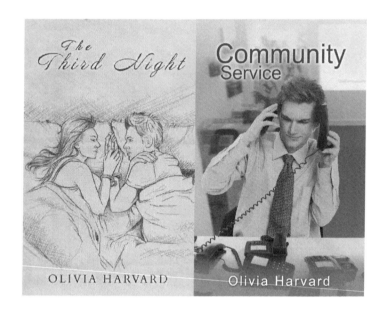

Get these two by signing up at
<u>olivia-harvard.awesomeauthors.org</u>

Here is a sample from another story you may enjoy:

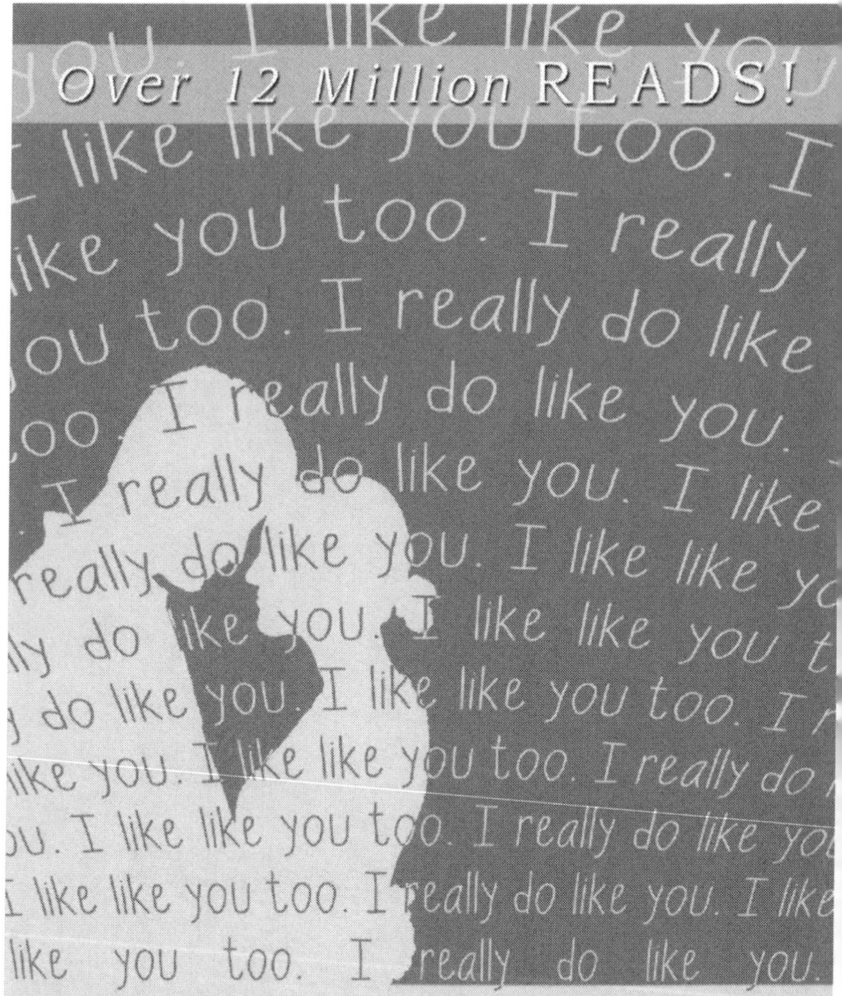
Over 12 Million READS!
MY BEST FRIEND'S BROTHER
M J THOMPSON

CHAPTER ONE
Real Home

Hope

I pulled up outside my sister's house. With a smile on my face, I opened the car door and stepped out. Before I knew it, I heard a squeal and fell to the ground.

"Arrr... I think an elephant fell on me!" I yelled, knowing it's my sister judging from the weight of her stomach on my back.

"Hey! I'm not that big," she said, confirming my suspicions.

I laughed joyfully. "In that case, can you please get off me? I can't breathe."

"Oh yeah ha, ha," her voice was laced with embarrassment and I felt her try to sit up and get off me, but to no avail. I could just imagine how we looked, me lying on my stomach with my heavilypregnant sister on my back.

It was so hilarious, I found myself laughing uncontrollably. At that moment, I heard the door of her house open.

"Oh crap, are you ok? What happened?" I heard Robbie say as he ran over to help us. He pulled up my sister before he saw me lying flat on the ground. He rolled his eyes knowingly and held out his hand and pulled me up, too.

"So?" he asked, trying not to laugh.

Kira looked at him, then to me as if to say, 'Say nothing.'

I gave a mischievous smile. "Well, Miss Turtle here decided to surprise me with a hug when I got out of my car and managed to knock us both over and she landed on me and I couldn't get back up," I said, effectively embarrassing her.

She blushed like a tomato, causing us all to laugh. After a moment, Kira hugged me again, but this time more carefully.

"I'm so happy you are finally living here for good," she said in a broken voice and with tears in her eyes. "And so is Robbie," she added, breaking the hug to poke her husband in the stomach.

He smiled and nodded. I returned the smile.

"But seriously," Robbie said to me, "we are happy to have our little sis around."

This remark made Kira's smile brighter. He had always been like an older protective brother. He's great and I'm glad my sister was married to him.

Robbie helped me get the stuff that I had brought with me from my car and took them inside to my room. I had lots of stuff at Kira's already, but there were more at my parents'. At that time, I thought, 'As I would be living there from now on, I should probably bring more with me.'

After somehow fitting everything in, we all went into the dining room where dinner was waiting for us. Sitting down, I smiled and said, "Thank you. But seriously, you shouldn't be jumping on people in your condition." I shook my head at Kira. Robbie readily agreed.

To lighten the serious mood around the table, I added, "You could really hurt the little one. Not to mention kill me."

The rest of the day was pretty much uneventful and so I decided to unpack my stuff. When I was done, I went to bed early after a long hard day. I wanted to be well rested for I'll be seeing Heather tomorrow. She was always hopping about full of energy, a lot like Kira before her pregnancy, not that it stopped her, much to Robbie's dismay.

Upon waking up the next day, I opened my eyes and screamed, falling off the bed.

"Ricky! What the hell!" I shouted.

My brother laughed and exited my room.

"I swear, this family is trying to kill me," I muttered under my breath before getting in the shower and changing.

I walked down the stairs and into the kitchen where everyone was eating pancakes.

I looked at Ricky and asked, "What are you doing here anyway? I'm happy to see you, of course, but shouldn't you be at college or something?" I sat down next to him and grabbed a spare plate of pancakes.

"It's the end of term," was all he said before wolfing down his breakfast.

"I heard you scream earlier," Kira said. "What did he do?"

I glared at Ricky, who was smirking as he chewed his pancakes. "When I woke up, this melon" – I poked his head – "had his face right in front of mine, scaring the hell out of me that I fell off the bed."

They all laughed. I love my family, but they can be such pains sometimes. I just rolled my eyes and continued to eat.

After breakfast, I walked out of the kitchen with Ricky.

"You got a new car this year?" he asked. I nodded and he hugged me. "Well, it's your big eighteen after all. We should have a party for you," he said, cheering me up.

"Yeah, but we'll have to ask Kira first," I told him just as she walked in.

"Ask what?" she said.

Ricky told her his idea and she agreed, but only if she could choose a theme.

"Alright, just try not to choose something too..." I stopped when I noticed Kira wasn't listening.

Kira had her thinking look on, her eyes looking up and her mouth partly open with her tongue slightly out. I looked at Ricky and he looked from Kira to me and we both laughed.

Kira jumped up. "I have the perfect idea." She grinned and looked so proud as though she made an important discovery.

We both waited for her to continue. "Yes?" I asked.

As if realizing she hadn't actually said anything yet, she slapped her forehead and said, "Oh yeah, I should probably tell you first." Her face was reddening, "How about a masquerade party? I've always wanted to have one."

Before Ricky or I could say anything, we were interrupted by a knock on the door.

"I'll answer that and give you a second to think about it." Kira smiled at us and walked, or more like hobbled, to the front door.

A short time later she returned with Heather in tow.

Ricky and I exclaimed "Hello!" at the same time. It was such a surprise to see her again.

Heather rushed over to me and Ricky, and like kids, we fell into a group hug.

"Hey guys," Heather said in excitement. "I missed you both."

The three of us spent so much time together growing up that she was more like another sister to us than a friend.

I rolled my eyes and exclaimed, "I've only been gone for just a week."

Heather sighed dramatically. "And it was the longest week of my life." This made us laugh. "Anyway," Heather continued as she took my hand in hers, "Kira was just telling me about her wicked party idea for you."

What was said next surprised me.

"Yeah, it's a great idea, isn't it?" It was Ricky who sounded so cheerful that I thought I might be imagining it.

I looked at him to see if he was being sarcastic.

"What?" he asked. "There will be lots of cuties around for me and I will have my mask on, so no one will ever know it's me and bother me afterwards," he smirked to himself.

I rolled my eyes in disapproval. "That sounds more like you."

We all moved to the living room and sat down.

"How long are you back for?" I asked him.

He shrugged, "Long enough," always the secretive one.
Heather scooted next to me and grinned, "The big eighteen soon?"

I grinned back and nodded, "Yep.Only fifteen days to go. Do you think that's long enough to invite a few new friends and some old ones to the party?"

"For sure," she said, nodding in return.

Kira, Heather, and I sat around talking about the party and what to wear, serve, and so on. After about ten minutes, Ricky stood up, clearly bored and perhaps out of place because of girl talk.

"I'll just head out to see some friends. See you all later," he said as he exited the house.

In the end, we girls decided on princess-inspired dresses and the boys would have to wear tuxes.

"It will be so great," Kira gushed, looking more excited than I was.

"Yep,we will look just like Cinderella," Heather added as she smiled at us.

I could see them now, dreaming about their Disney-inspired fantasies, but who wouldn't want a handsome prince at her party?

"Speak for yourself. I'll look more like Princess Fiona." I laughed.

They both frowned at me and Heather hit my arm.

"I've had enough of your self-loathing. We need to get you a boyfriend." She looked so serious that I laughed again.

Kira got up. "Why don't you two go to one of your friends' house or something?" She was trying to get us out of the house.

"If you want us gone, you just have to say so," I said to her.

"I'm sorry, honey, it's just for a couple of hours." She shooed us out of the house and closed the door behind us.

I looked at Heather and asked, "Where do you want to go?"

"Want to go to my house? Mom's cooking." She grinned at that, knowing how much I loved everything that her Mom cooks.

Her Mom was the best cook ever. I'm just glad she wasn't my Mom, because if she was, I swear I would weigh three hundred pounds.

I nodded and we walked over to my car.

"Nice car," Heather commented and whistled, "Birthday gift?"

"Yeah," I answered as I got into the car, shortly followed by her.

She lived only about a mile away, so we were there pretty fast. I guided my car into her driveway, parked, then stepped out. Following Heather into the house, I was almost knocked off my feet by the smell of something baking. I could feel myself starting to drool. I wiped my mouth as we made our way to the kitchen.

"Hi, Mom," Heather greeted, stepping into the kitchen.

Lanie turned around from what she was doing and smiled when she saw me.

"Oh.Hi, love," she said to me.

"Hi Lanie,it's nice to be back," I replied, trying to see what she was cooking.
She shook her head and pulled out a plate of freshly baked brownies and cookies. "You want some?"

I nodded eagerly and grabbed three at once. "Thanks."

Heather shook her head when she saw what I did. "Calm down and eat one at a time." And then she took one from me.

"Leave her be," Lanie scolded her daughter. To me she asked, "I've heard you're here to stay now and you're starting school here, too?"

"Yeah, I thought it was about time to settle in one place so I could finish my final year in peace, without interruptions," I told her. I looked around the kitchen and the living room through the door. "I haven't seen Dean in a while. Did he run away or something?" I was referring to Heather's younger brother.

I've spent a lot of time here, but for the last few months I didn't see even his shadow. He was a year younger than us and normally spent most of his time playing *Call of Duty* and *Halo*.

"He's about…" Heather said, unmindfully.

I looked in confusion between mother and daughter.

Lanie sighed. "Well, Dean has got some new friends and…" She trailed off when we heard someone come through the front door.

Heather stood up from the kitchen island where we were sitting and waited for the newcomer to show himself.

"Mom,we're home. Who owns the cool car outside?" I heard this being shouted by whoever it was that stepped into the kitchen.

CHAPTER TWO
Cookies

Hope

"Mom, we're home. Who owns the cool car outside?" I heard this being shouted by whoever it was that stepped into the kitchen.

A tall, dark-haired man came in, followed by another with similar appearance. They were really familiar, but I couldn't place them, until I thought about what they said, 'Mom.' 'So they're here, fantastic,' I thought to myself. I never thought about Matt and Nathan coming home. I should have really because of the fact that Ricky did so today.

'God, I'm so dumb,' I thought, turning back to the cookies and hoping they wouldn't notice me. I felt eyes burning into my back.

Lanie and Heather hurried over to them and pulled them into hugs. I just sat there munching cookies, happy that they were distracted.

"Hello lads. You're early," I heard Lanie say to the two.

"We wanted to surprise you, Mom." It was Matt.

Lanie squealed and jumped then I heard another set of footsteps.

"Mom, did you burn them again?" I heard another voice say, which I recognized as Heather's younger brother, Dean.

Unlike the two older boys, I actually quite liked Dean. He was a nice boy who would always try to get Heather and me to play on his game consoles with him and his little buddies.

"Oh. Hi," Dean said to his brothers, sounding a bit bored.

"And it's nice to see you, too," Nathan spoke, sounding annoyed.

"What happened to you?" asked Matt.

"What do they mean?' I thought. I haven't seen Dean in a while, but he couldn't have changed that much.

I was brought out of my thoughts when I heard Heather walk over to me while the otherstalked among themselves.

"Oh my god! How many did you eat?" she laughed.

I looked down on my plate and saw only a couple left.

"Oops! That would explain my sick feeling." Both of us laughed out loud, getting everyone's attention.

"Hey, I didn't see you there." I heard a very happy Dean rush over to us. I was shocked and started to laugh nervously when he gave me a hug.

"Hi. I missed you, too." I laughed again as I awkwardly patted his back.

Heather grinned at me and I mouthed, 'not a word.'

Yes, I have known for a while now that Dean had a crush on me, but I thought it was harmless. He would have a girlfriend soon and he would forget about his feelings for me. I thought it was kind of sweet in a way and Heather and his parents thought it was funny.

I pulled away and looked at him and was shocked by what I saw.

"What happened to your clothes?" I asked, but then realized it didn't sound very kind, so I tried to correct myself, but not before I heard a deep laugh behind me.

I tensed for a second before continuing, "I mean, you look nice but what happened?"

This made Dean smile. He was no longer in his old clothes. Gone were the blue jeans and sports shirts. He was wearing black combats, a black hooded top, high military-style boots and a bit of eyeliner on his eyes. I was shocked that my friend had taken such a drastic turn in a short time.

"I made some new friends, love," he explained, making me blush when he said the last bit.

Don't get me wrong. I have no romantic feelings for him, but it was always nice to have this kind of attention. On the other hand, I felt bad because it was like I was leading him on. I did speak to him about it once and told him my feelings and he said he understood, but now I'm not so sure he did.

Heather was just standing there laughing quietly.

"Hey, Dean," I heard someone say and walk over to where I was sitting. By this time, Heather was sitting beside me while Dean had moved to sit opposite me and would watch me when he thought I wasn't looking.

"Is this your girlfriend?" Nathan asked, looking at me.

"No!" I quickly answered without a second thought.

I looked at Dean, who didn't even seem to notice what I said, much to Heather's and my amusement.

"Leave your brother," Lanie admonished.

Nathan just grunted, "Ok," then he sat down on the empty seat next to me.

I tried my best to avoid his gaze. It may be childish, but I was still pretty traumatized by what I've gone through when I was younger.

"So, is that your car outside?" Nathan asked me.

Heather knew how I felt about them and gave me a look of apology.

"Yes," I said, turning slightly towards him and giving my best fake smile.

"Sweet ride," Matt butted in, from somewhere to my left.

Nathan gestured at his sister and asked, "How long have you known Heather?"

"Do you go to the same school?" Matt quickly followed.

I looked at Heather and saw she was as shocked as I was that they didn't recognize me. Have I changed that much?

I looked at Dean, who was now grinning at his brothers and muttering, "Idiots." The twins looked baffled.

I never thought this would happen. I didn't think they wouldn't recognize me because we've spent so much time together when we were younger. But it was pretty funny and so the three of us just laughed while the other two brothers looked confused. At about this time, Lanie was on the phone to tell her husband the boys were back. She walked in later on to see the three of

"We've been friends for a while now," I told them, grinning cheekily.

"Yeah, a long while," Heather confirmed.

"How old are you?" Matt asked as he stood to the side, giving me a toothy smile.

"Seventeen.Eighteen in a few days," I replied to them.

They smirked at each other and Matt said something under his breath so only Nathan could hear, but I was sitting close so I heard, too.

"Good."

I looked at Heather in confusion, but since she didn't hear them, she just shook her head and mouthed, 'I don't know.'

Lanie walked over to the oven and got another batch of cookies out and then looked at the plate where she placed the first batch and glared at Dean.

While the others were busy watching Lanie scolding Dean, Nathan moved closer to me and whispered in my ear, "Maybe you want to go out sometime?"

To say I was shocked would be an understatement. Here I was, a seemingly unknown girl, a friend of their sister and he was already trying to hit on me.

"No, thank you," was all I managed to say, still in shock.

Matt must have heard this because he laughed and said, also in a whisper, "She has taste,how about me instead?"

Nathan glared at his brother.

'These boys,really!' I thought.

I shook my head to say 'no.'

Nathan laughed and said, "Not so funny now, 'ey?" And then he looked at me and whispered even more quietly, while breathing down my neck, "Don't worry, honey. We won't give up." He made sure to use a deep, almost erotic sounding voice that sent a shiver down my spine, much to their glee.

I turned my attention back to the others who were arguing about something.

"What?" Dean asked with the last cookie in his mouth.

"Don't give me that. You ate all the cookies." Lanie grumbled at him.

"What? No, I didn't," he protested, looking at his Mom as though she accused him of something more sinister than eating all the cookies.

I looked at Heather guiltily and she smirked at me.

"What does it matter anyway, Mom? You have more," Heather said to try to pacify her.

But Lanie insisted, "That's not the point."

I sighed and was just about to confess when Dean grinned at me and looked at his mother. Pointing to Heather and me, he said, "If you want to know what happened to the cookies, Mom, why don't you ask them?"

Lanie looked at Heather, but before she had a chance, Heather almost shouted, "What? I only ate one." And then Lanie looked at me and I gave her an innocent toothy grin before Heather continued. "You saw me earlier telling her to slow down."

Lanie laughed at this.

"And as soon as we turned our backs, she ate a couple, which Dean finished," Heather said and Dean smiled.

"Oh. That's ok, then." Lanie answered smiling. It made Dean choke and caused the boys to laugh.

Lanie was always trying to fatten me up, saying I was too skinny.

"Hey, that's not fair," Dean protested as he scratched his head. "How come I get shouted at but it's ok if she ate all the cookies?" He even pouted to prove his point.

"Because you are big enough already," Lanie said. "Plus, Hope is a guest."

"But she's here more often than I am," Dean continued to protest but his mother wasn't listening anymore.

Dean was about to walk out of the kitchen, but before he could, I smiled at him and mouthed 'sorry,' then held my arms out for a hug. Heather laughed as his face changed from a frown to a smug smirk. He walked over and I gave him a brotherly hug, which Heather joined in on.

We broke apart and Heather said, "Good. Now we are all friends again."

Dean started to leave and asked if we wanted to play a game of C.O.D. We told him maybe later.

When he was gone, I looked at Heather and sighed, almost forgetting the two next to me.

"Can we have a hug now, too?" Matt asked, still grinning like a Cheshire cat.

Heather stood up and hugged them.

"That's nice," Matt said then pointed at me, "but I meant her."

Heather playfully slapped Matt's arm. "It's rude to point and she has a name."

Matt and Nathan were fraternal twins, so they would often speak for each other.

"He's sorry, honey," Nathan said, giving me a sweet smile.

'What happened to them while they were away?' I thought again.

"So, what's your name, love?" Matt asked, wearing the same smile.

Heather glared at her brothers. "You two are stupid."

I laughed at her.

"Why?" They both asked, confused.

Heather pulled me up from my seat and ignored them. "Let's go to my room."

We started to walk out, but I stopped momentarily and turned to Nathan and Matt who were still looking confused at each other.

"Nice to see you again, by the way," I said.

"Again?" Nathan asked.

Heather was growing impatient so she decided to show them something they would recognize. She walked closer to me and placed her hand on the back of my neck. She looked at me to ask if it was ok and I nodded.

"Are you lesbians?" Matt asked, smirking.

As if realizing how it looked, Heather jumped and shouted, "No! Just look!"

They both stood as Heather turned me and moved my hair up to reveal a nasty-looking scar at the edge of my hairline caused by one of their many pranks that went wrong.

I heard a gasp and Heather dropped my hair. "See now, stupid?" she asked.

I felt a hand on my shoulder, which made me turn around. I looked down on the floor, feeling old emotions resurface. I felt a couple of fingers under my chin as it was pulled up to look at the twins.

"Hope?" Nathan asked as he dropped his hand from my chin.

They both had looks of sorrow and regret on their faces, which surprised me because they never once did apologize. I nodded as tears started to fill my eyes. Never in ten million years did I expect what happened next, but neither did Heather.

They both said, "We're really and truly sorry for those things we did to you all those years." And then they both pulled me into a group hug, just as my tears started to fall.

I stood there frozen, not sure what was happening.

All Heather said was, "About time," and I heard her mother, whom I didn't realize was listening, agree.

I had no idea what happened to these two, but I sure wanted to find out.

If you enjoyed this sample then look for
My Best Friend's Brother

Our other books available on Amazon!!

A Unique Kind of Love
By: Jasmine Rose

★ ★ ★ ★ ★

"I remember reading it for the first time and falling immediately in love with it. Beautifully written with A Unique Kind of plot."– **Elena**

One Night with the Prince
By: T.M. Mendes

★ ★ ★ ★ ★

"I absolutely love this book! It has a great storyline with a really strong female lead who is not afraid to be herself and who does not fall instantly for the prince. This book also has great humor and it is just an awesome read that you just can't get tired of.." -**Paola Luevanos**

The Assistant
By: Elle Brace

★ ★ ★ ★ ★

"I love this story so much! To me it showed how a woman can grow in so many ways. I think every woman would agree with me, that we would like a man like him!..."–**Cassanderia**

Marriage by Law
By: N.K Pockett

★ ★ ★ ★ ★

"I fell in love with the chemistry of the charac- ters. This book is funny, charming, heart warming, and overall a great read. You'd be foolish not to read it too."-**Edimar Rodriguez**

Mars
By: Jasmine Rose

★ ★ ★ ★ ★

"Mars is one amazing and beautiful story about Amaryllis, a girl who falls in love with Logan Masterson, a boy dying with cancer. Mars is fascinating and even though I've read it more than a million times, I'd read it again and again…"-**Lucy iihoshi**

The Best Thing For Me
By: Lauren Jackson

★ ★ ★ ★ ★

"I reaaally like the storyline of this book, I read quite alot of books and can be very picky, so for me to continue reading a book after a chapter means that it is really interesting. congratulations on keeping my attention!" - **Meenzypenzy**

My Best Friend's Brother
By: MJ Thompson

★ ★ ★ ★ ★

"It was an amazing book full of passionate love. It was beautifully written and I cordially give MJ Thompson a round of applause for giving me one of the most romantic books I've ever read."- **LaMya Cowan**

Married to the Bad Boy
By: Letty Scott

★ ★ ★ ★ ★

"I would love to read more of your writings! Loved this series! I usually don't read young adult books but I couldn't put it down!"-**hope anne**

My Beloved
By: T.M. Mendes

★ ★ ★ ★ ★

"From fantasy to paper-bound! Simplify and honestly one of my favorite all time books! As a young reader, I was drawn to this book like a moth to the flame because of my favorite two aspects. Vampires and Romance..."
-Lilianna Meza

Unique, Different, Found
By: Violet Samuels

★ ★ ★ ★ ★

"I really enjoyed this book from start to finish. It made me so happy at some parts and at others I was crying my eyes out!..."
- Nichole

Hand-cuffs, Kisses and Awk-ward Situa-tions
By: Olivia Harvard

★ ★ ★ ★ ★

"One of the best stories I've read so far. I love the plot and how the story is filled with funny and adorable moments. Can't stop reading it once I start. This is really a book worth reading." **- Christina Li**

The Bad Girl and The Good Boy
By: Karla Luna

★ ★ ★ ★ ★

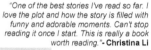

"This book was completely and utterly wonderful! I always found myself either smiling or laughing my butt off to the point of having tears running down my face! This book is worth every penny of your money and totally worth pulling an all-nighter just to finish the book! "
-D76

Of New Beginnings
By: Le-an Lai Lacaba

★ ★ ★ ★ ★

"Wow! I was finally able to find a collection of short stories that I liked. There were short stories in the book, all of which I liked. I felt like I was back in high school experiencing my first love. This book is a good read, I assure you, and I would definitely recommend buying it. Thumbs up to the author!" **-Martha Judds**

Psycho Sitter
By: Alexandra Ayers

★ ★ ★ ★ ★

"Most thrilling book that I have ever read! I have already bought the book and read it twice, that's how amazing this book is. I give major props to the author Alexandria Ayers for writing such a captivating story, especially at such a young age. Great job." **-Darlene boltz**

ACKOWLEDGEMENTS

There have been several people who have made this book possible. First of all, the biggest thank you to my family who have been nothing but supportive through my endless rants and out-loud brainstorming. A particular thank you to my parents, who have tolerated my indecisiveness and my constantly late appearances to dinner because I just *had* to write an idea down. You're all amazing.

Thank you to Morgan who has given me infinite amounts of patience and encouragement, not only through this book but through many other messy drafts. You were there throughout my entire writing experience; fangirling, laughing and crying with me, even at two in the morning.

Thank you to Danni for being both a friend and a consultant throughout my writing experience and who probably freaked out as much as I did when I received the opportunity to publish.

Huge thanks to the BLVNP publishing team, particularly to Grace and Kristine for all their patience throughout my endless annoying questions and for being so understanding throughout this entire experience. Honestly, what would I do without you two?

Lastly, thank you to all my readers who loved the story before I did and have been nothing but encouraging. You are *__all__* my inspiration. I may have written the story, but you were the ones who made it come alive.

Special thanks to these awesome people:

Delia Grace

Nasha Wa

peaches

Alyssa Howitt

Vivifirerune

Alina Marie Desiree

Sony Petal

Ashley Zerby

Kate hart

Naima.I.A

Madeeha

ifraah

Jood

Brigitta Nguyen

Joy Lew

Tiki Brown

About the Author

Olivia Harvard is an eighteen-year-old Australian author, publishing her debut novel 'Handcuffs, Kisses, and Awkward Situations' in December, 2014. She started writing when she was fifteen years old on the online writing community, Wattpad. Her first completed story was fortunate to receive an award and luckily enough, it was the start of many more to come, including:

2012 Watty Award Winner, On the Rise, Humour; 2013 Watty Award Winner, Most Popular, Mystery; 2014 iParchment Best Work; Shortlisted for the Young Writer's Short Story Competition hosted by Hot Key Books

Recently graduated from high school, she plans to attend university to complete her bachelor's degree in Business and/or Creative Arts. Aside from being a writer, Olivia is an avid reader, full-time dreamer, and professional procrastinator. But between reading and dreaming, she has future ambitions to travel the world, own a home library (currently owns four hundred physical books), and learn a new language.

Made in the USA
San Bernardino, CA
08 August 2015

Nora Montgomery's primary goal was to remain
seemingly unnoticed until graduation, and that
meant staying away from Ryder Collins. But
when both she and Ryder are se-lected to participate in the local police department's handcuff
demonstration, they find themselves inescapably
chained together. The tension between them is
thick; filled with unresolved issues from their past
friendship.

But things get a whole lot worse when the officer
loses the key and the pair are forced to accommo-
date each other until a re-placement is available.
Being handcuffed to the opposite gender was sure
to introduce some extremely uncomfortable situations.

Things are about to get awkward, right...

Cover Design by:
Junry E. Dela Torre

Published by:

ISBN 978-1-68030-068-0

9 781680 300680 >